TATSEA

TATSEA

by Armin Wiebe

TURNSTONE PRESS

Tatsea
copyright © Armin Wiebe 2003

Turnstone Press
Artspace Building
018-100 Arthur Street
Winnipeg, MB
R3B 1H3 Canada
www.TurnstonePress.com

All rights reserved. No part of this book may be reproduced or transmitted in any form or by any means—graphic, electronic or mechanical—without the prior written permission of the publisher. Any request to photocopy any part of this book shall be directed in writing to Access Copyright.

Turnstone Press gratefully acknowledges the assistance of The Canada Council for the Arts, the Manitoba Arts Council, the Government of Canada through the Book Publishing Industry Development Program and the Government of Manitoba through the Department of Culture, Heritage, Tourism and Sport, Arts Branch, for our publishing activities.

Cover design: Tétro Design
Interior design: Sharon Caseburg
Printed and bound in Canada by Friesens for Turnstone Press.
Second printing: September 2008

National Library of Canada Cataloguing in Publication Data

Wiebe, Armin.
  Tatsea / Armin Wiebe.

  ISBN 0-88801-281-0

  I. Title.
PS8595.I5311T37 2003   C813'.54   C2003-910746-9
PR9199.3.W465T37 2003

Turnstone Press is committed to reducing the consumption of old growth forests in the books we publish.

Mixed Sources
www.fsc.org Cert no. SW-COC-001271
© 1996 Forest Stewardship Council
FSC

For Sara Jane

TATSEA

DENENDEH, CANADIAN SUBARCTIC
CIRCA 1760 A.D.

CHAPTER ONE

"BUT EHTSI," TATSEA PROTESTED, "I JUST WISH TO FEEL THE wind and to breathe a mouthful of cool air."

"My granddaughter, you are a woman now," Ehtsi said. "You have a woman's power. You must not frighten the men."

"I know, Ehtsi, I could spoil the hunt if a man saw me." Tatsea crawled back into the menstrual hut. "But it's so hot in here and there's nothing to do."

"You are learning to be a woman." Ehtsi crawled into the hut after her. "A woman doesn't waste her power on foolishness."

Tatsea fixed up the spruce boughs on the floor, then tucked the hem of her caribou-hide dress beneath her as she sat down in the middle of the hut.

"Spread your skirt on the ground," Ehtsi said. The old woman gripped three sharpened sticks in one hand and a stone in the other.

"You don't need to use the sticks," Tatsea said. "I promise I won't go out again."

"Three times I catch you trying to run away. Two times when the boy with the big ears is nearby."

Tatsea spread her skirt out on the spruce boughs, avoiding her grandmother's eyes. Ehtsi had only caught her three times. She didn't know about the two times Tatsea had sneaked away through the shadows and met Dienda at the bathing place beside the big rock on the beach. What if Ehtsi or any one of the people had seen them splashing in the silvery water? But the cold water on her sweaty skin had been worth the risk, she thought. Besides, the people watching the handgame could not hear their splashing over the banging drums.

The old woman pounded the sharpened sticks through the hide skirt into the ground. Tatsea held her breath, wondering if Dienda would wait for her all night beside the bathing rock.

"There, my child," Ehtsi whispered, retying the hood over Tatsea's forehead, "we are all ehtsi, we women. We are creators, we make life."

Tatsea raised her head to peer beneath the edge of the hood into her grandmother's eyes. Never before had she noticed how the word for grandmother was the same as the word for create. *We are all ehtsi, we women. We are creators, we make life.*

Ehtsi slipped the scratching stick into Tatsea's hand. "Keep the flies from your hair. I will bring fresh water from the lake."

As soon as the flap closed after her grandmother, Tatsea rose on her knees. By stretching her skirt at one of the pegs she could put her eye to the tiny hole in the hide wall. But she didn't peep out now. Instead, she settled down between her kneeling legs and reached back with the stick to toss her long hair. She listened to the flies circle around her head. Then the flap opened and her grandmother set the birchbark water bowl on the ground beside the bag of dry moss leaning against a hut pole.

"Here, my child, drink," Ehtsi said.

Tatsea pulled the hollow swan's-leg bone from her sleeve. Her grandmother leaned over and whispered mischievously into her ear, "Just think of all the hides you do not have to scrape when you are here in the hut—and all the fish you don't have to gut. Men's fear of a woman's blood has its uses. So just be patient, my little hawk. You will find a way to fly."

Ehtsi slipped outside and Tatsea sucked through the drinking tube. Even fresh, the water tasted of bone. A woman at her first blood should not touch the water with her lips—or her hair with her fingers. What if the camp knew that she had touched the lake with her whole body while Dienda splashed right beside her? Little hawk and little squirrel playing together as they had every summer at fish camp here on the man's bones island, Do Kwo Di.

For a moment Tatsea slipped into an open-eyed dream. Resting in her moss bag on her mother's back, she gazed at clouds and circling gulls. Her mother's back rose and fell, twisted and leaned, as she reached for a fish, cut, sliced, pulled guts and tossed them to hungry ravens. Tatsea's view bounced from treetops to clouds to tops of tents. Twisting, her mother reached for another fish, swinging Tatsea's gaze to meet a pair of small, dark eyes peering at her. Baby Dienda gurgled from a moss bag tied to the back of the woman gutting fish next to her mother. Tatsea locked eyes with him in wonder.

The banging of a drum startled Tatsea out of her memories. The handgame, she thought, but then she heard her father's voice begin the song he always sang before he told a story to the camp. Tatsea pushed the water bowl out of the way and raised herself to peer through the hole in the hide wall. Ehke, her father, sat between two tents beside the cooking fire, tapping his new drum with a curved stick.

In the spring Tatsea had scraped the caribou hide so thin she could almost see through it, while Ehke carved the birch sapling with his sharpest flint knife and soaked it in the lake until he could bend it to make a ring. He tied the frame with babiche and with a sharp splinter of bone he worked holes through the wood, spacing them evenly around the ring. Tatsea had carefully twisted the strands of babiche, then held the frame while her father tied the cross-braces. Then he stretched the wet caribou skin over the frame and fastened it by lacing babiche through the holes. Tatsea remembered how the shrinking skin tightened as it dried.

Ehke's singing stopped and his drumming became soft like the heartbeat of a baby sleeping. Tatsea felt her dress pull at the pegs and she wrinkled her nose at the warm smell of the hides, the smell of her sweat and her blood. She felt the moss pad between her legs. Ehke's drumbeat changed, still soft but a little quicker, like the soft thrum of a hawk's wings. Tatsea wanted to tear up the pegs, to fly like a hawk and swoop down to scoop a fish from the lake. She raised her hood and pressed her eye to the peephole. Her father, Ehke, began to speak.

"It is said one time a large tribe of Dogrib people lived together on the west shore of this marten lake, Wha Ti. It was winter and one day the young men decided to cross over for ice fishing by Big Island, for the village was nearly out of food.

"In this village lived a young man no bigger than a small boy. His body had been covered with sores and scabs since he was born and his face was as bumpy as a frog's. The people looked down on him and felt sorry for him and they never allowed him to help with the work of the village because they thought he was too weak and too slow to work like the other young men. Even his own parents treated him as if he was no older than a child in a stinking moss bag.

"On this winter day the frog-faced boy cried and begged his parents to let him go fishing with the other young men. At last his mother gave in and the frog-faced boy followed the young men over the ice to Big Island."

Ehke paused in his speaking, drummed a little louder. He sang a few words, then softened the drumming again. Tatsea held her breath. Her eye staring through the peephole filled with tears, but she did not blink until Ehke spoke again.

"On Big Island the young men made a camp and left the frog-faced boy to keep the fire while they went out on the lake. They chopped holes through the ice with their stone chisels and dropped their hooks and lines into the water.

"The first big trout had just been hauled from the ice when Enda raiders were spotted sneaking toward them. The Dogrib men turned to flee but the Enda were too close. Soon the Enda were running beside the Dogribs, clubbing their heads so that their skulls broke and the tops of their heads flew onto the ice. Not one Dogrib young man made it back to the shore. The Enda killed them all and carried away the scalps of hair.

"Seeing the smoke on the shore, the Enda rushed on toward the camp. They saw the boy standing next to the fire. They shouted and ran faster, eager to close in for the kill. Then right before their eyes the boy became a frog and leaped into the spruce boughs he had spread around the fire.

"The Enda beat the spruce boughs with their clubs until only bits and pieces of green remained scattered here and there on the trampled snow. But they found no trace of the boy or the frog.

"The frog huddled in a hole in the snow, watching through spruce needles. He waited for a long time until he was sure the raiders had gone. Then he crawled out and became a boy again. He looked around the destroyed camp, then trudged out to where his companions lay dead on the lake. He could barely face the sight, but he remembered the people waiting for food, so he sang a prayer song and he pulled the rest of the fish out of the ice and headed back to the village with the two largest trout over his small shoulders."

In the hut Tatsea shuddered. She had heard of Enda raiders before, heard stories of her people killed for their hair, stories that happened far away, on the shores of the big water, Tindee. But this frog-boy's story had happened so close, here on Wha Ti. Last summer her father had set his nets near Big Island.

Tatsea squinted through the peephole, trying to see Dienda listening to Ehke's story. Was he frightened by this story? Then as she felt the tug of her skirt against the pegs she thought of the frog—the boy changing himself into a frog—and she wondered how he had done that. Could she turn herself into a hawk? She flapped her arms like wings and her hands cracked against the tent poles. She winced, then squinted through the peephole to see if anyone had heard the noise.

A short man stood with his back to her in the smoke drifting toward her hut. Her nostrils tickled and she sneezed, bumping her head against a tent pole. When she put her eye back to the peephole, the short man had turned to stare at her hut. Through the drifting smoke Tatsea saw the sores and scabs on the man's face. It was Ikotsali, who lived alone in a small tent at the other end of the camp.

Tatsea shivered. Was it right to tell the story of a man's power when he was right there listening? Bragging and boasting were wrong. Bragging about power was as dangerous as a woman's blood between her legs. Was Ikotsali really the frog-faced boy? Was he the same?

A soft tapping noise behind her cut into her thoughts. "Tatsea," a voice whispered at the bottom of the hut wall facing away from the rest of the camp. Tatsea laid her head on the ground and tried to peer through the narrow gap under the wall. "Tatsea, listen." What was Dienda doing, talking to her in the hut? If Ehtsi saw him she would chase him away with a stick. The people would mutter about him, give him dirty looks, maybe even refuse to talk to him.

"Tatsea, listen!" Dienda whispered, louder than before. His hand clawed through the gap. Tatsea pulled her hand back. "Tatsea, I'm going away."

"Aiyii?" Tatsea whispered, reaching out and grabbing the fingers, which wiggled at her like the legs of a bug fallen on its back.

"I'm going far away with my brothers to find the place where the Enda come from."

"No!" Tatsea said, louder than she wanted. Dienda gripped her hand tightly. Tatsea whispered, "You will never come back. You must not go."

"Don't be frightened for me. I will be with my brothers. We are not afraid."

"But the Enda will kill you."

"Not if we get thundersticks."

"Thundersticks? I do not understand." Tatsea felt real fear now. She had not heard of such things.

"Some Enda have sticks that kill with thunder. We must find the place where such sticks grow."

Tatsea gripped Dienda's hand more tightly. "Do not go," she whispered, "do not go."

"You are just a frightened girl," Dienda said. He started to pull his hand away, but Tatsea held on with all her might. Dienda stopped pulling.

Tatsea laid her cheek on his hand. "Wait! I must swim with you once more. I will meet you at the bathing rock in the dark."

A loud cheer from the handgame players drowned out Dienda's reply.

CHAPTER TWO

IKOTSALI, THE SORE-FACED MAN, HEARD EHKE'S DRUMBEAT begin as he tramped through the bush toward the camp. His heartbeat quickened for he had not heard the sound of another human for three days. He straightened his hunched back a little and slipped his hand between the tumpline and his forehead to relieve the pressure of his pack, heavy with fresh moose meat.

He smiled. If only he had had his canoe, he could have brought the whole moose into the camp at once. Wouldn't that have been something for the people to see?

He thought about the girl sneaking out from the menstrual hut to the bathing rock to splash with the big-eared boy. Would she have noticed him paddling past the bathing rock with a whole moose in his canoe? But he had chosen to walk into the bush, away from the camp, when the handgame started and no one had offered him a place in the row of drummers behind the players.

He had walked away into the bush alone to check his snares for small game, work usually done by women.

The sound of the handgame drums softened in his ears and he thought about the girl who played with the big-eared boy. If the girl were living in his tent she would be going into the bush to check her snares for hare and marten. In his mind he saw her kneeling in front of his tent sewing moccasins from moosehide he had brought her. The handgame drums had faded when Ikotsali noticed the thick moss covering the ground as he stepped into a clearing. In his mind's eye he could see the girl gathering moss with the other women. A gust of wind brought the faint pounding of the drums back to his ears. He glanced back toward the camp, even as he stepped forward. His foot sank through a layer of moss and he plunged into a hidden hole. Shamed, he scrambled out of the hole and fled the place. Later, as he slept hidden in a thicket he dreamed he was sleeping in the hole under the moss and that a bear plunged down on him.

Ikotsali had spent two nights away from the camp when he had spotted the moose in the swamp. Taking in the bush around him, he noticed how the well-worn path the moose used to reach the water ran between two sturdy trees. With his braided rawhide rope he set a large snare between the two trees. Then, with a bag of stones slung over his shoulder, Ikotsali waded quietly into the water behind the moose and tossed rocks at it, gently at first, just enough to annoy the animal and make him move in the direction of the trail.

Gradually, Ikotsali flung the stones harder so that as the moose neared the shore it was spooked enough to want to flee. Ikotsali hurled a few more stones and the moose clambered up the muddy bank and lumbered down the trail at top speed. Ikotsali struggled out of the water, then grabbed for his spear hidden beside the trail. The moose charged straight ahead, then jerked to a halt as the snare tightened around its throat.

Ikotsali sprinted to where the trumpeting moose struggled against the snare. With his spear ready he watched for the moose's soft underbelly to show itself. He didn't want to spoil the hide with bad spear holes. The perfect spot appeared and he drove the spear in hard. Blood splattered the front of his clothes. The moose stumbled, bawling as the life flowed out of it. Ikotsali hung on to the spear, kept it thrust deep, until the big animal stopped moving. Even then he waited until his heartbeat slowed before he pulled out the spear and looked at what he had done.

Ehke's voice cut through Ikotsali's memory. He was singing the storytelling song. Ehke was going to tell a story, a story about some great deed done in the past. Ikotsali straightened up and strode forward, thinking of his great moose and the young girl on the beach, and he felt good about coming back to the camp after three days in the bush without hearing another human voice. For a moment he felt a twinge of regret as he remembered the warmth of the moose's body. He had wondered if there were a way to touch a warm moose when it was still alive. Now he wondered what it would feel like to touch the girl on the beach. What if he visited Ehke in his tent? What if Ikotsali asked to be Ehke's daughter's husband?

Ikotsali stepped into the clearing and stopped. Ehke's story words came clearly to his ears—the story of the young men killed on the ice, and how he, Ikotsali, had escaped by changing into a frog.

His mind pulled back through time, Ikotsali heard again the shouts of the Enda raiders, the young men's blood-curdling screams as axes crashed through their skulls, sending the tops of their heads spinning to the ice. From the fire Ikotsali saw the young men fall, saw the Enda raiders gather up the scalps of his friends. He saw the Enda turn on their heels when they spotted him, small and puny, beside the fire. He heard the laughing shouts as the raiders stampeded toward the shore, toward his fire. Ikotsali, small beside the roaring fire, felt his blood shiver colder and colder and colder. His mind cried out, I will die, I will die. Fear made his mind and his body think small, small, smaller, smaller until his ears were level with the snow, hearing the raiders' trampling footsteps. Ikotsali's hind legs crouched, bent ready to spring with all the power of a frog a hundred times its size. He leapt through the air, landing on the spruce boughs he had spread beside the fire. Ikotsali's leap was so powerful he burrowed right through the spruce boughs, through the snow, through the frozen sand down into the frozen mud where the other frogs waited with nearly frozen blood for the summer sun to wake them.

Ikotsali waited, barely awake, barely alive. The raiders' clubs beat the ground above him, shaking the snow and the frozen sand and mud, bouncing him, filling his tiny head with the thumping of the clubs on the ground. He almost croaked a frog croak, but he was too chilled to make a sound. Once when still too young to have teeth, he tried to sleep on his mother's back, but a loud banging kept him awake. He had been shaken up and down and sideways while his mother danced in the circle inside the largest tent in the camp, people packed in around the wall and the drummers' drums beating right beside his tiny ears. He had looked out, frightened but unable to cry with the constant shaking up and down and sideways.

Then the thumping overhead stopped and Ikotsali, the frog, heard the trampling feet move away. When all was still he pushed himself up from the mud through the frozen sand and snow and crawled out through the broken spruce boughs. He hopped in a circle until he was pointed in the direction of the lake and as he hopped toward the bodies of the young men on the ice his small boy arms and legs came back and he ran to the dead.

The smoke from the fish-drying fires drifted towards Ikotsali, blurring Ehke and the story. His eyes watered, then a sneeze somewhere behind him startled him. He turned and saw the small hut, saw the movement of the girl inside pushing against the wall. An eye stared at him through a hole in the hide.

What did she see when she saw him? Had she heard the story, too? Did she know he spied on her when she splashed in the water with the big-eared boy?

His shameful fall into the hole flashed through his mind. What if the women had been gathering moss and had seen him fall? Then in his mind he saw the girl falling into the hole. Ikotsali shot out his hand to stop her fall, then hid it behind his back when he remembered where he was.

Ehke's voice stopped; the drum stopped. Ikotsali turned away from the menstrual hut. The men took their places for the handgame, forming two teams of two rows each. The players with their robes knelt low in front, the drummers kneeling high behind them. Ehke placed a pile of scoring sticks in the space between the two teams.

Ikotsali stepped closer. He had never been invited to join in the game with the rest of the men. Once, a few months after the Enda raiders killed the young men on the ice, Ikotsali tried to take his place on one of the teams, but no one even noticed him when he pointed and guessed correctly the player on the opposite team who had the stone hidden in his left hand. No one noticed him now either, the man they had just heard a story about. Even though he knew all the songs of the people, he had never been asked to join the drummers when the people danced. Once he had joined the circle of dancers, but tripped and fell, causing two old women to tumble down on top of him. The people all laughed at him and he feared to join the dance again. It was easier to slink about in the flickering shadows of the campfire.

With his parents dead, few people spoke to him. Ikotsali spoke so seldom that when he tried to speak his voice was dry from disuse and his words came out like a squeak or a squawk. People looked at him strangely and snickered behind his back, or turned from him in fear of his frog medicine.

Ikotsali slunk away from the camp, the pack of fresh moose-meat still on his back. He trudged along the pebbled beach until he saw Dienda, the big-eared boy, lurking in the shadow of the bathing rock. He is waiting for the girl, Ikotsali thought, as he dropped his pack at the water's edge and began to strip off his clothes. He ignored Dienda, who watched him for a moment, then hurried away after the frog-faced man waded into the water.

In the water up to his waist, Ikotsali bent over and washed the pus from the boils off his face. Even after living with the sores for all his life he still winced each time the water touched the sores. He raised his head and wiped his face with his hands. As always his face in the water startled him. It was not the face he felt from inside; even the pain of the sores on his face was not the pain he saw when he looked into the water. The small, small body he saw attached to the face was not the body he felt when he was walking. The weakness others saw was not what he felt in his mind when he was alone, when he was setting his snares, when he skinned a caribou or a moose he had caught in a snare all by himself without the help of the other men. Despite his small size, he was not as weak as the people made him out to be, or as weak as he felt himself to be when he was with the people, when he was with the other hunters.

Ikotsali bent close to the water and splashed his face again, but he couldn't wipe the young men's bloody heads from his eyes. Every time he heard someone tell his story the bloody snow came back, and not even memories of the starving villagers cheering him when he arrived with the two trout as tall as himself over his shoulders could wipe the blood away.

Ikotsali finished washing, but instead of leaving he stood in the water for a time, listening to the handgame drums and the cheers as a team guessed the hiding place of the little stone. He listened, too, for a soft, furtive footstep on the pebbled beach.

A streak of light pierced through the trees on the north shore and brightened the water at his waist. Ikotsali's boil-covered face looked up at him. That is what the girl in the menstrual hut would see if she crept along the beach to the bathing rock. If she did come, would he change into a frog and leap into the water?

The light faded, leaving the lake in the pale darkness of a summer night. He sensed something behind him. Slowly he crouched, then spun around. Neck deep, squatting in the water, a woman grinned. Ikotsali grinned back and reached out toward her open arms. The woman gasped, stopped a scream with her hand. Flinging a handful of water at him, she whirled about and staggered toward shore.

Ikotsali watched her pick up her clothes from the beach, then scurry into the shadows. The handgame drums still echoed over the camp as he stumbled out of the water and pulled on his sweaty clothes, stinking with moose blood. Then he picked up his pack and tramped into the bush, wondering if the girl would get back to her hut without getting caught. Then he wondered what would have happened if he had not turned around. What if he had waited until she reached him? What would she have done then?

Ikotsali tramped through the night—brooding, wondering—lugging the fresh moosemeat. He began to dream and in his dream he saw himself trudging through deep snow, meat heavy on his back.

CHAPTER THREE

HER HEART POUNDING LOUDER THAN THE HANDGAME DRUMS, Tatsea wriggled her dripping body into her hide dress. Frog-faced Ikotsali, naked in the water. And she had wanted to throw her arms around him! Embarrassed, seething, she tiptoed through the trees at the edge of the camp, her leggings and moccasins clutched under her arm. Had Dienda seen her he would tease her about this for the rest of her life.

A hand clapped over her mouth; an arm squeezed her chest. Tatsea's heart stopped. The Enda had come and she was going to die. A head pressed against hers; breath tickled her ear. Before she could fight back a voice said, "So you go swimming with frog-face Ikotsali?"

Dienda! Relieved and furious, Tatsea elbowed Dienda's belly, but now her greatest fear again was to be discovered outside the hut.

"You sure looked funny running away from the frog man," Dienda said. "Good thing your Ehtsi wasn't there to see."

Dienda slipped his hand off her mouth and relaxed his hold so Tatsea could turn to face him.

"Why didn't you stop me if you could see?" she said, a touch of fury in her voice.

"It was too late, you were already in the water."

"You should have seen the look on Ikotsali's face, it was frightening and funny at the same time. He reached out for me, he smiled like he wanted me." Tatsea wrapped her arms around Dienda's back. "When you grabbed me I thought it was Ikotsali or Enda! What if he comes when you are gone?"

"He was more frightened than you, I think." Dienda hugged her close.

The drumming at the handgame stopped and for a few breaths the whole camp was silent. "You better go back into the hut," Dienda said, "before your Ehtsi catches you."

"Wait," Tatsea said, "I will give you something to keep you safe. Don't move." Tatsea let go of Dienda's hand and untied the string of babiche that fastened a small bag to the waist of her dress. The handgame drums started beating again.

"You mean you got power now?" Dienda whispered in a teasing voice.

The bag was narrow at the top and wide at the bottom. Ehtsi had showed Tatsea how to make it from the feet of a swan. The swan's claws clasped each other like hands. The bag was so new Tatsea had not put anything inside it yet.

"Take this with you." Tatsea tucked the bag into his hand. "Promise you will keep it."

"I will carry it for you, but you must go now." Dienda nudged her toward the hut.

Tatsea slunk back to her hut, suddenly fearing Ehtsi's anger. Caught again, Tatsea would be sure to feel her grandmother's stick. She lay down on her spruce-bough bed and while the handgame players drummed her to sleep, Tatsea kept seeing

Dienda's face drifting before her in the smoky air of her dream. Sores would appear on the boy's face and then, as the smoke cleared, Tatsea would be reaching out for Ikotsali bending over in the water. Tatsea's eyes would open and her heart would flutter as she stared up into the darkness until the drums lulled her back into the smoky dream and the vision began all over again.

The sun was high in the sky when Ehtsi entered the hut with a roasted moose rib, still warm. Ehtsi said nothing about the stakes Tatsea had pulled out of the ground so she could sleep more comfortably. Instead, Ehtsi's eyes twinkled as she watched her granddaughter eat. When Tatsea noticed her grandmother's look, she stopped eating.

"Aiyii?" she said, looking into Ehtsi's eyes so directly Tatsea frightened herself.

"The boy with the big ears has gone away with his brothers."

Tatsea looked away.

"Before the sun had climbed over the trees someone came to visit your father. He brought your father a gift. Meat from a moose, freshly killed."

Tatsea looked at Ehtsi again. Ehtsi gazed at her, amusement still in her eyes.

"Big bull moose, it has a big hide." Ehtsi reached out and caressed Tatsea's cheek. "The hide is too big for your mother to scrape alone. I believe the time of the power of your blood is past. There is work to be done."

Tatsea finished gnawing the flesh off the bone, then crawled past her grandmother to toss it out through the tent flap. She hesitated, then took a deep breath and poked her head out into the sunlight. Behind her Ehtsi said without expression, "It may be that someone will be asking your father for a wife."

CHAPTER FOUR

TATSEA'S LEGS ACHED. SINCE BEFORE FIRST LIGHT SHE HAD BEEN tramping after her father through the soft snow. She sank past her knees each time she stumbled off the trail Ehke was breaking ahead of her. She thought it was good that the snow was not yet winter deep. For three days now she had trampled through the snow carrying her father's spear and they hadn't seen a fresh caribou track. She was a woman; she should be at home in the camp, sewing and cooking.

Cooking what? The families from the fish camp had missed the big caribou herd before the snow came. The caribou had not come to the usual place and with Dienda and his brothers gone on their long journey the camp had only a few hunters and they had found only a few stragglers before the caribou scattered into the bush. Tatsea thought Ehtsi, her grandmother, had given her a strange look when Ehke and Dienda's father decided to go their separate ways for the winter, even though that meant Ehke would be one man hunting to feed three women. One family was easier to feed than two. And so Tatsea was following her father on the hunt, as if she were a man.

Ikotsali, the frog-faced man, had brought gifts of fresh meat to her father three times after Tatsea was allowed out of the menstrual hut. Each time Tatsea had shuddered at the thought that this man would ask her father to let him have Tatsea for a wife. Each time Ikotsali had looked like he wished to speak, but in the end he always set the meat in front of Ehke's tent and walked away without saying a word.

Ikotsali had not been seen since the caribou hunt failed.

Ahead of her Ehke stopped. He signalled her to keep still. Then he crept forward. Tatsea shifted her backpack to relieve the pressure of the tumpline strap across her forehead as she steadied herself with the spear. Ehke prepared his bow, drew two arrows from his quiver, notched one. He waved for Tatsea to follow, then crouched and crept forward into a clearing.

Tatsea followed in his tracks and watched him steal toward a caribou bull digging with its hoof to the moss beneath the snow. Dry, velvet strips dangled from one of the bull's antlers; the other had splintered into a sharp point.

Ehke crept into range, using the luck of the wind to get close for a good shot. Tatsea watched him draw back his first arrow and aim for the soft belly below the ribs. She held her breath. Ehke let the arrow go. The bull stumbled down on its front knees, then reared up and spun around, swinging its antlers from side to side. It saw Ehke kneeling on the ground, notching the second arrow.

"Bring the spear!" Ehke called, but before he could release the second arrow the bull charged and gored him and flung him across the snow. Bone cracked when Ehke landed.

The bull charged again. Tatsea's scream drowned out her father's scream. Tearing the tumpline from her head, she lunged at the bull with the spear. Blood gushed where the arrow stuck in its side. Tatsea shrieked to distract the bull, gripping the spear with both hands, raging. She could not let her father die.

The bull stumbled in the snow. Tatsea charged and drove the spear into its side. She felt the point hit a rib, then slip sideways into the soft guts. Blood spattered all over the front of her parka. The bull sank to its knees. Tatsea held on to the spear, driving it in deeper and deeper until the bull collapsed on its side.

Tatsea hauled the bloody spear out with both hands, ready to plunge it in again if the bull moved. She watched the blood seep into the snow, heard a gurgle from the bull's throat. She began to tremble so much she had to stick the spear into the snow and cling to it to keep from falling.

Her father moaned in a heap in the snow, his right leg bent beneath him like a branch broken by lightning. Tatsea stumbled to his side. She tried to move him, to straighten out the leg, to make him more comfortable, but Ehke screamed with such suffering Tatsea couldn't bear to touch him again.

Fire! she thought. I must build a fire! I must keep my father warm. She rushed to the edge of the bush and kicked through the snow for fallen branches. Quickly, she gathered an armful. Back and forth she went, gathering dry twigs and branches and finally a log thick as her leg.

The wind gusted across the clearing while she built the pile of wood the way she had been taught. She wanted to move her father into the trees, but the sound of his moaning made her believe that the fire must come first.

Tatsea reached inside her parka for the fire bundle at her waist. She knelt beside the woodpile and opened the bundle. Beside the two firestones lay three sheets of birchbark and a small bag of dried birch-tree knots, ground into a powder. Tatsea made a bed of dry twigs on the snow, then laid a sheet of birchbark on top. With trembling fingers she poured the powder onto the birchbark. Would there be enough to catch a spark?

With her fingers she scraped the powder into as deep a pile as she could make. Then she picked up the two stones and struck the black stone against the white. A tiny spark flicked off into the snow.

Again and again she struck the stones. Some of the sparks hit the powder but each vanished before Tatsea could blow it into a flame. Beside her Ehke moaned in a rhythm that seemed to match the beat of Tatsea's striking of the stones.

The wind sharpened, chilling her fingers, but she dared not stop to warm her hands in the mittens dangling from the babiche around her neck. Again and again she struck the stones, sending sparks in all directions until one large spark landed on the powder and glowed, but as Tatsea leaned in to blow it into a flame a fierce gust killed the spark. Before Tatsea could strike again another gust scooped up the birchbark sheet and scattered the powder all over the snow.

Frantic, Tatsea scraped up the powder, but her fingers only soaked the powder with the snow.

Tatsea spread another sheet of birchbark on the bed of twigs and peeled bits of bark into a pile. To keep the wind from blowing the bits away, she built a little fence of twigs around the tiny pile. Then she struck the firestones again, hoping for a spark to catch the thin bits of bark.

Ehke moaned quietly in rhythm with the striking stones. Fear shivered through Tatsea's body: her father's moaning was like a song, like the song Ehtse, her grandfather, had sung last winter. *Her father was singing the death song. If she couldn't build a fire he would die.* She struck the stones harder and faster, sending sparks everywhere except to the pile of birchbark bits.

In the darkening clearing Tatsea saw her grandmother's eyes accusing her of not respecting the power of a woman's first blood. Tatsea cringed, remembering how she splashed in the lake with Dienda when she should have remained hidden in the menstrual tent. First the caribou herd had not come to the usual place, and now her father would die. Then her mother and her grandmother would die unless she could make her way back with meat from the bull.

The bull lay still. They had killed the bull. She thought of the frog-faced boy who had saved the village with two large trout. But she could not leave her father to die. Ehke, a man who needed a son, had not left her to die that hard winter when she was born. She could not leave him to die. She would not.

Tatsea heard a change in her father's moaning. She turned to him. He wasn't singing the death song. He was calling her. She crawled over to his side. "What is it? What are you telling me?" Her father gripped her hood and pulled her down to his face. At first she couldn't understand his murmuring words. Again and again he mumbled the words until she figured them out.

"Use my fire bundle," he said.

In her panic Tatsea had forgotten her father's fire bundle. "Yes, Father, yes, I will try again."

Ehke did not cry out when she rummaged through his clothing. But she found nothing. There was no little bag filled with dried birch-knot powder to catch the spark from the firestones. "Father," she cried, "where have you hidden the fire bundle?" But her father was moaning again, chanting, and though she screamed in his face he did not respond to her, he just chanted with his eyes closed, chanted the death song. Louder and louder she screamed, screamed like the hawk she was named for.

She choked in the middle of a scream. A shadow moved beside her. A man knelt at her woodpile. In the rising moonlight the shadow man laid out a bed of twigs on the snow, covered it with a sheet of birchbark; then with a steady hand he poured birch-knot powder onto the sheet. With a sharp thrust he struck firestones; the first spark fell on the powder and glowed. The shadow man breathed it into flame and gently added twigs.

Tatsea couldn't move or speak. She was dreaming, she thought, watching a spirit build the fire, but then she felt the warmth from the flames. In the firelight the man's face turned; she saw the scabs.

Ikotsali's eyes shone at her. "Wood," he muttered, and shook his head in the direction of the bush. Tatsea remained frozen for a moment, then scrambled to her feet and ran to the bush. Near the edge of the clearing she grabbed her backpack. She stooped to sling the tumpline across her forehead; then she gathered an armload of dead branches and hurried back to the fire, now roaring and crackling in the wind.

Ikotsali had shifted his attention from the fire to the injured man. He had laid Ehke flat on his back and was slowly straightening out the broken leg even though this made Tatsea's father scream out in such pain Tatsea stumbled and spilled her firewood all over the snow. Tatsea grabbed up the wood again and staggered to the fire.

Ikotsali looked up from her father's leg and Tatsea feared he would scold her for her clumsiness, make some comment about a Dogrib woman who could not even make a fire. Looking out from his scabby face, Ikotsali's eyes seemed almost gentle, filled with concern for her father's pain.

"Skin it," he muttered in that abrupt way men spoke to women, jerking his head toward the dead bull. Then he focussed on Ehke's broken leg.

Tatsea fumbled for the pouch at her waist, slipped her hand under the flap, and felt for the larger of the two flat stone knives she carried there. Back at the camp her mother had reached into her own pouch and pulled out her best knife. Her mother hadn't spoken when she handed the knife to Tatsea, but her eyes had made plain the responsibility she was passing on to her daughter.

Tatsea gripped the quartzite blade between her thumb and fingers and set about hacking through the thick hide. Although her mother had freshly sharpened the cutting edge, Tatsea found she had to repeat her slashes to cut through the hide before she could strip it away from the still warm flesh.

Ikotsali edged her father closer to the fire and covered the injured man with his own coat. Then Tatsea noticed him rummaging in the snow until he had gathered a heap of fist-sized stones, which he placed in the fire. She was relieved when Ikotsali brought out his own blade and joined her in skinning the caribou.

Even in the near darkness, Tatsea felt as if they moved as one as they worked. Only once did they bump into each other, and Tatsea thought she heard Ikotsali laugh softly.

Ikotsali pulled the hide free and gestured for Tatsea to help him wrap it around her father. Then he muttered at Tatsea to cut some meat and cook it for her father. "Gather what's left of the blood to make soup," he said. Tatsea obeyed each order without question. She felt her own hunger but she made herself wait, not even daring to reach into her pack for a tiny piece of drymeat.

Tatsea cut out the bull's stomach, then hesitated, thinking how tasty the contents of the stomach would be after the stomach had hung beside the fire, turning, cooking slowly for most of a day. But Ikotsali had said to make blood soup. Her father needed soup. So Tatsea scraped the stomach clean, and set it on a bed of sticks beside the fire.

By this time the smallest cooking stone glowed faintly in the fire. She filled the stomach pot with snow and blood and morsels of meat. With two sticks she picked up the stone and dropped it into the pot, listened to the sizzle as she quickly closed off the opening and tied it with a strand of babiche Ikotsali handed her.

While Tatsea added hot stones to the pot and returned cooled ones to the fire, Ikotsali stripped the skin from the bull's legs. Then he set about fashioning a sled with the long strips of hide. At last, the soup in the stomach pot began to bubble and Tatsea looked around for something to dip it with. Ikotsali reached into his backpack and drew out a tiny birchbark bowl. He dipped it into the pot and then dripped the steaming soup into Ehke's mouth. Ehke swallowed, then moaned. Again and again Ikotsali filled the little bowl and poured the soup down Ehke's throat until the injured man closed his eyes and fell asleep.

Tatsea took the stirring stick out of the pot and Ikotsali dipped the bowl once more. She turned away, expecting the sore-faced man to drink the soup himself. Instead, he nudged her elbow and held out the bowl. Tatsea looked at him with questioning eyes. Ikotsali smiled. Her hand trembled when she reached out for the bowl. The soup tasted more delicious than marrow sucked from a bone. She handed the empty bowl back to Ikotsali and he filled it for her again. After the second bowlful Ikotsali said, "Cut meat. Fill your pack." Then he dipped the bowl again and slurped the soup.

With her mother's knife Tatsea hacked at the meat, groping the bull's carcass in the moonlight for the heart, the liver, and the kidneys. The bull had begun to freeze so she had to chop and saw at the more solid meat.

Ikotsali spread out the sled beside Ehke. When her pack was full Tatsea helped Ikotsali slide her father onto the sled. Then she tied on her snowshoes and hung the tumpline across her forehead, settling the meat on her back. She carried more than half her weight in meat on her back.

"You break trail," Ikotsali said, stepping inside the strap he had tied to the sled.

Tatsea tramped through the snow, sometimes stumbling off the trail into snow so soft and deep she sank to her waist and floundered while Ikotsali waited wordlessly for her to struggle back up to the trail and resume the lead. She felt guilty at her clumsiness, guilty for her failure to kill the caribou before her father was hurt, and she feared this sore-faced man who had come to her rescue. Would he cause her mother and grandmother to blame her for her father's accident? Would her grandmother say she caused it by leaving the menstrual tent during her first blood?

Tatsea wished she had never gone hunting with her father and then she wondered if her father could have been hurt anyway, and what would have happened then? Would Ikotsali have found her father in the snow if she hadn't been screaming while she tried to make the fire?

The moon and the stars had moved into near morning positions by the time they stumbled into the camp.

Ikotsali laid her father beside the fire in her mother's tent, spoke a few words, did not blame Tatsea for anything. Then, after a short rest and a piece of drymeat, he nodded at Tatsea and they tramped back through the bush to get the rest of the meat before the ravens got to it. They packed all they could carry on their backs, following the dark trail faintly lit by the stars and the moon, a sliver like a knife.

And at last, inside her father's warm tent, chewing morsels of hot caribou, Tatsea crawled inside her sleeping robes beside the fire. Ehke was sleeping, moaning from time to time, but mostly sleeping peacefully.

Then, just as Tatsea felt herself entering a dream, Ikotsali spread his robes beside her and lay down to sleep. All night long Tatsea felt the mound beside her, though it never touched her once.

CHAPTER FIVE

TATSEA SHIVERED AND STARED UP AT THE DARK BOTTOM OF THE baby swing strung on two ropes across the tent. A raven squawked outside, then Ikotsali's breath beside her touched her cheek. She shivered again when she felt his hand resting lightly on her shoulder. The end of a spruce bough dug into the small of her back but she didn't move. Tatsea didn't want him to wake up yet.

On the other side of her husband she heard her father's faint snoring and her mother's whistling breath. Smoke from the green wood smouldering under the dryfish racks curled in through the open flap. The swing twitched as the baby coughed. Tatsea held her breath, waiting for the first morning cry. Then she breathed in the stink of her baby's moss bag.

Her husband's hand moved from her shoulder. Tatsea quickly closed her eyes. She stiffened when Ikotsali's lips brushed her cheek like a flick of her baby's eyelashes. Her heart drummed and she felt sticky as he slipped away from her side and tucked the bearskin cover around her before he crept out through the flap. Squawking and a flutter of wings told her that Ikotsali had chased the birds away from the toilet log. Tatsea took a deep breath and wiped the stickiness from her cheek.

A raven squawked on the peak of the tent and the baby's cough erupted into a loud cry. Without opening her eyes Tatsea reached up and pushed the swing with her foot. The crying faded and Tatsea tried to snuggle into a warm dream. Maybe he would be gone before she had to get up.

But the baby started to cry again. Another push with her foot cut off the cry, but just long enough for a gulp of breath.

"Bebia yewaedi," her mother scolded from the other side of the tent. Feed the baby.

Stumbling to her feet, Tatsea felt her milk leaking against the soft hide of her dress. She tried not to breathe in as she lifted the baby out of the swing and kissed her little brow. Then she grabbed the bag of dried moss hanging beside the flap and ducked outside into the morning air.

No one else stirred in the camp. Smoke mingled with the mist over the still lake, streaked by the sun shining through the treetops. Tatsea carried her little daughter between the other tents and the racks of drying fish to the log at the edge of the camp. The ravens protested her approach and flapped up to a tree. Tatsea glanced around, but Ikotsali was nowhere in sight.

Kneeling beside the log, she pulled the baby out of the bag and laid her on the grass. "Bebia goma," Tatsea said. "Stinky baby." The baby smiled, kicking and waving while Tatsea dumped the dirty moss. She would need to gather more moss today, she thought, wiping the baby with a clump of dry moss. For a few moments she watched her little daughter kick and wave in the fresh air. When the baby rolled over in the grass, showing the blue spot on her little bottom to the sky, Tatsea slipped her back into the bag and packed moss around her bottom, carefully leaving room for her daughter to kick her legs.

"Bebia nezi," she said. Nice baby. The baby gurgled, then shoved her fist in her mouth.

Tatsea sat down on a log beside the firepit to nurse her baby. Her mother would mutter at her later for not building the fire first to heat up the fist-sized cooking stones piled neatly beside the stomach pot resting in a hollow on the ground. Tatsea glanced at the tent, shrugged, then gazed into her daughter's eyes until they closed in contentment. She let her own eyes close while the baby's hungry mouth made her body tingle like she was in a special dream.

A sound soft as a breath of wind stroked her ears. Tatsea opened her eyes and tightened her grip on the baby. Ikotsali, small and hunched, walked toward her from the lake. Huge boils on his face and neck made him look like a giant frog from the time of the long-ago stories. Tatsea tried to hide her dread, but she couldn't stop the shiver that ran through her body. Even the baby stopped sucking for a moment.

Tatsea looked at the ground while her husband pulled a strip of dryfish from her rack. He sat down on the other side of the firepit, smiling at her as he pulled the dried flesh off the skin with his teeth. Tatsea forced herself to smile back, embarrassed at her reaction to Ikotsali's face. She couldn't help it. Even though she had known the frog-faced man since she was a little girl, each time she saw pus leaking from the boils on his face she felt her stomach pinch. Would she ever get used to having such a man for her husband?

"Our daughter has a big hunger," Ikotsali said, when Tatsea moved the baby's mouth to her other breast.

"I have much milk," Tatsea said, pleased at Ikotsali's interest in the child. If only his face wasn't so ugly.

Ikotsali threw the fish skin at a raven stealing toward them. He reached for his pack and stuffed in a few pieces of dryfish.

"I must go for birchbark and wood for paddles and axe

handles. I know a good place on a little island. I will check the nets on my way back to camp. We will need much food with such a hungry daughter." Ikotsali bent to pat the baby's head, thick with black hair, then reached out and brushed Tatsea's cheek with his fingers, so lightly Tatsea would have thought they were butterfly wings if her eyes had been closed. It took all her strength not to turn away from his touch and she was glad it was proper for a woman to look down to the ground in the presence of a man.

"Be careful when you go for moss," Ikotsali said. Pus from a boil beside his left eye oozed down his cheek. "I saw a bear swimming yesterday when I lifted the net. If a bear comes after you, run for the hole under the moss."

Tatsea tried not to shudder. Almost she had forgotten the fear she had felt the day Ikotsali had taken her to the clearing to show her the hole under the moss. At first she had just been confused. Why was this man showing her this hole? Then Ikotsali had walked backwards to the edge of the clearing. Without warning he had run at the hole and leaped over to the other side. He had showed her how to make the shortest jump, but then, when she landed on the other side, how to skip sideways to trick the bear into crossing at the widest part of the hole so it would fall in.

On that day, Tatsea had barely been aware that she would be having a baby, and she hadn't played with anyone since Dienda had gone away with his brothers in search of thundersticks, so she tried the jump many times until she thought she could do it with her eyes closed. She had been amused by Ikotsali's playful mood. Usually he was so serious she was afraid to speak to him. Usually he seemed like an old man, but on this day as they leaped over the moss-covered hole he had seemed like a boy.

After Tatsea landed another jump over the hole, Ikotsali caught her in his arms. For a moment, she thought she would wrestle with him, but he pointed at a pile of sticks he had hidden under a bush. When he pulled the sticks out Tatsea saw they were as straight as arrows, but thicker. Ikotsali pulled out his knife and picked up a stick. He cut away at the tip until it was as sharp as a spear. He gestured to Tatsea to pull out her knife to help him. Tatsea, still flushed from the playful jumping, worked at his side without even wondering why they were doing this.

Ikotsali said nothing, even when all the sticks had been sharpened at both ends. Then he picked up the sticks and carried them to the edge of the hole. He lifted up the layer of moss over the hole and Tatsea saw that thin branches had been laid over the hole to hold up the moss. Ikotsali slipped down into the hole and began shoving the pointed sticks into the ground, so they stood straight with sharpened points up. Then Tatsea understood, and she shivered. What kind of man was Ikotsali that he would think of such a thing? Tatsea wanted to shut her eyes, but her eyes wouldn't blink. Wide-eyed, she watched Ikotsali crawl out of the hole and arrange the moss over the branches so that the hole could no longer be seen. Would Ikotsali make her leap over the hole now?

As if he sensed her fear, Ikotsali gazed at her for a moment, then he planted two sticks on each edge of the hole to mark a path. Without warning he ran up to the sticks on one side and jumped. Tatsea nearly died until she saw him running away on the other side of the hole.

Now, after hearing Ikotsali's advice, Tatsea looked down at the toe of her moccasin, until Ikotsali turned away and carried his paddles down to the canoe. She had wanted to forget the sharp sticks under the moss. She had wanted to forget the Ikotsali who had put them there. When she couldn't see his sore face she almost loved her husband, his gentleness, his warm arms on dark winter nights. Ikotsali hadn't complained when the baby was a girl. He even seemed proud of their daughter's hunger.

Ikotsali pushed his canoe off the pebble beach and nimbly stepped in without wetting his feet. He waved at her, then with a few strong strokes paddled around the curving shore of the island, out of sight.

Tatsea shuddered then, reminded of another meaning for her

husband's words. In a hard winter when the caribou didn't come, a baby daughter's big hunger could be too much for a camp. Was Ikotsali thinking such thoughts? What did a man with such a sore frog face think? Were the whispered stories about his medicine power true?

The summer sun burned the mist off the lake. Tatsea heard Ehke snoring in the tent, and she thought about her father's twisted leg, how Ikotsali had pulled Ehke back to camp on the sled after being gored by a caribou. A crippled man's family needed a hunter, so her father had not refused when the man who had saved his life moved into their tent and took his daughter as wife.

The other tents were still silent. Ikotsali always got up early, no matter how late the sun stayed in the sky the evening before, no matter how late the handgame or the drum dance. Tatsea, too, liked the quiet of the morning, the aloneness before the work began. She glanced over at the half-scraped caribou hide stretched on the frame beside the tent. Her legs still ached from yesterday's hours of kneeling while she and her mother had scraped the hair off the skin. They would have to finish this hide today, before Ikotsali brought more fish to cut up and hang to dry.

The baby stopped sucking and grinned at her with a milky mouth. Tatsea wiped the baby's face and hugged her tightly for a moment, rubbing her nose against her baby's cheek. Her daughter burped milk over the quill pattern on the shoulder of her hide dress. Tatsea frowned, wiped the milk away, then tied the baby to her back. She picked up the two birchbark pails beside the firepit and set off to the water.

When she reached the pebble beach, she looked back. There was no sign that anyone was ready to get up. Here was her chance. Tatsea hurried along the curving shore, soon out of sight of the camp.

The water lapped against a large boulder half in, half out of the water. The baby had fallen asleep in the moss bag on Tatsea's back and didn't wake when she hung it on a spruce tree branch.

Listening for voices from the camp, she quickly hung her dress beside the baby and waded slowly into the lake until she was in waist-deep. After ducking under she washed quickly, for even in midsummer the water still felt very cold. Then she hurried to shore and slipped back into her dress.

The sun was well above the trees now, warming her where she sat on a rock squeezing the water from her long black hair. Tatsea ran her fingers through the damp strands to straighten out the tangles. Then she shook her hair to spread it over her shoulders to help it dry.

Tatsea leaned back and looked up. The sky was clear, not even a wisp of cloud in sight. A hawk circled above her. Hawk. That's what her name meant. What would it feel like to fly, to look down? The hawk circled lower, then swooped to the water and flew off with a fish in its beak. Tatsea shuddered, waiting.

A strange thunder cracked the air. She looked up at the cloudless sky and sniffed. She couldn't smell rain. Another thunder, like dead trees breaking.

The baby cried out in the moss bag. Tatsea jumped up, froze when a scream echoed from the camp. Thunder cracked again and something ripped through the branches over her baby's head.

CHAPTER SIX

TATSEA GRABBED HER BABY FROM THE BRANCH AND STUMBLED through the trees. The strange thunder cracked again. She stopped and nuzzled her baby's forehead to stifle a cry. She looked up through the branches to the patch of blue sky. She thought she heard laughter.

Tatsea took a few steps toward the camp. A woman's scream pierced the air. She looked down at the baby in her arms. Ikotsali had warned about a bear. She turned away from the lake, away from the camp. She knew a tree, a tree she had once climbed when she gathered moss.

When she reached the tree she climbed up and hung the baby in its moss bag on a sturdy bough so it rested on a fan of branches.

From the ground she had to squint hard to see the brown hide showing through the green needles. The baby whimpered and

Tatsea clutched the tree, but before she could begin to climb back up, the strange thunder cracked again. Then an even stranger sound rumbled from the camp, a deep growl, laughing. A bushman, Tatsea thought. Never had she heard of a bushman coming to a camp in midsummer, in daylight. But then never before had she heard thunder out of a clear blue sky.

She looked up at the patch of brown showing through the green branches. Should she climb up and hide with her daughter? But what about Ehke and her mother? How could Ehke fight the bushman with his crippled leg? And if a bushman came in daylight bringing thunder from a clear blue sky, what could her mother do? Why had Ikotsali gone for birchbark today?

She reached for two branches at eye level and tied them into a crude knot to mark the tree, even though she was sure she could easily find it, for she knew this bush well. Her family had camped here every summer for as long as she could remember.

Tatsea sneaked through the bush toward the camp. What if the bear Ikotsali had warned about was attacking the camp? Ehke once said to take a burning branch and touch it to a bear's nose to drive it away and in her mind's eye Tatsea looked about the camp for a branch she could put into the fire to get a good flame burning on the end.

A dry stick cracked under her foot, cracking like the thunder that came from a cloudless sky. She froze, looking ahead of her through the green needles of the spruces and pines. She tiptoed forward, her feet feeling each stone and clump of earth, each layer of fallen needles, brown and dry, slippery, and she felt the breeze brush her face. A raven squawked and for half a breath the bush fell more silent than the lake on the night of first frost.

Another scream echoed from the camp, so piercing and high-pitched it hurt Tatsea's ears. A roar followed, a roar half bear, half man, and Tatsea picked up a dry stick, a dry stick to catch fire quickly, and she rushed toward the camp, past the sticks marking the moss-covered hole hiding the sharpened sticks.

Tatsea quickened her step, crashing through twigs, letting

branches whip her face, no longer worried about silence. She heard another scream when she caught her first glimpse of the tents. Tatsea stopped short. It was her father's voice, more tortured than when the caribou broke his leg. She heard another crash of thunder, then a deep laughing voice bellowing strange words. This was not a bear.

She looked back in the direction of her baby hanging on the tree. She wanted to run back, but the strange laughing voices made her go forward. She could not leave without finding out what had happened to her family and the others in the camp. She stepped out into the clearing.

In one glance she saw the strange canoes pulled up on the beach, the strange men dragging her people from their tents, saw a man drag her mother by the hair, heard her mother scream, saw the flash of something covered with shiny blood, saw the man pull her mother's hair from her head, saw him rise up and lift the long, black, silver-streaked hair high in the air. Then she heard the man's laugh, roaring, deep and low like a bear's. Tatsea shrieked, then turned and began to run. But her shriek had cut through the deep laughter and the man pointed and hollered and bent to pick up a strange long stick from the ground.

Tatsea plunged through the bush, stepping on sticks and stones and slippery needles, her lungs gulping. Her body wanted to run for her baby, run for the tree and climb up to hug her baby in her arms. Her body wanted to do this, but then she heard Ikotsali's voice in her head, *watch out for the bear, watch out for the bear*. She turned sharply.

Behind her she heard the big man's growl; she felt him gaining on her, shouting, laughing like evil medicine. Tatsea pushed her legs faster until the trees blurred at the corners of her eyes. A deafening crash blasted her ears and something whizzed over her head and crashed into the tree ahead of her.

Tatsea stumbled, pretending she didn't know where she was going; for a moment she forgot where the hole was and she looked over her shoulder. Her pursuer stood still, surrounded by strange-smelling smoke. He held up his strange stick with both hands, the thick end of it pressed back against his shoulder. Then he lowered the stick, leaned it against a tree and pulled a bloody axe from his belt.

I can't die, Tatsea thought. I have a baby! I can't die! She darted ahead. Then she saw the sticks marking the hole under the moss. She looked back.

Her pursuer stumbled on a root, went down on one knee. Tatsea pretended to stumble, too, but as soon as the man rose she dashed forward, but a little slower, allowing him to catch up. He got so close she felt his fingers claw the back of her dress. Tatsea reached the sticks. Abruptly, she leaped forward, spreading her arms like a hawk in flight, peering ahead past the sticks where she would land, refusing to look down at the soft moss stretching over the hidden hole. Her feet began to run before she touched the ground and she fled without looking back. A yelp behind her, then a shriek and the cracking of sticks. A snarl and a roar, then a screeching yowl that faded into a moan.

I'm free, she thought. I can go to my baby now! But another man stepped out from behind a tree and before she could flee, her neck was locked inside a very strong arm.

Tatsea kicked and screamed but the strong arm cut off her breath and then a bloody hand appeared before her eyes, gripping the most threatening knife she had ever seen. A knife not bone or stone.

Tatsea closed her eyes to dream about her baby hanging on the tree in the bush all alone.

Then the arm around her throat relaxed a little and the man laughed. The knuckles of the bloody hand clasping the knife stroked her cheek and the man spoke words she couldn't understand. He laughed again, stroking her neck with the bloody hand; Tatsea thought of Ikotsali and wished she was back in the tent feeling Ikotsali's lips on her skin, wishing she could feel the pus from his ugly boils.

Her captor put away his knife and, with a movement so quick she had no time to struggle, he gripped her wrist and twisted her arm behind her back until she cried out. He laughed and shoved her in the direction of the camp.

Moaning sounds drew her eyes toward the hole under the moss, but she was too far away to see over the edge. The man who gripped her wrist didn't even pause to check on his companion. He just spoke words into her ear in a tone of voice that seemed almost respectful. For a few breaths his free hand stroked the hair over her ear. Then he pushed her forward again, stopping only to pick up the strange stick her first pursuer had abandoned against a tree. The man laughed when he saw the puzzled look on her face. He jerked her arm and touched the thin end of the stick to her cheek. Tatsea squirmed at the heat. The stick did not feel like wood or even a hot rock; it smelled of strange fire.

Then she was pushed from the trees into the smoke of the burning camp. Flames gulped at most of the tents; the raiders carried armfuls of dryfish to their canoes. Tatsea tried not to see when she was shoved past the bodies on the ground, the bloody heads, but her eyes would not close, her head could not turn away. She had to look at each bleeding scalp, at each dead and dying face. She had to look for sores beneath the blood. She had to know if Ikotsali had come back.

When the raiders spotted her they cheered and hooted and one of them, still a boy, ran up brandishing his knife in her face, but her captor spoke sharply and the boy slunk away to a canoe.

Tatsea's captor shouted a command and all the raiders scurried into the canoes. Tatsea was shoved toward the canoe where the boy waited with his knife. In her mind's ear she heard her baby crying from the tree in the bush and she tried to scramble out of her captor's grip. But the man was too strong and before she could kick or bite or scream she was flung into the canoe, face down on a pile of hair. Before she closed her eyes she saw the silver strands in the top scalp and the tiny yellow feather her mother had tied to her hair with a string of babiche.

CHAPTER SEVEN

IKOTSALI LOVED THE SEASON OF DRYFISH, THE SEASON OF THE long sun. It was the time of making new things—willow nets and birchbark canoes. With his new family he needed a bigger canoe for the time when they moved camp. He remembered Tatsea's soft warmth next to him under the sleeping robe while he paddled to a spot where bushes hung down over the water. He thought of their hungry baby as he pushed his canoe in behind the branches so no one could see it from the lake. In his mind he saw the toes of Tatsea's moccasins and he remembered how she had stared at them after he had told her to run for the moss-covered hole if a bear came. He wondered now if he had frightened her. Should he go back? But he needed birchbark.

Ikotsali took his axe out of the canoe and walked into the bush without a sound. Soon he came to a stand of birch trees. He stood silently for a moment, studying the trunks for large sections of unbroken bark. Then he chose a tree and set to work. With the knife his father had made from stone found at the place where the long-ago man, Yamozha, was born, he cut through the bark and carefully stripped it from the tree. He worked steadily, soundlessly, but in his head he sang an old song. He thought of Tatsea back at the camp with the baby. How his life had changed since Ehke broke his leg. Ikotsali felt like a man now; he was no longer alone. He had a family and his sore face and hunched body didn't matter.

Or did it? Even now Tatsea rarely spoke to him, rarely looked at him, and he could sense how she stiffened whenever he touched her. When he whispered to her in the darkness under the sleeping robes, when he told her about what he had seen that day in the bush, he was never quite sure if she was listening, for she never replied, never asked a question. Sometimes he imagined that her breathing changed when he told her about having seen an eagle or a hawk riding the wind.

Ikotsali wanted to tell Tatsea many things, things from his dreams, things from deep inside himself: how it felt to change into a frog, how it felt to be so alone that he wanted to throw his arms around a moose's neck just to feel another living thing. Sometimes he felt as if Tatsea wanted to hear about these things, but he could never make himself speak of them. Always something interrupted the moment—Tatsea would scratch herself, Ehke would cough, the old woman would thrash around in her robes, trying to find comfort for her aching bones on the sprucebough bed. Perhaps if he took his wife and child out alone for a few days they would be able to talk.

The caribou that crippled Ehke had also come too late to save Ehtsi, the grandmother. While the hot broth from the bull helped Ehke heal, Ehtsi had grown weaker and weaker, refusing food. This had frightened Tatsea, made her seem like a ghost even while Ikotsali kept her warm through the long, cold nights. She did not refuse his touch; rather, she seemed hardly aware of his presence, and when Ehtsi died, she wept for four days and then kept silent, not even speaking to her mother when the old woman scolded her about not having completed some task in the tent. Ehke seemed pleased to have a son—the old woman, too—there was someone to provide for them. Ehke's leg healed so he could stumble about with a stick, but he would never hunt again.

Ikotsali worked without stopping until he had a large stack of the white bark piled beside him. Then he loaded as much as he could on his arms and carried it to the canoe. The birchbark was light but he had cut so much that he had to make two trips.

On his way back for his second load Ikotsali heard a sound just a little different from the many other little sounds that make up the silence of the bush. It was a faint sound, like a whisper so soft he wasn't sure it was outside in the bush or just a thought inside his brain. He turned in the direction the sound had come from and stole through the trees so lightly he could have stepped on a worm without squishing it. He stopped at the edge of a small marsh. He heard a flap of wings, then a bird's cry, almost like a gull, but with more sounds. He peered between willows just in time to see a huge white bird, wings spread wider than a man's arms, set down in the shallow water beyond the tall grass growing at the edge of the marsh. For a few breaths he saw the red head moving above the pointed tips of the grass; then the head sank out of view.

Ikotsali's heart thumped so loudly he thought it would frighten the bird. A whooping crane nesting! Such a big bird would be much to eat, a change of taste from fish and caribou. He looked around the edge of the marsh until he saw a spot beyond the reeds where the trees grew to the water's edge. The air was still. Ikotsali moved like a shadow through the growth along the shore until he reached a point where he had a clear view of the shallow water. A whooping crane sat on a nest built of marsh plants on a spot where the wet ground rose slightly out of the water. A second crane, the bird that had just landed, stood facing the crane on the nest, tucking in its wings. A fish hung from its beak.

The first crane rose from the nest and its partner settled down in its place. Ikotsali expected the standing bird to fly away in search of food, but the bird stayed near the nest for a while, as if having a conversation with its mate on the nest. Then it strutted toward the shore until it faced the spot where Ikotsali hid. For a short breath Ikotsali thought the bird might attack him as it leapt into the air, but instead of darting at him with its long bill ready to snap, the whooping crane whirled in mid-air and flapped its wings, although it had no intention to fly. Instead, it repeated the movement again and again, adding twists and turns, wing movements and the occasional cry. Ikotsali wanted to laugh; the whooping crane made him remember a drum dance when Ehke, with two good legs, danced alone, circled by all the people in the camp. All alone the big white bird danced, unaware of Ikotsali's staring eyes. The crane was not dancing for its mate on the nest—its mate was facing the other way. The crane danced all alone, for itself, just for fun!

The dance continued until Ikotsali felt his foot prickling, gone to sleep. Then abruptly the dance ended and the crane waded back into the water, dipping its bill while it searched for food.

Ikotsali had lost all desire to kill and eat the big birds. Instead he felt a warm need to return to camp. He wanted to tell Tatsea about what he had seen.

CHAPTER EIGHT

THE YELLOW FEATHER FLOATED IN FRONT OF HER EYES EVEN though Tatsea kept her eyes pinched shut. She didn't move, didn't even twitch her nose pushed down into her mother's hair—and her father's and all her people's hair—except her baby's and Ikotsali's and Ehtsi's.

For a few breaths she heard her grandmother's death song, then Ehtsi's whisper, *We are all Ehtsi, we women. We are creators, we make life. Play dead and the bear will leave you alone.* Ehtsi had taught her this when she was still little. Had she played dead, would she still be with her baby daughter? Should she have stayed in the tree with her baby? Should she have waited while her family was killed? Was she wrong to have wanted to help?

If only she could fly like the hawk she was named for, flap her wings and fly from the canoe, fly to the tree where her baby hung in its moss bag. She felt her wings floating on the wind, tipping back and forth, riding up and down. She saw the moss bag through the spruce branches and heard her baby's tiny cry.

A knee thumped down between her legs, another on the outside of her left leg. She felt the canoe move over the water, gently tipping from side to side as the men shifted their weight with the movement of their paddles. Tatsea didn't move, even though a hard ankle pinched her right foot against the canoe frame.

Play dead. She heard Ehtsi's long-ago voice softly telling her how to play dead, how to let her body go soft and heavy, how to stay limp even when she was picked up. Again and again she had played the dead game until Ehtsi could pick her up and she still stayed soft and heavy.

Tatsea listened to Ehtsi's soft voice now, let her body go soft and sink into the pile of hair, into the ribs of the canoe. Her pinned foot softened until she barely felt the enemy's shin bone pressing on it. The motion of the canoe gave her the sensation again that she was flying, riding on the bumpy wind, flying to her baby on the tree.

A hard, flat object pressed against her arm; she recognized its shape. *Play dead, but don't fall asleep*, she heard Ehtsi's laughing voice. One day Tatsea had played dead so well she had fallen asleep. Tatsea let her body stay soft, but her arm remained hard even as she floated over the lake to the trees on the island.

Gusts of wind buffeted her hawk's wings. Then shouting from another canoe, shouting from her canoe. The canoe tilted as all the paddlers dug their paddles into the water on one side. She felt the canoe turn.

The men shouted, "Astam! Winsisk! Astam! Winsisk!" Tatsea's fingers rubbed over the cold, flat hardness, then found the wood. She did not take the time to wonder at the strange smoothness of the axe handle. She raised her head and saw the other enemy canoes giving chase to a small Dogrib canoe paddled by a small man.

Ikotsali!

She must not let them get Ikotsali! If he got away he could

find their baby! It was not just her baby, it was *their* baby! He must get away!

Without a thought to her own safety Tatsea raised the small axe. Before she could chop through the birchbark bottom a paddle clipped the side of her head. The world went dark and she didn't feel her face meet the pile of her people's hair, her body softer than if she had been playing dead.

CHAPTER NINE

WHEN HIS CANOE WAS LOADED IKOTSALI GOT IN AND EASED OUT past the branches. The water was still, like ice. Too quiet. Not even the cry of a seagull. Yet his neck tingled as if he had heard something. All around him the sun glinted off the water. Ikotsali scanned the spruce trees on the islands to his right, looking for eagles.

With strong strokes Ikotsali paddled back to the camp. Near the curve in the shore that hid the camp from his eyes, he caught a glimpse of Big Island in the distance. He lifted his paddle and let the canoe drift around the curve. His back stiffened at what he saw.

Two strange canoes were just pushing away from the camp. Each canoe held four men. One man held something up on a stick—the long flowing hair of a woman. Enda raiders!

A shout echoed when the Enda spotted him. Two raiders in

the nearer canoe threw down their paddles and then seemed to pick them up again and hold them in a way Ikotsali had never seen before. From a distance they appeared to be holding the blades of the paddles against their shoulders and pointing the handles at him. Thunder cracked. Smoke billowed around the canoe rocking on the still water. Ikotsali felt a strange wind overhead, then something splashed in the water behind him. He shuddered, feeling evil power at work. Another raider raised his paddle to his shoulder. Before Ikotsali could turn to flee a raider in the second canoe shouted and stood up. He raised his paddle high, then smashed it down on the water. His companions laughed, digging their paddles into the water to steady the canoe against the force of the blow.

Ikotsali didn't see the third canoe, didn't see Tatsea raise the axe, didn't see the paddle hit her head. He didn't see the third canoe turn and head off in the other direction.

The Enda laughed behind him, their huge canoes getting closer. Four strong paddlers in each canoe against one frog-faced man.

Anger gripped Ikotsali's heart, anger at the Enda who had slaughtered his people. His anger cried out to his spirit. He felt his legs tighten and wonder flashed in his brain at how like a frog a man was and he prepared to feel himself shrink. Could a frog swim all the way to shore from the middle of the lake? Would he need a leaf to float on, or maybe a log or a bit of birchbark? Should he throw his paddle overboard so he could leap onto it and float to shore?

Ikotsali felt the power move in his muscles, but he didn't shrink. Instead, his arms bulged until the hide of his sleeves tightened and almost stopped his blood. Wondering questions faded, and his mind calmed like the strangely still water around him. Ikotsali gave himself up to the power the way a canoe gives itself up to the rise and fall of water. He dug his paddle deep, but with such a lazy stroke not a ripple disturbed the water surface. The Enda raiders didn't notice how Ikotsali's canoe had surged away from them until it veered sideways and vanished among a cluster of tiny islands in the same moment the water from below heaved their canoes and spilled two men into the lake.

Ikotsali planned how he would circle back to the camp to take care of the dead, to play the drum to send his family's spirits home to the sky. Then he changed his thoughts. Getting away was not enough. He had to do more.

Ikotsali slowed his canoe and, holding his breath, he listened for the shouts of his enemies. He opened his ears as wide as he could. He heard their shouts, their paddles dipping furiously in the water. Ikotsali closed his eyes and with his dream eye he saw the enemy canoes on the other side of an island some distance behind him. With lazy strokes he paddled out from between two islands so they would be sure to see him.

Even before he glanced over his shoulder, he heard the strange shouts, "Astam! Winsisk!" He pretended to paddle hard while the canoe moved as slowly as the moon through an endless winter night. The Enda paddled viciously, closing in, their shouts echoing across the water, "Winsisk! Astam! Sacre bleu! Sonumbitch!"

Ikotsali let the raiders get so close that a lucky hunter's arrow could have reached him, then he put on a surge of power again. But as soon as he disappeared out of reach around the point of another island, he lifted his paddle to let the canoe drift. When the Enda rounded the point, they saw him slumped over his paddle, as if he needed to rest after each burst of speed.

Ikotsali had just dipped his paddle into the water again when thunder shattered the air. Before he could look over his shoulder something whistled over his head and plopped in the water ahead like a stone just dropped in. Over his shoulder he saw smoke surrounding the front canoe. In the second canoe a raider shoved a thin stick up and down into the handle of his paddle. Ikotsali's muscles bulged with each paddle stroke. He knew now he would have to keep a greater distance between himself and the strange Enda thundersticks. He thought of Tatsea and the burning camp and such a pain shot through his heart he almost dropped his paddle. Then he thought he heard his baby cry and the power surged through his muscles again.

Ikotsali led his pursuers across a wide expanse of water with no little islands. A small side wind stirred up the waves and Ikotsali seemed to be using the force of the wind to head for the point of a long arm of land reaching far into the lake. The Enda raiders started to gain on Ikotsali's canoe. Abruptly, Ikotsali turned his canoe into the wind, struggling to aim his canoe at the middle of the arm of land. Fighting the waves, the Enda raged behind him, then, drawing nearer to his canoe, cheered and laughed as they spotted what Ikotsali was heading for—an opening in the land the width of two canoes.

The Enda paddled with all their might, chanting like sick ravens—caw, caw, caw, caw. Ikotsali appeared to lose power, his canoe slowing, the Enda a mere canoe-length behind. Ikotsali struggled to guide his canoe into the gap. The Enda yelped like wolves leaping on a stumbling moose.

Ikotsali's light canoe skimmed over the shallow water of the gap. He heard the heavy Enda canoe scrape on the pebbled bottom, then snarls from the raiders forced to jump ashore to save their canoe.

Ikotsali led the Enda across a bay, deking in and out among tiny islands where the water was so shallow even he frequently struck rocks with his paddle. Then he hit the open stretch with the tall spruce tree on a point of land in the distance. All the branches, except for the crown, had been cut from the tree to mark the mouth of the river where the water was so shallow even Ikotsali's small canoe could not float there.

The Enda saw Ikotsali pick up his canoe, make a quick portage, then disappear around a bend in the river.

The Enda carried their canoes over the portage so fast that when they reached the water again half the men stumbled and fell into the river.

Down the river they chased to a small lake, where they found

Ikotsali waiting. Then Ikotsali streaked across the lake and disappeared around some islands and into the river again.

The Enda paddled harder and harder, eagerly rounding each bend, thinking only of the man they wanted to kill. Twice Ikotsali's little Dogrib canoe shot through rushing rapids that stopped the large Enda canoes dead. After they threaded their way through the rocks like a crippled hand sewing moosehide with a dull bone needle, they would see Ikotsali lazily paddling away on the other side of the rapids.

On and on they pushed, faster and faster, on and on. They chased Ikotsali over a long portage, sending runners ahead of the canoes, sure they had him. But again, Ikotsali was back in the water paddling calmly away.

Then once more they spotted Ikotsali disappearing around a large island in the middle of the river covered with swans. The Enda paddled harder, followed the current toward the side of the island where Ikotsali had disappeared. The sinking midsummer sun glanced off the swans, nearly blinding the raiders. Then they saw Ikotsali slumped over, one arm dangling over the side of the canoe. The Enda raced on. The first man in the lead canoe raised his paddle ready to strike. A second pressed his paddle blade to his shoulder and peered along the handle at Ikotsali. With a rushing noise that filled the air, the swans rose from the island, their wings gleaming white against the evening sun.

The Enda canoe was only a paddle-length away, but Ikotsali didn't move. It seemed he couldn't hear the enemy in the rushing noise of the swans' wings. The raider smashed his paddle down to break the Dogrib's head.

Ikotsali flashed into a small creek, hidden by willows. The Enda still heard the rushing noise even though the swans were gone. They dug their paddles deep to stop, but the river's force knocked the paddles from their hands.

The Enda howled as their canoes shot over the first waterfall, and then the gorge gaped before them.

The first canoe smashed on the rocks of the second fall,

hurling men into the raging water below. The second canoe charged over the falls, flipped in the air, and flung the raiders into the white spray, down deeper than the length of two tall trees.

A grim smile creased Ikotsali's face while he crept up to the bank overlooking the falls. Two raiders clung to rocks, their legs buffeted by the plunging water. One by one their fingers slipped from the wet stones. Screams echoed from the walls of the gorge. Ikotsali shivered until the roar of the falls washed all Enda voices from his ears.

CHAPTER TEN

TATSEA RODE THE WIND HIGH IN THE AIR, LIKE A LOG ON A WAVE rolling against the shore over and over again. She couldn't fly forward, forward to the island, forward to the tree where her baby screamed in her moss bag. Pain throbbed in her head, her wings pinned to her tail, legs joined at her feet. She couldn't move herself forward. She could only ride the wave of the wind, rolling into an invisible shore in the sky.

Looking down, she saw Wha Ti. She began to fall. Then she saw three canoes. Two canoes chasing one. Chasing Ikotsali. She cried out, her voice a raucous hawk screech.

Then she felt the hide strips binding her hands behind her back and the braided rope pressing her ankles together. Face down in the hair, she breathed in the smell of grease and blood. She heard paddles dip in the water, felt the canoe riding on the gentle waves. A man's knees loosely held her feet between them, knees covered with a strange kind of skin. She could feel the roughness through a hole in her legging between the top of her moccasin and the bottom of her dress.

The man's leggings scratched her skin like animal hide covered with short bristly hair. Tatsea remembered now what she had been too frightened to notice when she was fleeing through the bush. Her captor's leggings were the colour of the sky on a day without clouds. What strange animal grew hide the colour of the sky—a sky that brought thunder without the help of a single cloud?

With the strange thunder echoing through her mind, Tatsea saw her baby hanging alone on the tree; she wanted to tear her bonds; she wanted to roll and thrash around like a fish out of water; she wanted to tip the canoe and spill these killers into the lake, spill herself into the water.

But before she could move, before she could invite another paddle blow to her head—softer than a butterfly's wing, a breath on her ear stopped her; Ikotsali's face across the morning fire talked proudly about their daughter's great hunger. For a short breath in the dark of her closed eyes she saw Ikotsali stealing through the trees like a shadow.

She must live, she thought, she must live for her baby and for Ikotsali. As she let her body go soft, playing dead, she felt a faint cramping pain down in her belly and she heard Ehtsi's whisper, *"Men's fear of a woman's blood has its uses."*

But were these killers men? With their strange sky-coloured leggings, with their sharp knives and axes, their hard hot sticks smelling of strange fire? Were they men? Or were they Nahga, bushmen?

A paddler at the front of the canoe shouted a strange word. The men stopped paddling and shifted their weight. The canoe slowed and wobbled. The pile of hair rose and fell under her face. Tatsea raised her head slightly and opened her eyes.

Blood! She dropped her face into the darkness of the hair again. Was her head bleeding behind her eyes? She felt a bump over her ear where the paddle had hit her but she felt no pain in her eyes. She looked again without raising her head. All she saw was the black of hair.

Slowly she raised her head. She saw the red—but it was not blood. It was the back of the man in front of her. The kneeling paddler's hide-covered legs stuck out from a coat the colour of freshly spilled blood. Curved animal horns hung from straps on each side of the man's hips.

What strange creatures these killers were. They hunted people for their hair and killed animals with hides the colour of the sky and the colour of fresh blood. What strange land could they be taking her to?

The canoe slid along the water, the paddlers resting, chattering to each other. Tatsea raised her head a little higher to see over the edge of the canoe. She caught a glimpse of trees moving by. Then a hand slipped under her dress and grabbed the back of her leg just above the knee. Tatsea dropped her face back into the pile of hair and played dead. The hand stayed on her leg until Tatsea felt the canoe touch ground and stop. Then the hand moved away and she felt fingers undoing the knots that tied her wrists. Her arms slipped off her back to her sides and then she felt the fingers loosening the knots at her ankles.

"Astam!" the man said, prodding her side with a moccasined foot. Tatsea struggled to her knees but her numb legs and arms collapsed. The man prodded her again. "Astam! Winsisk!" This time she rose on one leg but stumbled, almost throwing the paddler with the red coat off balance. The man behind her laughed, then grabbed her dress at the shoulders and waist, lifted her easily and threw her over the side to the shore. Tatsea struck the ground, cried out, then played dead, listening to the men laughing while they unloaded the canoe. Then she heard footsteps approaching and she scrambled to her feet. She didn't want to be kicked.

The man with the blue leggings, her captor, walked up and grabbed her dress at the throat and raised his fist. He smiled at the fear in her eyes, then, instead of striking, he gently caressed her cheek with the back of his fingers. But before her fear lessened he shoved her away and pointed to a heavy pack on the ground. This Blueleg spoke roughly, his words strange, but Tatsea understood what to do. She knew what a woman was for.

Tatsea crouched beside the pack, bent forward and slipped her head inside the tumpline. She stood up and the pack, stuffed with dryfish from her people's camp, fell into place on her back.

Tatsea had barely found her feet when Blueleg added another pack to her load, a pack stuffed with the hair she had been lying on in the canoe. She stumbled sideways and her spine wrenched as if the dead lay heavy on her back. The voices of the dead cried out to her with such force she pitched forward. She reached out to break her fall. Eyes closed, on hands and knees, she listened to each voice, listened for the voice she did not want to hear.

Grunting sounds forced her eyes open. Tatsea struggled to her feet and saw the man with the red coat and a boy about Dienda's size pick up the canoe and balance it on their shoulders.

The men carried the canoe toward a trail through the bush. Tatsea started after them but Blueleg's voice stopped her. She waited, looking down at the ground, but out of the corner of her eye she watched Blueleg bend over a pile of four strange sticks. Animal horns, like Redcoat's, hung at his hips. He picked up two sticks, each with a belt attached. Blueleg looked at her, looked at the other two sticks on the ground, looked at the large pack beside them. He shrugged his shoulders and laid the two heavy sticks across her back, slipping the belts over her head so they crossed in front over her chest. Then he shoved her toward the trail.

With the strange sticks the load weighed more than a pack of meat, and the ends of the sticks pointing up caught on overhead branches until she learned to keep bent low enough to avoid most of them. But this added strain to her back and even though she had been carrying loads all her life she soon had a terrible backache.

At first Tatsea kept her eyes on the ground ahead of her, careful not to trip, careful to keep ahead of Blueleg with his long sky-coloured legs. She saw only the faint trail with an occasional caribou print left in a spot of mud or the scuff of a moccasin dragged through brown spruce needles. Once in a while she brushed mosquitoes away from her face. Then, where the almost invisible trail bent around a boulder, she noticed a patch of ground covered with caribou hair and she caught a glimpse of a piece of bone washed white from many rains. She broke her stride and turned her head to get a clearer look.

Behind her, Blueleg laughed his deep laugh and she immediately picked up her step, but now her eyes no longer focussed on the ground just ahead of her feet. Instead her eyes took in the details of the bush on both sides of the trail, details that looked familiar, as if she had been here before.

Then she remembered.

She had been hardly old enough to talk, but too big for her mother's back. Her father, Ehke, had killed a woodland caribou with huge velvet antlers while berry picking. Later, when her mother was scraping the hide, Tatsea wanted to help and when her mother put down the scraping bone to step away from the camp to relieve herself, Tatsea picked up the scraper and tried to scrape the hair off the stretched hide the way her mother had. When her mother wanted to take the scraper back, Tatsea ran away and her mother chased her around the camp until Tatsea tripped and skinned her knee. Her mother hugged her until she stopped crying, then picked up the scraper from where it had fallen. Later, her mother sewed new moccasins for her little girl.

Now Tatsea realized where she was. Her captors were taking her down a trail of her people to Tindee, the big water. If she could escape somehow she could easily find her way back to Wha Ti and Do Kwo Di, where her baby was hidden in a tree.

Tatsea risked a glance over her shoulder. Blueleg's mouth opened into a grin. With teeth missing on both sides of his top front teeth, he looked like a beaver. Tatsea returned her gaze to the trail before her. Had he noticed how she had been observing the bush? As if he could read her thoughts, Blueleg laughed his deep laugh even louder than he had before and he took a few big steps, closing in so that his breath seeped through the hair on the back of her head.

Redcoat and the boy had built a small fire at the end of the portage on the shore of a small lake. When she stepped into the little camp and lowered herself to the ground, the boy looked at Tatsea with hungry eyes. She barely had time to slip the heavy sticks off her shoulders before he rushed up to her and snatched a hunk of dryfish from the pack still on her back. Blueleg growled a few words and the boy backed away, but he watched her like a wolf circling a caribou, his teeth scraping a mouthful of the dried fish from its skin.

Emboldened by his fear of Blueleg, Tatsea glared into the chewing boy's eyes. He glowered back, raising the fish skin to tear off another mouthful. A fish bone pricked his cheek and he had to turn away to spit it out. Blueleg growled a laugh. The boy gritted his teeth and turned his back on the fire.

Tatsea hid a smile as she slipped the tumplines of the two packs from her forehead and, without a thought to her safety, she ducked into the bush to relieve herself. She listened to the men talking in low tones, but no one seemed to follow her. Could she lose these strange men in this bush? A twig cracked and when she looked toward the noise she saw Redcoat crouched behind a bush, chewing on a flap of dryfish, staring at her with unblinking eyes.

When Tatsea stepped back into the little camp, Blueleg lay stretched out beside the fire alone. He grunted and pointed to the pack with the dryfish in it. Tatsea pulled out a piece and handed it to him. He took it and gestured for her to take some for herself. She pulled another piece from the pack but after she took her first nibble she felt her breasts, heavy with milk, leaking against the hide of her dress. She almost choked on the dryfish as she cried out inside for her hungry baby crying in the moss bag on the tree on Do Kwo Di. Tatsea's heart stung; she whirled around and fled back down the trail. She ran without fear for herself, without fear of the men at the camp behind her, without thought about what she would do when she got back to the river without a canoe.

She heard Blueleg's deep laugh behind her at the camp, but he didn't seem to be following her. She ran past the spot covered with caribou hair. The dryfish flapping in her hand, she ran without thinking how far she would have to run or how she would last with her lungs already aching with each new gulp of air.

The boy stood at the riverbank, gazing up the river, chewing on dryfish. He held one of the strange sticks at his side. Tatsea stumbled, gasping for air. The boy spun around, fear on his face. Then his hungry look returned. Before she could flee he rushed at her and knocked her down. One of the animal horns swinging at his side struck her cheek. Exhausted, she kicked weakly while he pinned her to the ground and tore at her clothes.

A shout cut through the bush and the boy scrambled off, his knee crashing down on Tatsea's thigh. He grabbed for the strange stick he had dropped to the ground.

Blueleg strode up, holding his strange stick. He spoke roughly to the boy, pointing to Tatsea and then to himself. Tatsea belonged to Blueleg.

Then the older man spoke to the boy in urgent tones and pointed up the river. The boy shrugged his shoulders and shook his head. Then Blueleg raised his strange stick, resting the wide end against his shoulder, pointing the hard narrow end toward the sky. He put his finger through a ring and looked up along the stick. Thunder cracked and a cloud of smoke surrounded the man. Thinking the thunder would come again, Tatsea covered her ringing ears. Her nose stung from the smell of strange fire.

The two men cocked their ears, listening, then looked at each other and shook their heads. Blueleg looked at Tatsea still lying on the ground. "Astam!" he said. Tatsea struggled up from the ground. The boy raised his thunderstick and pointed it at her face. Tatsea shuddered. Blueleg laughed his deep laugh. The boy lowered his weapon, but Tatsea understood the threat in his eyes. She stumbled after her captors and never once looked back in the direction of her baby.

CHAPTER ELEVEN

IKOTSALI CROUCHED BESIDE THE FALLS. HIS EYES STARED, BUT HE saw nothing. His ears barely heard the water plunging over the cliff. He had seen too much; his head had no room for him to see more. Ikotsali rested in a black world, rested his eyes for the sight he had not yet seen.

The sun glowed low in the sky when Ikotsali's open eyes saw the world again. Like a shadow he slipped back to his canoe hidden up the tiny creek. He pushed the canoe into the river and with gentle strokes he paddled upstream, leaving the roar of the falls behind him.

No power filled his muscles now, just a slight ache when he dug his paddle against the current. Ikotsali didn't think about where he was going. He didn't worry about the sun setting behind the trees. He didn't see the flock of white swans settling on the wide marsh along the river's edge. He didn't notice his empty stomach or the birchbark still piled in the front of his canoe. His head only allowed him to see enough to keep the canoe moving up the river.

For a while in the silvery light of the midsummer night, a pair of beavers swam alongside the canoe. Ahead of him a loon called each time he switched his paddle from left to right. Frogs sang in the pools of still water where the willows hung over the shore. Near the rapids a moose stepped out of the bush to drink. Ikotsali set down the canoe many times during the portage past the rapids. A few times he stumbled when his foot caught on a root. Once he fell. The canoe crushed a clump of cranberry bushes. Ikotsali's fingers trembled as he caressed the birchbark, feeling for damage.

Back in the canoe, with the rushing water dragging him back toward the rapids, for a few heartbeats his paddle seemed made of stone. Then all the aching muscles in Ikotsali's body woke to force the canoe across the current to quieter water. Each stroke sent jabs of pain through his shoulders, but he felt alive again, and his paddle soon found a rhythm like the beat of a slow drum.

When Ikotsali reached Wha Ti, the rising sun caught the single tall spruce tree at the end of the point of land that divided the two shallow bays he needed to cross before he got to the big lake. Ikotsali's father had told him that it was his father's father who had first stripped off the branches halfway to the crown so the tree could help people find their way. His father had told him, too, that the Barrenland people piled rocks to mark their trails because they had no trees. These thoughts floated in Ikotsali's head while he paddled through the shallow water, occasionally hitting his blade against an underwater rock. These thoughts were there, but they were just part of every other thought stored in his head in his lifetime. Ikotsali made no attempt to harness any of his thoughts to make power.

The sun blazed overhead when Ikotsali rounded the silent curve of Do Kwo Di. Not even a raven squawked in his people's camp. Not a wisp of smoke rose from the firepits. The fish racks lay splintered on the ground and only Ikotsali's own tent still stood upright. The others leaned in charred collapse.

The frog-faced man let his canoe drift on to the pebbled beach and then he sat for a moment, eyes closed, clearing his head for what he would have to see. Then he stepped ashore and walked softly up the slope to his tent. His eyes took in the bodies scattered about the camp, but he didn't allow himself to look too closely. He wanted to see Tatsea and the little one first.

Tatsea's mother sprawled face up beside the firepit. Ikotsali hardened his eyes when he saw the bloody top of her head where her hair had been. Ehke lay crumpled in front of the tent flap, his bad leg bent beneath him. Ikotsali crawled into the tent. The baby swing hung limp in the dim light. He rummaged through the sleeping robes.

Ikotsali crawled out of the tent and forced himself to face each bloody body. He turned over those who had fallen face down and studied each face. Three times he checked each corpse. Then he searched the edges of the camp and followed footprints to the bathing rock. He remembered his last glimpse of Tatsea and the baby kneeling beside the fire. The last words he had spoken to his wife echoed through his head. *Be careful when you go for moss.*

Ikotsali crouched on the beach beside the bathing rock and studied the footprints. Footprints in the pebbles were hard to read but he followed a set of impressions up from the water until he spotted a birchbark pail tipped over beneath a tree. He noticed a freshly broken branch a little higher than a person's head. Down on the ground a moccasin print pointed into the bush. Perhaps Tatsea had gone for moss before the Enda raiders came.

Without bothering to look for more footprints, Ikotsali set out for the moss patch the women usually went to.

He broke stride when he spotted the ragged gap in the moss, then stole nearer until his eyes made out the bloody tip of a stake poking through a man's back. Circling the death hole, Ikotsali noticed the man's neck impaled on another stake. A glint from the bottom of the pit drew his eyes to the dead man's arm, dangling with fingers spread as if reaching out. Ikotsali crouched, and as he squinted into the shadows he saw an axe with a shiny edge lying below the dead man's hand. From the look of his clothing, this man was a stranger and the axe was not like any axe Ikotsali had seen before.

But Ikotsali had other concerns, so he rose to his feet and stepped back to peer at the stranger impaled on the stakes. He noted the direction the man had fallen. He must have been running. He must have been chasing someone from the camp, someone who knew where the hole was. Tatsea knew. He had taught her how to lead a bear over the hidden hole. Had the raider been chasing his Tatsea? Had their daughter been on her back?

Another look along the body revealed scrape marks in the mossy ground beyond the dead man's head. Ikotsali walked his eyes along the scrape marks, then stepped around the hole and followed the scuffs of running feet through the trees until the marks stopped.

Ikotsali leaned forward with his hands on his knees to scan the dry leaves, fallen needles, and low cranberry bushes for a sign of the runner's trail. No sign caught his eye, but when he straightened up he heard a cry so faint that at first he thought he had heard it only inside his head. But the cry came again and again and as Ikotsali followed his ears, his eyes were drawn upward. The cries grew louder, started and stopped, leading him between trees and around bushes. Keeping his eyes on the branches above him, he stumbled into trees, tripped on stones and roots, turned in circles. Then he spied a brown lump showing through the green boughs of a spruce tree. The brown lump did not look like a nest. The cry came again. Ikotsali needed no more. He shinnied up the tree.

Mosquito bites covered the baby's face but Ikotsali could see that she was his daughter. For a long time he hugged her, stroking her tiny head, singing a soft song his mother had sung long ago. The baby's tiny mouth sucked at the air as she looked at Ikotsali's face with wide eyes. His touch calmed her but she could not sleep. Ikotsali felt the baby was keeping her eyes fixed on him as if she feared he might disappear.

Then the baby cried out with hunger again. Ikotsali hung the moss bag around his neck so the baby rested on his back and he crept down the tree and hurried back to the camp.

With the baby on his back he shifted Tatsea's mother and father away from the tent and the firepit, murmuring a few words to promise the spirits he would take care of the dead, but first he must take care of the living. Then he built a fire in the pit and set the cooking stones in the fire before he picked up a bark pail and walked to the water's edge.

On his back the baby woke up and cried when he set the pail beside the fire. Ikotsali thought of Tatsea's breasts filled with milk. This baby had tasted no other food. This baby had no teeth. Ikotsali picked up the pail and tipped it to his mouth. He held the water in his mouth until it was warm. Then he lifted the baby from his back and dripped water into her crying mouth.

She stopped crying, startled at the strange taste. Ikotsali leaked more water into the baby's mouth. The baby swallowed. When his mouth was empty Ikotsali grinned at his daughter's staring black eyes. Then she burped up the water all over the front of his shirt and began to cry again.

Ikotsali hugged the baby close to his chest, confused and afraid. The baby nuzzled his shirt, trying to fasten her mouth to a nub of hide sticking out from his shirt like a nipple. *Whitefish*. He heard Ehtsi's old-woman voice speak in his ear. The grandmother of his wife had died in her sleep five nights after Ikotsali and Tatsea had brought Ehke home with his broken leg. *Whitefish*. The old woman whispered like water lapping the sand of a beach.

Ikotsali acted decisively then. He fastened the baby to his back, making sure she was secure. Then he ran for his canoe. He paddled harder than when he had been chased by the Enda. He knew exactly where his net was. Without even squinting against the sunlight sparkling off the lake, he saw the dark tops of the poles sticking out of the water.

With practised hands he lifted the willow net. He eyed each fish for signs of life before he pulled it from the net. The net had not been lifted for two days. Ikotsali needed a fresh fish, a fresh whitefish still flopping around. By the time he had lifted the whole net he had three large whitefish, still fresh.

Back at the camp Ikotsali built up the fire in the pit and piled the cooking stones in the flames. He rinsed out the birchbark cooking pail and filled it with fresh clean water. He gutted and skinned the whitefish, then cut the white flesh into small chunks and dropped them into the pot. Patiently, he brought the water to a boil, pulling the cooled stones out and dropping them back into the fire, picking up the hot stones and slipping them gently into the pot. From time to time he stirred the fish in the pot with a stick.

The baby's hunger was not so patient and Ikotsali almost gave the baby some of the fish soup long before the water boiled, but he remembered words from his mother, words about a baby dying from fish that was not well cooked. Still, the baby's crying made him feel uneasy, so he placed the baby under his shirt against his bare chest and helped the tiny mouth find his nipple.

The baby was still asleep when Ikotsali decided the white milky soup had cooked long enough. But how to feed the soup to the baby? Ikotsali looked at the tiny face nuzzling his chest. He thought of Tatsea's full breasts. Then he remembered the sneeze in the menstrual hut, the eye watching him through a hole in the hide wall.

He looked around the camp. Tatsea's hut was no longer there. What did a woman do with the tools of her first blood? Did she save the hood, the scratching stick, and the drinking tube? Ikotsali knew of the bundle Tatsea always made sure she packed each time they moved camp.

He rummaged through the tent. Under a corner of the sleeping robe he found it, a smooth stick and a hollow swan's-leg bone wrapped in soft hide. He hesitated for a moment, fearing to disturb a woman's power. Then the baby cried again and he picked up the hollow bone and returned to the fire.

Holding the bone between his teeth, he dipped a cup into the soup. Then, with the baby in position at his nipple, he sucked up some soup with the drinking tube. Slowly, he dribbled the milky liquid over his nipple into the baby's sucking mouth. At first he twitched when the baby's gums closed on his nipple and he had to force himself not to move. After a few refills of the tube, however, a pleasant tingling spread all over his body, lulling him into closing his eyes, and he had an amusing thought that he was becoming a woman. What power that would be. Then the baby clamped her gums down hard to remind him she needed more soup, and he jerked open his eyes and refilled the tube. He repeated this until the baby's stomach filled and she fell asleep in his arms. Wide awake then, Ikotsali waited through the starless night, listening for his baby's every breath.

CHAPTER TWELVE

BLUELEG DID NOT TIE HER UP WHEN THEY CRAWLED BACK INTO the canoe. Instead, he handed her a paddle. At first Tatsea knelt in the canoe, loosely gripping the paddle blade like an ignorant woman who had no idea what to do with it. Blueleg snarled behind her and yanked her hair. Tatsea fumbled for the correct end of the paddle and with huge body movements splashed the blade around in the water, rocking the canoe from side to side. Behind her Blueleg growled his loud laugh, then jabbed his paddle butt hard into her ribs. Tatsea shrieked, then paddled properly, painfully matching the rhythm of her enemies.

By the time they crossed the lake and headed down a small river, Tatsea decided she preferred paddling to lying trussed up with her nose buried in a pile of scalps. By and by the sun hung low in the sky and Tatsea expected the men to make a camp for the night. But they kept on paddling. When the sun had slipped behind the trees, Blueleg muttered an order and Redcoat pulled dryfish from the pack, tossed pieces at Blueleg and the boy, then flung another so it slapped Tatsea's chest. Tatsea dropped her paddle and tore at the fish with her teeth to make sure she ate it all before a poke in the ribs forced her to paddle again.

The summer sun slipped behind the horizon just far enough to dim the golden glow while leaving enough grey light to follow the river ahead of them. At first Tatsea thought how cruel of these men to push on without sleeping, but after the boy turned and glared at her Tatsea wished they would never need to stop to make a night camp.

Then she dozed off and she knelt inside Ikotsali's tent, cradling her baby girl inside her dress, enjoying the sucking mouth on her breast. Ikotsali watched from his sleeping robe, his head propped up on one elbow. His eyes shone in the small firelight, his sore-splotched frog face the most pleasing sight she had ever seen.

A shout startled her from her dream. Tatsea shut her eyes again to keep the enemy canoe from spoiling her dream world. The dream was so real even her breasts felt empty from suckling her child. More shouts erupted from the men's throats. Then she felt the canoe slow and she opened her eyes before she might attract another jab in the ribs from behind. The current was drawing the canoe toward the mouth of the river. The big water, Tindee, lay before them, waves rolling under the early morning sun as far as her eyes could see.

At first Tatsea thought the men would land at the mouth of the river, but a shout from Blueleg set the others back to digging their paddles into the water. Tatsea joined them, still feeling the bruise in her side from Blueleg's paddle butt. The lake was much rougher than the river and Tatsea felt her empty stomach rise and fall with the roll of each wave.

She had only visited the shores of Tindee a few times in her life and never had her family ventured far out onto the lake. Her people seldom followed this particular river to the big lake.

Mostly her people travelled the Whati Dee river past the big waterfall to Golo Ti Dee river heading north to the Barrenland. For a moment she wondered if the other enemy canoes had chased Ikotsali down Whati Dee. Had they caught him? Her strangely empty breasts rubbed against her hide dress and hope crept through her body. Tatsea did not understand why she felt this hope but she knew that she must get away. She must get back to her baby.

The sun hovered overhead when Blueleg shouted an order to head toward shore. When Tatsea stepped ashore she scurried into the bush to relieve herself.

No one appeared to follow her so with soft steps she stole away through the trees, sidestepping dry sticks and crackling leaves. Only her beating heart disturbed the stillness. Tatsea dared not look back, dared not let fear stop her. In her mind's eye her baby snuggled in Ikotsali's arms beside a small fire. The bush air hung hot and still. Flies and mosquitoes swarmed around her but Tatsea dared not even swat at them for fear of rustling branches with the swing of her arm.

She hesitated as she peered through leaves into a clearing, then froze. Three woodland caribou and a calf grazed on the short grass. Instinctively, she reached to her waist for the pouch carrying her knife, the knife she would have carried had she had time to prepare for a journey. Just when she realized that the knife wasn't there, she felt a weight slide over her shoulder beside her right cheek.

A warning grunt kept her from moving as the end of the thunderstick pushed out past her nose. The stick exploded. Her head turned to stone. Through the stinging smoke she watched one caribou fall, while the others darted into the trees without a sound. The thunderstick shuddered. Tatsea felt Blueleg's laugh, but heard nothing. Blueleg drew the thunderstick back past her nose. Smoke curled into her nostrils, setting off a sneeze that knocked the thunderstick off her shoulder. The sneeze popped open her ears, and the groans of the dying caribou mingled with his laugh.

Blueleg shoved her roughly toward the fallen caribou. Blood gushed from a hole in its side; Tatsea looked about for an arrow or a spear. Blueleg snorted at her puzzlement, then he put his hand into a pouch at his waist and pulled out a small black pebble, round like a berry. He held it up to the hollow end of the stick, then moved his hand to show how the ball could shoot out of the stick to the caribou to pierce the hide. Tatsea looked at the dead animal, thinking about the other three animals who had fled the thundering noise. A silent arrow or spear could have killed all the animals for a hungry family.

Then Blueleg pulled his sharp knife from his belt. Sunlight glinted off the shiny edge of the blade. Blueleg knelt beside the caribou and plunged the knife into its throat, then slit the hide down to the spot between the forelegs. Tatsea had never seen a knife cut so easily, so cleanly. Blueleg growled grinned at her wide eyes, then held out the knife to her, blade first.

She stumbled backward a step, fearing the magic of such a knife. Blueleg laughed, then flipped the blade in the air. He caught it by the blade, then offered her the handle. Hesitantly, she reached out and took the knife. He spoke and gestured toward the caribou. Then he picked up the thunderstick.

Tatsea knelt beside the caribou and set to work skinning the animal. Once she got used to holding the handle, the strange knife cut easily. For a while she was so enthralled with the work of butchering the animal she almost forgot her captors. She had just finished peeling back the hide from the rib cage when she paused to catch her breath and realized that she was alone in the clearing.

Ikotsali and her baby appeared in her mind's eye again. At first she saw memories—the baby in its moss bag up in the tree, Ikotsali paddling frantically away from two Enda canoes. But then she saw scenes she didn't remember—Ikotsali huddled inside a dim tent with the baby inside his shirt; the baby crying on a tattered bearskin beside Ikotsali heating stones in a fire. Tatsea felt her milk dripping inside her dress. She must escape. She looked at the blood-covered knife in her hand. With such a knife she could easily survive in the bush while she made her way back to Wha Ti and Do Kwo Di.

Tatsea started to get to her feet, but a crack of killing thunder echoed from the bush behind her. She remembered how the caribou had fallen. She looked at the half-skinned animal in front of her. She saw the hole in the meat. Now was not the time to run. The men had their thundersticks. How far could the killing power of the thundersticks reach?

Instead of trying to escape, Tatsea set about gutting the animal. With her practised hands and the sharp knife, she separated the stomach from the intestines; then she cut out the heart, liver, and tongue. She heard brush crackling and the sound of grunting and laughing. She looked up to see Blueleg and Redcoat dragging another caribou from the bush. The boy followed with the thundersticks over his shoulders.

The men dumped the caribou beside Tatsea. Blueleg gestured at her and then at the animal. He barked a command and the boy scrambled to gather firewood. Blueleg and Redcoat pounced on the heart, liver, and tongue, which Tatsea had set aside. At first Tatsea thought they would eat the raw flesh the way the Barrenland people did, but instead they cut it into strips. The boy built a roaring fire and the men sharpened sticks they stuck in the ground at an angle over the fire to roast the meat.

Tatsea noticed the spit dripping from the men's mouths as they eyed the cooking meat. If they eat until their stomachs want to burst, they will get very sleepy, she thought. That would be the time to escape. She could even steal their canoe.

As she cut the stomach out of the second carcass, an idea popped into her mind. Cradling the stomach, she stood and held it up. Blueleg barked an order and Redcoat grabbed the stomach from her hands and bolted toward the lake. The boy gathered fist-sized stones and arranged them in the fire. Tatsea knelt to her task again, cutting meat into tiny pieces.

Redcoat returned with the washed stomach filled with water. Blueleg arranged the cooking stones in the fire while the boy gathered more dry logs to keep the fire going. Tatsea found a small hollow in the ground near the fire and rested the water-filled stomach in it. She cut a length of intestine from the pile of guts and squeezed out the contents and laid it on the grass near the stomach pot. After a while she noticed the first stones turning red in the fire. She pointed them out to Blueleg, then spread open the top of the stomach. Blueleg, using two sticks, picked up a hot stone and dropped it into the stomach. Tatsea quickly closed off the opening to keep in the steam from the hot rock sizzling in the cold water. Blueleg picked up another rock and they repeated the procedure. After half a dozen rocks, Tatsea tied off the top with the length of intestine and let the stomach sit.

Blueleg handed her a stick with a piece of roasted heart on it. Tatsea chewed it slowly, savouring the taste.

Soon more rocks glowed red in the fire. Tatsea carefully opened the stomach just enough to allow Blueleg to fish out the cooled rocks. Then he quickly dropped in red-hot ones and Tatsea tied off the stomach again.

It took a long time for the water to come to a boil and even longer to cook the meat inside. But while they waited for the stew to cook, they munched on roasted bits of tongue and heart and liver. Tatsea continued to cut the meat into chunks that could easily be packed into the canoe. She knew how to feed men and by the time the stomach pot nearly burned her fingers, all three men leaned back lazily enjoying their filling bellies. By the time they had eaten their fill of the delicious stew, Tatsea didn't think they would be able to move.

Tatsea ate her fill, too, but like a well-behaved woman she did not eat too much. Blueleg had made no effort to take his knife back from her, so when she set about wrapping the chunks of meat in the hides, she slipped the knife under her dress into the belt that held up her leggings.

When she finished wrapping the meat, the sun settled behind the trees, leaving the clearing with a silvery light. The boy lay on his back with one arm over his stomach, the other laid over his face. Redcoat and Blueleg sat near the fire, now just a patch of glowing coals. Tatsea rested on her knees beside the wrapped meat, pretending to be sleepy. Loons called each other on the lake. Redcoat lay back and then rolled over onto his side. Blueleg lay back, too. His eyes appeared to close. Tatsea waited, listening to their breathing. Hardly daring to take in her own breath, she sat so still she looked like she was asleep.

One of her captors began to snore, then two. Tatsea waited to hear the third man join in. It took a long time. At last, as Tatsea felt herself dozing off, she heard three separate snores going on at once. Tatsea wiggled her toes, tightened and relaxed her muscles to get the blood flowing through her cramped legs. Then she stood and tiptoed away from the fire.

An arm's length from the trees she was grabbed from behind and pushed to the ground. Blueleg sat on her stomach while he tied her wrists above her head. He dragged her to a tree and tied the end of the rope around the tree. With another rope he quickly bound her ankles. Tatsea didn't even bother to scream. No friend would hear her and a struggle would only invite a beating.

Blueleg stood up and looked down at her, the dim light revealing just the whites of his eyes. He turned away, then suddenly crouched beside her and fumbled under her clothing. Tatsea held her breath, expecting the worst. Then his hand found the handle of his knife at her waist. He drew it out, caressing her skin with the blade until she shuddered; then he lay down nearby, leaving Tatsea to stare at the summer night sky that was too bright for stars.

CHAPTER THIRTEEN

IKOTSALI SPENT A DAY AND TWO NIGHTS FEEDING AND CRADLING the baby in his arms before he set about the heavy task of taking care of the dead. He feared to leave the baby alone for even a moment. Since the baby had been left alone on the tree, Ikotsali believed it was vital to have her feel his presence at all times.

Then on the morning after the second night, he emptied the baby's moss bag and stuffed it with fresh moss. He tucked her inside and tied her to his back the way a woman would have, and he took his axe and began to build stages for the dead. It took three days until he had all the bodies from the camp laid out respectfully on the stages. Using his stone knife he cut strips of hide from what was left of the tents and tied them to the stages so they could flutter in the wind to keep the shadows of the dead from abandoning their resting places and losing their connection with their land.

In the tent spared by the raiders' fire, Ikotsali found Ehke's drum, safe in its bag. After feeding the baby with the drinking tube he beat the drum softly, singing a mourning song for each of the dead. He drummed and sang all night long until the sun climbed back into the sky. Then he fed the baby again and built a large fire in the middle of the camp. He burned all the possessions of the dead, the tents, the sleeping robes, the clothing. He dragged the smashed canoes up from the beach and laid them on the fire. Then, with the baby tied to his back, he picked up the drum, and he beat the carved stick against the thin tight drumskin, shuffling his feet in a slow dance around the fire, around and around and around until the fire died down to a layer of glowing coals.

Then the drumstick took hold of his hand and changed the beat of his drumming. He felt his tongue move, a force gripped his voice, and a new song sang from his lips, a song he had never sung or heard before—a song about Tatsea, the hawk. On his back, the baby woke up without crying, and seemed to sing along with his new song about her mother, and Ikotsali saw, just for an instant, Tatsea stumbling toward him through deep snow on snowshoes.

Ikotsali continued to sing and dance around the dying fire for a long time, but the brief vision didn't return. At last his voice and legs could not continue the dance. He sat down beside the cooking pit and heated up the baby's food, and after he nursed her with the drinking tube he cradled her inside his shirt until they both fell asleep.

When he woke Ikotsali gathered up a few cooking pots, his axe and knives, his bow and arrows, his harpoon, and loaded them into his canoe. He was about to push off and leave the camp when he remembered the enemy raider impaled on the sticks in the hole. Warily, he stole through the trees. Crouching beside the hole, he saw the axe on the bottom. He reached in and pulled it out. Then a sheath at the man's waist caught his eye. He reached in to pull out the knife and discovered a pouch filled with strange black pebbles. The Enda raider's medicine bag, Ikotsali thought, so he dumped the pebbles out of the bag onto the man's body. He decided not to touch the curved animal horn hanging from a strap around the man's neck and shoulder.

For a moment he considered covering up the man with dirt and leaves, but then thoughts of all the killing that had been done convinced him that the man deserved to hang from the stakes, like meat on a stick. So he took the knife and the axe and returned to the canoe.

Singing softly to the child gazing up at him from the canoe bottom, Ikotsali paddled with steady strokes, searching for another camp of Dogrib people.

CHAPTER FOURTEEN

IN THE MORNING BLUELEG SLASHED TATSEA'S BONDS AND SHOVED her into the canoe where Redcoat and the boy already waited. She couldn't even rub her sore wrists and ankles before a sharp jab in her back signalled her to pick up the paddle and set to work. Exhausted, her arms ached. Every time she had moved in her sleep the rope tied to the tree tightened around her wrists. Breathing so slowly she thought she might die, she had waited for Blueleg to begin snoring so she could wriggle closer to the tree to relieve the strain on her arms stretched out above her head. In the night silence her body's dragging on the ground had grated as loudly as a canoe's rubbing on sand; her heartbeat had echoed like a drum. And then, when she had felt almost comfortable, she had slid onto a sharp root poking up from the ground.

The morning sun blazed hot even after they had left the shore behind. No clouds hung in the sky and the breeze hardly cooled their faces while they dug their paddles into the rolling waves.

For the first time after days of following the northern shore, the men appeared to be heading south, away from shore, farther out onto Tindee, the big water, than they had ventured before. Tatsea didn't notice at first. She concentrated on the rhythm of the paddling, trying to keep time with the men, trying to move in the least painful way for her aching body. From time to time she felt her head turn to stone, and for a few paddle strokes the world would be silent as death. Then her ears would open to the paddle dipping in the water. Tatsea cringed from the touch of the thunderstick resting against her kneeling leg. During one moment of deafness a pause in the paddling made her look up and she shuddered. On all sides of the canoe Tindee's waves stretched as far as her eyes could see.

Then Tatsea noticed that her captors were shielding their eyes and peering to the south at a group of islands barely visible across the shimmering water. After some discussion the men dug in their paddles with new energy, the islands appearing to be within easy reach, but after relentless paddling in swelling water Tatsea saw no lessening of the distance. Her arms ached and the kneeling cramped her legs so she could barely wiggle her toes to keep the blood moving. The light breeze brought no cooling under the burning sun; Tatsea's hide clothing heated up so hot it nearly burned her skin. Only the coolness of the canoe bottom gave any relief to her cramped legs.

On and on they paddled over the rolling lake, the rhythmic strokes as regular as breathing. After a while the glittering water burned Tatsea's eyes and she closed them without disturbing the rhythm of her paddling, shifting from side to side at the barely audible signals from Blueleg behind her. Tatsea felt herself drifting away even as she paddled. The regular movement of her dress against her breasts took her back to the camp on Do Kwo Di. The sucking baby seemed so real that Tatsea prepared to let go of her paddle to cuddle her daughter and shift her little mouth to the other breast. Her mother's face floated in the dim light of her eyelids, and Tatsea felt a tear seep down her cheek when an understanding overwhelmed her—both she and her baby had lost their mothers on the very same day.

Heat seared in front of her face. A horrendous crash. Tatsea's eyes flashed open to a blackening sky. Wind blasted her face; thunder cracked louder than a thunderstick beside her ear. The heaving waves doubled in size, lifting the canoe high in the air. The men wrestled with their paddles.

Her aching arms forgotten, Tatsea pitched into the struggle. Lightning flashed, setting off thunder like a giant old man clearing a throat as big as the sky. The canoe rose and plunged, rose again so high the boy screamed; the canoe slipped sideways off a wave, but before the wave could collapse and swamp the canoe, another wave heaved them up again.

Many times Tatsea feared she would be flung from the canoe, but Blueleg behind her and Redcoat in front seemed to know just when their weights needed to be shifted so the canoe worked with the waves, not against them. Blueleg shouted commands; Tatsea obeyed, without knowing his words. Still, water splashed into the canoe and she knelt in water beside the bag of scalps getting soaked. She wanted to throw her people's hair into the lake, but she didn't dare let go of her paddle, didn't dare to break up the paddling to shove the bag over the side. She could not drown yet.

Then, as suddenly as the squall had come up, the wind stopped and the sky cleared. With aching muscles and wet clothes, they lurched to the nearest island, reaching a stony beach in the light of the sun hovering low in the northwestern sky.

The men stripped off their clothing and hung it on trees to dry. Then they spread out the scalps on the ground. Tatsea turned away, but not before she glimpsed the little yellow feather in her mother's hair. What did these strange men want with her people's hair?

She stripped off her moccasins and leggings and hung them on a branch to dry. The little stones tickled the soles of her bare feet on her walk back to the water's edge. She crouched to dip a handful of water from the lake and raised it to her lips. The men laughed behind her, so she glanced over her shoulder. Redcoat and the boy lay on the ground face to face, each gripping the other's hand, trying to push the other's arm to the ground. Blueleg crouched beside them, naked except for his breechcloth and his sheath with the sharp knife. Tatsea turned away to drink more water.

The knife clattered on the stones beside her. Tatsea didn't move. She didn't glance back. Blueleg growled, "Astam!" She turned to look at him. He pointed at a bundle of meat lying beside the drying scalps. Then he kicked at the naked boy still straining against Redcoat's hand. The boy scrambled to his feet and bent to gather dry wood from the ground. Tatsea picked up the knife and tiptoed to the meat bundle. She kept her eyes to the ground in front of her, but she felt the boy's eyes, and Redcoat's, watching her kneel to unwrap the meat.

Tatsea made no attempt to hide the knife under her dress after she finished cutting the meat into strips. She wrapped the hide around the remaining meat and laid the knife on top of the bundle so it would be handy if she needed to cut more meat. Redcoat had stuck a circle of sharpened sticks in the ground around the fire. As Tatsea impaled the strips of meat on the sticks, she saw Blueleg casually slip the knife back into his sheath.

The toe of Blueleg's moccasin nudging her bare leg roused her from a dream of sleeping in a tent beside Ikotsali with the baby in the swing above them. Blueleg, still almost naked, stood covered in mud from his feet to his waist, his axe in one hand. "Astam," he growled quietly, waving for her to follow him. Redcoat and the boy still slept, clawing half-heartedly at mosquitoes settling on their sweating skin.

Tatsea followed Blueleg through the bush into a swampy area, until he pointed to the crumpled body of a freshly killed bull moose. Laughing his rumbling laugh, Blueleg rocked his head to show her how the moose had tried to shake him off with those menacing horns. Blood still oozed from the throat where Blueleg had slashed the windpipe. If only she could escape with that knife, she thought. With that knife she could get back to Do Kwo Di and her baby.

Tatsea helped Blueleg roll the moose onto its side. She didn't blink when he handed her the knife; she grasped the handle and knelt to skin the large beast. The sharp knife cut so smoothly and cleanly that Tatsea thought only about the hide and the meat, of the things she could make, how careful cuts would let her use every bit of the hide. She hardly blinked when Blueleg chopped off the moose's antlers and then the head.

For three days they camped on the island. Redcoat and Blueleg each killed another moose—cows, smaller than the bull, but still larger than caribou. Blueleg ordered the boy to help Tatsea scrape the hair from the hides with a leg bone sharpened with Blueleg's axe. The boy muttered in protest, and instead of picking up the scraping bone he reached for a thunderstick and attempted to sneak off into the bush. A sharp word from Blueleg stopped him, but he argued, pointing at Tatsea. Although she did not understand the boy's words, she knew he was complaining about having to do women's work. Blueleg grunted, amused, then landed a quick backhanded slap on the boy's cheek. The thunderstick dropped to the ground and the boy sullenly set to scraping the hide stretched on the frame next to the one Tatsea was working on.

Blueleg and Redcoat slipped into the bush with their axes and knives. Tatsea watched the boy warily out of the corner of her eye. Under her dress her sharp bone knife scraped against her belly. When Blueleg had handed her his axe so she could cut a scraper from the legbone, she had stealthily crafted a bone knife as well.

But the boy didn't try to attack her. Instead, he annoyed her by tossing small stones at her or by coming up behind her and dropping a handful of moosehair on her head. If she turned to look at him he would be busy scraping his hide. Once he made an animal sound and when she looked he was relieving himself in her direction. Then Blueleg and Redcoat returned with their arms full of birchbark and the boy attacked his hide so fiercely Tatsea thought he might push his scraper right through the skin.

While Redcoat set about repairing the canoe, damaged in the storm, Blueleg shaped a large bowl out of birchbark. With almost as much care as a woman, Tatsea thought, her captor sewed the edges with strips of sinew, then sealed the seams with spruce tree gum. Then he cracked open the moose skulls and scraped the brains into the bowl. He cracked open the larger bones, too, and scraped the marrow into the brains. Then he mixed in the softest fat from the animals and stirred the mixture with a stick into frothy liquid like the foam from waves left on a lakeshore.

Tatsea had removed nearly all the hair from her hide when Blueleg knelt beside her with the mixture. With his axe he helped her finish. Together they took the skin down from the frame. He folded the skin into her arms and nodded at the bowl.

For a moment, Tatsea trembled. She had never done this part by herself. She had only watched her mother and her grandmother, Ehtsi, soak hides in the brains mixture. Then she shrugged her shoulders and carried the hide to the bowl. Tatsea had watched women do this ever since she could stand on her own two feet.

Tatsea pushed the hide into the bowl until the creamy liquid covered it. While the hide soaked she gathered some thin poles to make a drying frame beside the fire.

In the meantime, Blueleg had set about scraping the third hide. The boy was nearly done scraping his hide when Tatsea decided her hide had soaked long enough. She drew the hide out of the bowl, squeezing and wiping the brains mixture back into the bowl, wasting not a drop. Then she stretched the hide on the frame to dry in the smoke. Proud of herself, Tatsea walked up beside the boy and pointed out bits of hair he had missed on his hide. The boy shook his scraper at her, but a growl from Blueleg quickly set him back to finishing the job. When Tatsea was satisfied, she helped him unlace the hide from the frame.

The brain-soaked hides dried over the smoking fire for three days. Tatsea kept busy cutting meat into thin strips and hanging it to dry near another fire. When the meat was all hung, Tatsea sat to catch her breath. Blueleg's knife was still in her hand. She picked up a bone, cut a sliver from it, then began carving a needle. Redcoat worked on the canoe. The boy circled about, gathering firewood, though this gave him plenty of opportunity to tease Tatsea.

Blueleg squatted beside the scalps drying in the sun. He examined each scalp carefully, and untangled the hair with his fingers. Then he sorted them into piles, bundled them up and tied them with babiche. Tatsea watched him with horror and curiosity. Why would such men carry people's hair across the land?

The needle finished, Tatsea began to mend her clothes, sewing up holes with strips of babiche. Before long, Blueleg dumped his clothes on her lap and then Redcoat and the boy did the same. Tatsea shrugged and finished mending the seam she was working on, then set about mending the men's clothes. The hide clothes were similar to her Dogrib people's clothes, though the design was a little different and the stitching was unlike any she had seen before. What was really strange, though, were the red coat and the blue leggings. She kept stroking the scratchy surface, trying to determine the kind of animal these strange hides had come from. One thing she was grateful for was the ease with which the needle pushed through this hide.

Blueleg didn't tie her up at night. Tatsea was glad of this. Besides, how could she escape from this island, exhausted after scraping and cutting and sewing all day? She was kept so busy she hardly thought about Ikotsali and her baby. But when she closed her eyes she was back on Do Kwo Di in the tent with her baby in the swing above her, Ikotsali at her side, brushing her cheek with his lips. Tears trickled down the sides, of her head into her ears, the ache inside her more painful than her sore arms and hands. But the dream offered her hope and she let herself slide into the dream completely, feeling Ikotsali's lips on her face, then her mouth, his hands fumbling gently with her dress, slowly moving his body up onto hers, and then Tatsea felt a bony knee press down on her leg. She opened her eyes. The boy pressed his body down on her, his face grinning in the dim light.

Tatsea cried out, kicked, and tried to push him away. The boy slapped her face, then pinned her to the ground with a hand over her mouth. Then she heard Blueleg growl and the boy was pulled off her. Blueleg's arm lashed out at the boy's face again and again and again until the boy slumped to the ground, whimpering like a small animal caught in a snare.

Blueleg lay down beside her without touching her. Tatsea listened to the boy's whimpering and to Blueleg's breathing. What kind of man was this who protected her like a wife, made her work like a wife, but never touched her like a wife?

CHAPTER FIFTEEN

IKOTSALI TURNED HIS FACE AWAY FROM THE FISHY BREATH tickling his nostrils, then rolled over on his side. A sharp rock poked up through the spruce boughs and dug into his hip despite the double layer of his sleeping robes. He shifted and a warm arm slipped off his shoulder. For a moment he thought of settling back into place, reaching for the fallen hand and placing it back on his shoulder. Then he remembered whose hand it was. He held his breath, listened to his heartbeat.

He rested his head on his arm, dipping his nose into the sour spot where the baby had burped up fish soup onto his sleeve after he finished feeding her. He shifted his hip off the rock, lay back, and opened his eyes. The two dark shapes of the baby swings hung from the braided hide ropes strung between the tent poles. In the dim light he saw one twitch slightly.

Don't wake up yet, he thought. Please let there be silence a while longer. Since Ikotsali had joined this camp of Dogrib people from Sahti, Bear Lake, the sound of human voices seemed never-ending. Only at night were the voices stilled and even then the noisy widow had talked into his ear after he was floating away into a dream. Dagodichih, the noisy duck. Her husband had broken through the ice when he was chasing a caribou across the lake in the spring. Ikotsali could believe the joking men who said that Dagodichih's husband had not really been chasing a caribou; he had been running away from his wife's endless chatter.

Ikotsali had often wished Tatsea would speak to him, tell him what she was thinking. But in the time since he had taken her for a wife, Tatsea had never actually spoken to him. She had obeyed his commands, shrugged or grunted at his questions, but she had never spoken to him. And when he spoke to her she seemed to shrink and disappear inside herself somewhere so that Ikotsali almost feared to speak to her because she might vanish. To hear her voice he had had to sneak out of sight and listen to her play with the baby or argue with her mother. There were times when he thought she behaved like a slave woman obeying her captor so she could keep her life.

Tatsea, a slave woman. What else could have happened to her? The Enda raiders must have liked her beauty enough to keep her alive. Ikotsali shuddered as he remembered a slave woman brought to his camp when he was a small boy. He remembered the bruised face, the frightened eyes, a broken person even little girls could boss around. What was happening to Tatsea now? What would she think of his living in Dagodichih's tent?

The people of the camp had listened to his story, had seen a man with a nursing baby, and directed him toward the young widow's tent, the widow who gave birth after her man plunged through the ice, a woman who would be willing to share her milk with the child of a man who had lost his wife. And Ikotsali had not refused. His infant daughter needed a mother's breast. Fish soup from a man's nipple would not keep a child alive for long, he had thought.

Dagodichih had been seated in the doorway of her tent, nursing her baby. Ikotsali's breath stopped and tears came to his eyes as the sight took him back to Do Kwo Di and the morning he last saw Tatsea. Dagodichih seemed not to notice his sore face—saw only the infant in his arms.

"Bebia, ayii?" she said, showing him all her teeth in a big smile.

"This man has lost his wife. Enda!"

"I have lost my husband, too. He fell through bad ice. I miss him so much, I have no one to hunt for me," Dagodichih said.

"Ejiet'o?" Ikotsali asked, shyly. Milk?

Dagodichih's smile grew even bigger and she reached out for Tatsea's child with her free arm. "Wekwi ejiet'o deghaa." I have enough milk.

Ikotsali shuddered with joy and with sadness when he placed Tatsea's child in Dagodichih's arms and helped the hungry mouth find the overflowing breast.

But Tatsea's daughter refused the noisy widow's milk, howled relentlessly until she was inside Ikotsali's shirt again, sucking ravenously while her father dripped warm fish soup from the hollow swan's-leg drinking tube.

A man who would nurse his own child was as curious a sight for the people of the camp as a man with a knife as sharp as an eagle's beak and an axe harder than stone. Ikotsali was a wonder and if he were shrewd he could become the most powerful man in the camp.

And Dagodichih was a strong woman who could give him many children. She sewed very well, too. Even now she had almost completed a new shirt for him, a shirt more intricately sewn and more beautifully adorned than any he had ever worn before. He could be known as a rich and powerful man. Might this not be the best thing to do for Tatsea's daughter?

Yet—each night his dreams showed him a hawk circling overhead, waiting to pounce on its prey, and then he would glimpse Tatsea stumbling through deep snow. And when he was feeding the baby, when the baby was sucking most vigorously, he would feel himself float out of his body to the other side of the fire, and through the flames he would see his little daughter tugging at Tatsea's breast.

Ikotsali crawled out of the tent. The camp was so quiet it seemed dead. Stars twinkled in the brightening sky. When he had last seen Tatsea, the night sky had been too bright for stars, the lake water warm enough to bathe in. Now frost coated the ground and rimmed the plants. Ice covered puddles near the river.

Ikotsali stole away from the sleeping camp up a hill with no trees. He felt like a giant—the tallest thing in the world.

When he reached the top of the hill Ikotsali looked out over the Barrenland. He could see far to where the sky touched the ground. He looked east to where the sun peered over the edge of the land, reddening the clouds like bloodstains in the folds of a caribou hide. He looked north and saw how the light chased the dark away to the west over the rise and fall of the treeless land. He looked west and in the retreating darkness saw tiny trees braving the open sky. He looked to the south and in the rising sunlight marvelled at the patches of small flowers still blooming among the yellow grasses and brown bushes that covered the ground. Then he looked again. Turning, he looked all around the Barrenland circle, the circle that was the sky. The circle that was the earth.

Then movement caught his eye. A movement way out in the east. Something. The Barrenland moved a little. Ikotsali rubbed his eyes. He looked again. Something was really moving.

Then he heard a very quiet click click click coming from out there on the Barrenland.

"EKWO!" he shouted. Then he turned and ran back to the camp shouting, "EKWO! EKWO! EKWO!" The men scrambled out of the tents. Dagodichih's brother tripped as he jumped out of his tent still half asleep. "EKWO! EKWO!" Ikotsali shouted again, pointing to the hill where he had seen the caribou.

The chief ran up the hill and looked out over the Barrenland. Then he ran back to the camp calling everyone, men, women, and children.

Before Ikotsali could get back to the tent to pick up his baby, he saw Dagodichih tying his daughter to her younger sister's back, a girl too young to be part of the hunt. Her own child already rested on the back of another small girl. "Ekwo!" she called when she saw him. He took one worried look at his daughter, then turned to hurry toward the fence they had built to guide the caribou to the lake crossing. Dagodichih ran up beside him and together they joined the people pulling off their outer clothes and hanging them on the sticks that made the fence to the lake.

Ikotsali pulled off his shirt. He shivered in the cool morning air, but then he forgot about that while the sound of the caribou came nearer—the click, click, click of the animals' hooves crashing over the Barrenland. Everyone was lining up between the sticks with the clothes on them—everyone except the young girls who stayed at the tents with the babies.

Dagodichih and some of the women lined up at the end of the fence closest to where the caribou would come. Ikotsali saw the chief and Dagodichih's brothers get into canoes and paddle out into the lake.

The ground shook. The caribou thundered. The women on the hill raised their dresses with spread-out arms. Then the caribou thundered around the hill. The women waved their clothes. The caribou rushed in between the fences. Ikotsali stood in the line as if he was frozen. Even though he had done this many times, he shuddered while the wall of antlers flowed by, close enough to touch. But he didn't move.

Hundreds and hundreds of caribou clicked by. They plunged into the lake and began to swim. The men in canoes paddled to the caribou to harpoon the swimming animals. The caribou kept pushing into the water. They pushed at the canoes so the men didn't have to paddle and could use their free hands to harpoon caribou after caribou after caribou. In and out plunged the sharp harpoons. Blood splashed over the harpoons, over the hunters, over the canoes, over the water.

But the caribou kept on moving. They had to get across the lake. Wave after wave of caribou splashed into the lake, swimming into the waiting harpoons.

Ikotsali stared frozen at the wall of caribou racing past him. He heard the people shouting. He felt the wind stirred up by the rushing animals. Then he shouted, too. He shouted as loud as he could.

Then, as quickly as it had begun, the rush of the caribou ceased. The last cow and her calf floundered in the water. The caribou herd had crossed the lake, leaving the dead ones floating in the water like many tiny little islands.

The men in the canoes gazed at the floating caribou. The people on shore stared, too. Then the chief shouted and everyone moved again.

The rest of the men rushed to their canoes and paddled out to the floating animals. For a long time the boys and men in canoes pushed the caribou to the shore and pulled them up the bank where the women waited with their bone knives. Ikotsali stood with the women, his Enda knife and axe ready. With his special tools he would be more useful on shore than in a canoe on the water.

He cut the head off a big bull and put it upside down on its antlers. Warmth caressed his face like breath while he slit the skin all the way down the belly. Next he opened up the belly and before he reached in to remove the guts he paused for a breath or two to ponder the inside of the caribou. As his eye passed over each organ he felt a twinge inside his own belly as if his body were recognizing parts of himself.

"Good full stomach," Dagodichih said beside him.

"Good heart, liver, kidneys, too," Ikotsali said, deftly cutting out the heart. He took a deep breath when he handed the heart to Dagodichih. The smell of blood in the cold air made him feel alive. He looked into Dagodichih's eyes. She smiled. His eyes blurred and he was looking into Tatsea's eyes. He blinked, and turned to cut out the liver and the kidneys, handing them to Dagodichih to put in a big cooking pot. Then he peeled the skin off the caribou, cutting carefully to avoid piercing holes in the skin. These hides would make the clothes and tents for the people.

All day the people worked, cutting up the caribou. Ikotsali worked at Dagodichih's side, the noisy widow almost like his own arm, they worked so well together. After a while, though, Dagodichih's sister brought him the baby and without thinking he handed the widow his sharp knife, took the baby, and returned to the tent to feed his child the whitefish soup. Ikotsali had grown so used to feeding his child that he did it even while he thought about the hunt. In his mind he was still at his place beside Dagodichih, cutting up the meat, doing his part to prepare for winter. People who passed by smiled at him warmly as if there was nothing strange about a man nursing a child. For the first time in his life, Ikotsali felt like he belonged to a camp.

When the baby was fed, he returned to the butchering, but he let Dagodichih keep the sharp knife while he set to work with the Enda axe.

That night the people feasted. Hearts, livers, and kidneys roasted over the fire. Ikotsali ate along with the others until he felt like his belly would break open.

Then the men brought out the drums. Dagodichih's brothers warmed up their drums over the fire first. Then the drumming began, bom-boom, bom-boom, bom-boom, bom-boom like a heart, beating like a heart.

First the chief rose to dance around the fire, moving his feet to the beat of the drums. Then another man, then a woman, then another and another round and round the fire. Ikotsali stood beside Dagodichih, watching the dancers. Their babies slept on their backs, twitching to the bom-boom, bom-boom, bom-boom of the drums. He felt the drumming in his ears, then his nose, all through his head and bones.

Dagodichih bumped his hip, then stepped out to join the line of dancers shuffling around the fire. For a breath Ikotsali remembered people laughing at him when he had tried to dance before, but then the bom-boom of the drums reached his feet and he shuffled after the noisy widow and joined the dance. Round and round the fire like the sun going around the world. Around and around like the Barrenland in the morning. Bom-boom. Bom-boom. Bom-boom. Everyone danced to the drums. The oldest grannies, bent from a life of carrying loads, danced with the same energy as the young boys and girls; even the youngest babies danced on their mothers' backs. Ikotsali's baby danced on his back. He heard her voice, but his daughter was not crying; she was singing along with the drummers.

On and on and on the drummers beat their sticks on the hide drums, starting a new song as soon as an old one ended. On and on and on the dancers shuffled around the circle, a new dancer skipping into place the moment any dancer stepped out of the circle to rest. Ikotsali danced and danced and danced. He took his turn at the drum. He didn't stop until the sky in the east was very red.

During the next few days the people took care of the meat. Much meat was cut into strips and hung over the fires to dry. When the meat was dry, some of it was pounded into powder and mixed with dried berries to make pemmican.

Ikotsali felt content. Even Dagodichih's endless chatter no longer annoyed him. His daughter also seemed to enjoy the widow's attention—as long as she didn't try to nurse her. Soon the child would eat chewed food. The whitefish soup would no longer be needed.

At last the meat was all taken care of. The people packed the meat and hides into the canoes. The men talked of moving in the direction of Sahti, following when the caribou scattered through the trees to where, sheltered from the blasts of Barrenland wind and snow, they would find the lichens and mosses and buried bushes that would feed them. Like the caribou, the people wanted to be back in the trees for the winter.

CHAPTER SIXTEEN

TATSEA LOOKED UP FROM THE MOCCASIN SHE WAS SEWING. HER eyes blurred a little when she looked past Redcoat's shoulders at the tree-lined shore skimming by. She thought she saw a white-headed eagle settle on a treetop in an open space on the shore dotted with the black trunks of burned trees. Purple-pink fireweed covered the ground. Tatsea searched through her mind for a story about this fire, but she could find none. She shivered at the thought.

Until her captors crossed Tindee and paddled up this river, Tatsea had felt like she knew where she was, that she could easily find her way back to her baby, back to Ikotsali. Even when the canoe had entered the river, Tatsea remembered a story about Yamozha, the wise man, who had come down from the river Hatl'ode to the big water, Tindee, to make the world safe for people. But she couldn't be sure these men were taking her up the river in the story. She couldn't feel any stories at all for this river.

The river appeared to be leading south and east, more east now than it had for the long days since they left the island on Tindee. Maybe the river was no longer the same. Had the last portage taken them to a new river? She had not noticed any rapids to explain the portage. Tatsea felt confused now. The river had so many bends, they seemed to be travelling in all directions.

Blueleg and Redcoat appeared to know exactly where they were going. At the head of the canoe the boy paddled sullenly, the bruises from Blueleg's beating still swelling his face. The boy hadn't come near Tatsea since that night, but a few times when they camped and Blueleg slipped into the bush, Redcoat and the boy had huddled together, speaking in low tones, eyeing her threateningly. Only their fear of Blueleg protected her.

Tatsea had done little paddling since they left Tindee. Each morning when they settled in the canoe Blueleg pointed at the bundle of hides and gestured that she was to busy herself sewing. When they camped for the night he handed her his knife, and when she had cut the meat for cooking she would spread the hides on the ground and cut the pieces she would need for sewing the next day.

Her busy hands filled in some of the emptiness she felt at the loss of her baby. During the days on the island while she prepared the hides, soaking, stretching, rubbing them into softness as they dried, she had almost been able to dream that she was at home in her people's camp. During her sewing in the canoe she made the task more bearable by dreaming that she was sewing for her husband and her child. She sewed with great care, making each stitch as neat and tight as she could with the bone needle. When she passed a finished moccasin to Blueleg for his inspection, he grunted his approval, though he did have a questioning look on his face when he pointed to his own moccasins to show her how they were different. Then he grinned at her and reached out to caress her cheek with the new moccasin.

Blushing proudly, Tatsea picked up the pieces for the other moccasin and took even more care. The more Blueleg liked her work, the safer she would be.

A shout startled her. Blueleg jabbed his paddle toward the shore. The sun was still high in the sky—much too early to make camp. Since leaving Tindee they hadn't put to shore in the middle of the day except to make a portage. But here the river was straight as far as she could see in both directions with no sign of any rough water ahead. Nothing on the shore suggested that this was a good place to stop.

It was a brief stop. Redcoat, the boy, and Tatsea barely had time to relieve themselves before Blueleg returned to the canoe with a bundle of fur. When they pushed back out onto the river, Tatsea pointed to the fur and then pointed to the moccasin she was sewing, showing how she could use the fur to trim the tops. Blueleg grinned, but shook his head. Tatsea was confused. What good was fur from small animals if you couldn't use it for making clothing? Was Blueleg taking the fur to another wife somewhere? But what kind of wife needed men to bring her fur?

Among Tatsea's people only the women and young boys set snares for the small animals. Men were much too busy hunting the caribou and moose, or sometimes a sleepy bear in a winter den. Ehke, her father, had once told of hunting the long-haired hozi ejie, the muskox, far out in the Barrenland, but her family hadn't ventured that far after Tatsea was born. Sometimes hunters venturing south of Wha Ti would bring home the meat of dechita gojie, the wood buffalo. But hardly a man bothered with a rabbit or a beaver or a marten unless the big meat was very scarce.

Why, Tatsea wondered, would men carry her people's hair and bundles of animal skins on a long journey in a canoe? What strange medicine did they have that gave them knives and axes so sharp they could cut meat like it was lard? What strange trees gave them thundersticks? What animals gave them hides, red and blue?

Redcoat spoke with a question in his voice. He lifted his paddle and pointed to a spot on the shore where willows hung down over the water. Blueleg growled back at him and dug his paddle in hard, causing the canoe to swerve, but Redcoat spoke again, his voice more certain. He pointed to the shore and the boy in front began shouting. Blueleg stopped paddling and when Tatsea glanced back at him he laughed his rumbling laugh.

This stop on shore was not rushed like the last one. Blueleg couldn't find the furs right away. After hiding the canoe in the willows, all three captors searched the bush around an old campsite, but found nothing. Blueleg muttered menacingly and Redcoat and the boy muttered back. Tatsea stayed near the hidden canoe, not sure what they were looking for and having no idea how to help them look.

Blueleg stomped out of the bush and he waved Tatsea toward the canoe. He shouted at his companions over his shoulder. There was no response for a moment, then a shout from Redcoat and then another from the boy. Redcoat stumbled out of the bush with a large bundle of furs on his shoulder. The boy was right behind with another. They chattered to Blueleg as they dropped the bundles on the ground.

Blueleg shouted at Tatsea, gesturing for her to load the bundles into the canoe. Then her three captors stumbled back into the bush.

Tatsea picked up one of the bundles of fur. She recognized the skins of marten and weasel and lynx. For a moment she had a vision of a wonderful coat she could sew for Ikotsali with all these furs. Then she heard a sound from inside the bundle. A watery sound. Like waves lapping. Something was moving inside the bundle, moving like water. What strange furs were these?

Curious, she set the bundle down on the ground. She checked over her shoulder for the men. They were still in the bush. She couldn't hear them. Trembling, Tatsea untied the babiche and opened the bundle. She jerked her hands back when her fingers touched something hard and woody. There was no sound, no movement from inside the bundle. Her heart beating against her ribs, she reached for the furs again. She peeled them away from what looked like a short, fat log. She had never seen such a log. The bark was smooth with straight lines and strange bands seemed to hold the log at each end. The ends of the log were flat. A knothole with a stubby piece of branch in it stuck out of one end.

Wondering if she dared to touch this strange log, her nose picked up a scent she had never smelled before. On her hands and knees she bent to sniff the log. She smelled a strange sweetness, like the smell of rotting berries. Why would men wrap a rotting log in a bundle of fur? What strange medicine did these men have?

A stick cracked in the bush behind her. Tatsea scrambled back from the fur bundle, then reached to wrap up the log and rush it to the canoe. But she was too late. A bundle of fur dropped beside her. Blueleg shouted and scooped up the log, raising it high above his head. His deep laugh rumbled through the bush. Redcoat and the boy dropped their furs on the ground and danced around Blueleg, reaching up for the log.

Tatsea cringed on the ground, waiting to be kicked for opening the bundle. But her captors had eyes only for the strange log. Puzzled, she watched Blueleg slowly lower the log and cradle it against his waist. Redcoat and the boy watched, their tongues hanging out like dogs circling a chunk of meat. Blueleg gripped the stubby branch sticking out of the end, wiggled and twisted until it popped out. Tossing the plug away, he raised the log to his lips and drank water that poured from the hole.

After a couple of swallows Blueleg lowered the log and bellowed like a starving bear. Then he passed the log to Redcoat, who drank from the log, too. The boy, so eager for his turn he spilled some of the water in his face, choked and coughed after his first swallow. The log nearly dropped when Blueleg grabbed it from him.

Redcoat cuffed the boy on the side of the head, but the boy

staggered back into place and reached out for the log again after the two men had had their drink. This time the boy didn't spill a drop, but Tatsea saw him grimace while he passed the log on to Blueleg.

Blueleg turned to Tatsea, his laugh like a knife. She tried to shrink away as he crouched before her and held the log in front of her face. The smell stung her nostrils. Blueleg grabbed her chin and with his strong fingers forced her mouth open. The strange water burned her mouth and she spluttered some all over Blueleg's hand. The water burned like fire all the way down to her stomach. Blueleg and his companions laughed, then forgot all about her, intent only on each getting their share of the fiery water coming out of the hole in the log.

Her captors sat down on the ground, laughing louder after each drink, singing bits of strange songs, shouting. They seemed to forget everything around them as if the only important thing was the log with the burning rotten water in it. Even the bundles of fur had lost their importance.

Stealthily, Tatsea moved back, away from the men. They didn't seem to notice. Could she sneak to the canoe and paddle away before they saw her?

Blueleg took the log from the boy, holding it out for a moment as if checking how heavy it was; then he growled at the boy, and struck him hard on the ear with the back of his hand. The boy yelped and fell back sprawling in the grass. Blueleg drank from the log and passed it to Redcoat. Redcoat drank and passed the log back to Blueleg. The boy watched, then sat up and reached for the log after Redcoat had drunk again. Blueleg hit him harder this time, bloodying the boy's nose.

Tatsea cringed, afraid to even think about escape, afraid what might happen to her if she stayed. The boy crawled away, whimpering. Just before he disappeared into the bush, Tatsea saw his knife flash as he pulled it from his belt.

Unconcerned, Redcoat and Blueleg kept drinking from the hole. Tatsea watched the two men's eyes follow the log as it passed between their hands. They weren't laughing, or singing, or shouting any more. All that seemed to matter was the next sip.

An arm tightened around Tatsea's throat and yanked her to her feet from behind. She managed a short scream before her breath was choked off. Then she was flung to the ground, the boy dancing and yelling out a challenge to Blueleg, who was trying to drip the last drops of the fiery water into his mouth. The boy had cut off his hair close to his scalp; the knife glinted in his hand. He repeated his challenge, pointing to Tatsea sprawled on the ground. He raised his knife hand and hurled the knife so the blade struck the ground barely a hand's width from Blueleg's knee.

Blueleg jumped to his feet. He flung the drinking log down, striking Redcoat's foot, and whipped his own knife from his belt. His hand moved so fast Tatsea had no time to blink before the knife stabbed the ground a bare finger's width from the boy's foot. The boy jumped aside, then screamed in embarrassed rage. Blueleg hooted and sneered and turned away to bend down for the log Redcoat was tipping to his mouth.

Too angry to feel fear, the boy rushed at Blueleg, jumped on his bent back, grabbed his long hair. Blueleg stumbled, but didn't fall; with a quick shift of his foot he whirled around. The boy's legs swung out, but he kept his grip on Blueleg's hair, forcing the man to scream when he fell backwards and landed on the boy's chest.

Redcoat huddled, ignoring the fight, trying to suck another drop of fiery water from the log.

Tatsea kept one eye on the fight. The boy's arm now clenched Blueleg's neck, choking off his breath. Blueleg tried to force the boy's arm away.

Tatsea watched, puzzled. Why was Blueleg having so much trouble fighting off the boy? Blueleg was bigger and stronger. He had drunk much more of the burning medicine water than the boy had.

Her other eye focussed on Blueleg's knife still stuck in the ground.

Blueleg reached back and clawed at the boy's head but couldn't grip the short hair. He shrugged his body sideways, chopped his elbow hard into the boy's stomach. The boy yelped, let go of Blueleg's neck. Blueleg rolled over, scrambled to his knees, and pounced on the boy.

Tatsea's fingers closed around the knife handle and she pulled it free just as Blueleg's fist smashed into the boy's face.

Redcoat staggered to his feet, the drinking log still in his hands. He tipped it to his mouth again, roared when he found it empty. He raised it high with both hands and stumbled toward the fighters. Blueleg landed on the boy's stomach with a bent knee; Redcoat smashed the log on Blueleg's head. The log burst into clattering pieces. One of the bands holding the log spun through the air and landed at Tatsea's feet. Redcoat collapsed on top of his companions.

Tatsea didn't wait. Gripping Blueleg's knife, she fled, not looking back while she shoved the canoe into the water, not pausing to choose a direction. She paddled with all her strength, paddled without stopping until long after the sun had disappeared behind the trees, leaving her alone on the silvery water, breathing silvery puffs into the frosty air.

CHAPTER SEVENTEEN

THE BABY'S SCREAMS BEGAN AFTER THE PORTAGE, TWO DAYS' travel from the caribou crossing. Until then the child had travelled well, watching the shoreline from her father's back while he paddled the canoe laden with meat and hides. Tatsea's daughter had stared wide-eyed at the world flowing by, gurgled with delight when Dagodichih shifted her child to her chest so the two babies could see each other. From time to time Ikotsali would break into song as they paddled and Dagodichih would join him, their voices blending into a quavering sound that set both babies giggling.

But after the portage Ikotsali's child screamed before one hand's count of paddle strokes had been made. At first Ikotsali thought the child had been hurt, that a fish bone in the soup was choking his daughter. Never had the baby screamed so loud, never kicked so violently in the moss bag. Tatsea's daughter seemed to be in a rage.

Ikotsali laid down his paddle and took the child into his arms. He tried to console her inside his shirt. Nothing seemed to work. Dagodichih stopped paddling, too—tried to help, took the baby from Ikotsali to see if the child was choking.

With no one paddling it, the canoe soon drifted around and when it touched the shore it faced the opposite way. Suddenly, the baby ceased screaming and smiled, seemingly happy again. They all had a good laugh, then set out again to catch the other canoes, which had vanished around a bend. No sooner had they paddled a handful of strokes in the direction of their journey when the baby began screaming again. Again they dropped their paddles to see what was tormenting the child. The screaming stopped when the canoe turned the opposite way.

"Ets'aetla," Dagodichih said. Turn around.

Ikotsali didn't understand at first.

"Ayii? Yegho naxo?a," Dagodichih laughed. Maybe we can trick the baby?

"Trick the baby? Ayiha?" Ikotsali creased his forehead. Why?

"Yeniwo hanide," Dagodichih said. She wants to go that way.

"I'll try it." The canoe rocked when Ikotsali turned around to sit facing Dagodichih and the way they had come. Sure enough, the baby calmed down. The child even allowed Dagodichih to hold her while Ikotsali paddled, as long as she was faced away from the direction in which they were travelling. In this way they caught up with the other canoes just before dark.

Ikotsali remained silent while he set up the tent. He listened to Dagodichih telling the story of his daughter's strange behaviour in the canoe. The story sparked much laughter among the other women. Ikotsali tried to feel the laughter, too, but his daughter's behaviour worried him. The baby's rage had been greater than her rage at the taste of the noisy widow's milk. What could such a little one know?

After the cooking fires heated up the stones and the whitefish soup, Ikotsali fed the baby and laid her in the swing in the tent. She seemed peaceful enough and went to sleep almost as soon as he set the swing moving back and forth in the darkness. He held his breath for a few heartbeats, listening to the faint rubbing of the ropes against the tent poles, listening to the wisps of breath passing through the tiny nostrils. Perhaps his daughter had just been uncomfortable in the moss bag. The bag had certainly been stinky enough by the time they made camp.

Ikotsali stepped out of the tent and sauntered over to where the men hunkered around one of the fires. The men were talking about Enda and some of the strange things they had. One of Dagodichih's brothers asked Ikotsali to show them his knife again. Without speaking he pulled it from his belt and held it out for the men to examine. The widow's brother told of some Dogrib men who had crossed the big water, Tindee, with some Tets'ot'i people who had bragged of making a long journey to trade animal skins for thundersticks and pots that would not burn. Two winters had passed since these men had been seen.

"Perhaps these men were won by Tets'ot'i women in fights," joked Dagodichih's other brother, the one said to scare away animals because he always found something to laugh about wherever he went. "It is said Dogrib men are so attractive that Tets'ot'i women will scratch each other's eyes out to win such men."

"It is good that we go to Sahti for the short days," said the chief. "Tets'ot'i do not come to Sahti."

"Enda do not come to Sahti, either," added another man.

But Enda came to Wha Ti, Ikotsali thought.

Faint stars still glimmered in the sky when Ikotsali pushed his canoe out onto the glassy water of the lake. The baby lay asleep on the tent hides at the front end of the canoe. Puffs of Ikotsali's breath wafted into the cool air. His back leaned against the bundle of winter clothing Dagodichih had made for him. As he dipped his paddle silently, he shivered. But he did not look back to the sleeping camp.

A loon called out over the water to Ikotsali's left. Two strokes later another loon answered from his right. He heard a flutter of wings and when he looked up, he thought he saw the swoop of a hawk, but in the dim light he couldn't be sure.

Ikotsali paddled with strong, steady strokes. He wanted to be out of sight before his absence was discovered. He wanted to be far enough away before he had to stop to feed his baby. Dagodichih's brothers might decide that he had mistreated their quacking duck sister and give chase. Ikotsali had only a small fear of this since the men of the camp, even Dagodichih's brothers, ridiculed this noisy woman and would probably laugh at her for having driven away another man with her chatter. Yet one never knew how men would react if they thought one of their own had been wronged. After all, Ikotsali had shared her tent during the journey to the Barrenland, worked by her side during the big hunt, shared in the feasting, and had accepted the clothes she made for him. Dagodichih's people had accepted him when he arrived at their camp with a motherless child. Ikotsali hoped that the people of the camp feared his power, the power of the sharp knife and axe, the power of a man nursing a child, feared it enough to make them think better of pursuing him. Perhaps they would even be relieved that he was gone.

It would have been so easy to stay, to push the past horror out of his mind, to accept the warmth the widow offered him and his child. It would have been so easy—except for the dreams the darkness brought him. Since the canoes had begun their journey in the direction of Sahti, his sleep had been tormented by dreams of Tatsea. In one dream Tatsea lay on top of him under the sleeping robe, murmuring, her hands exploring the skin under his shirt, her hips rocking lazily against his. In another he saw her through smoke, suckling a child at her breast. But then the smoke cleared to reveal that the child was a full-grown man. Some dreams made him watch Tatsea lying sprawled on the ground, while strange men fell on her, thrusting as she screamed. And each dream ended with a hawk diving to the water and flying away with a fish in its beak.

As well, the child had been seized by fits of weeping that wakened the noisy widow and her child and even sometimes people in the other tents. The child fought all arms except those of Ikotsali and the only way he could silence the child was to turn his back on Sahti.

The loons called again when the canoe pushed into a band of mist hovering over the still water. The stars had faded into the silvery sky. From far behind him Ikotsali heard the screaming voice of an angry woman—or maybe two ravens squawking over the guts of a fish. Ikotsali quickened his paddle stroke and cleared his mind of the camp he was leaving behind. He left room only for the dream vision of Tatsea tramping through deep snow on her snowshoes.

CHAPTER EIGHTEEN

TATSEA FELT HER EYES CLOSE. SHE LOOKED AT THE DIM LIGHT seeping through her eyelids. She opened her eyes again and lifted her paddle from the water. The canoe drifted forward, the river straight as far as she could see with the sun setting behind the spruce treetops along the bank. Tatsea rested her paddle across the canoe. Her knees had been bent for so long she hardly felt her legs. She tried to wiggle her toes. It seemed to take a long time for the power of her thought to travel along her legs. Her eyes closed again. Tatsea did not resist.

For two days now she had not left the canoe. When she tired of paddling or when sleep overcame her, she drifted with the flow of the river. She dared not stop until she had put enough distance between herself and those men. She could not be sure that they had killed each other. Who could tell what strange power the fiery medicine water from the bursting log might give to such men? Men who could kill with a thunderstick might well be able to travel like lightning, too. Even a few swallows of the fiery water had given the boy the courage to attack Blueleg, a man twice as large as he. And the boy almost succeeded in his attack even though Blueleg had swallowed much more of the strange water than the boy had. What if she had not escaped? What terrible things might the boy and Redcoat have done to her?

Tatsea felt the canoe slip sideways slightly, then straighten out. Her head had turned to stone again, but she did not open her eyes. The light through her eyelids dimmed. Her head slumped forward until her chin touched the hide of her dress. A hawk hovered in the dim sky at the edge of her eyelid vision. Then she saw her baby daughter being placed at a woman's breast—another woman's breast. She saw her baby suck for a moment, then turn away and scream. A man's hands pulled the baby away from the woman.

The canoe jerked and Tatsea's head flipped back. A rushing roar struck her ears. The canoe flipped in the air and she plunged into turbulent water. Her hip struck a rock and then water covered her head and she felt herself pulled along by the racing stream. She kicked and clawed. Her foot touched bottom and she jumped. Her head broke into the air and she gulped for breath just before the river knocked her over and pulled her under again.

Kicking and clawing, fighting to the surface for gulps of air, her body slammed into huge, round stones again and again until she discovered that if she stopped struggling, she hit fewer rocks and the water lifted her to the surface so she could breathe. Still she was sure she would die when she slammed into a huge, dark rock.

Then as suddenly as the rapids had appeared the water calmed, though the current remained strong. Tatsea felt herself sink and she kicked her feet down. She sank to her chin before she touched bottom. Feeling life given back to her, she kicked and clawed sideways across the current until she reached the shore. In the light of the rising moon she shivered, her breath puffing in huge clouds.

Thick bushes lined the shore where she landed, the darkness black even with the moonlight. Her soaked clothes chilling in the cool air, Tatsea knelt and groped in the darkness for dry wood. Her fingers found a few sticks. She scraped together a small pile of dry leaves and needles and broke the sticks in half before she laid them on top of the leaves. She reached inside her dress and pulled out her little bag with the firestones inside. Water oozed from the bag when she opened it and pulled out the two precious stones, too wet to start a fire. She would have to wait until they dried.

Rivulets of water ran down her dress inside and out and dripped off the fringes along the hem. Drops of water rolled down her stomach. Her leggings clung like a second skin. Tatsea shivered. She had no fire, but she had to dry her clothes.

In the darkness she found two roots spreading out from the foot of a tree. Carefully she laid her precious firestones in the hollow between them. Then she groped up along the trunk until she found a branch. She pulled off her dress and twisted it in her hands to squeeze out as much water as she could. Over and over she twisted and squeezed until she couldn't feel a drop more. Then she spread it out and hung it on the branch.

She rubbed her body with her hands to warm herself and to wipe off all the water she could reach. Then she set about opening the wet knots that tied her leggings to the belt at her waist. Her bone knife pressed against her hip. Blueleg's sharp knife had been lying on the bottom of the canoe. Now it lay at the bottom of the river. At last she opened the knots and stripped off the leggings and her moccasins. She wrung them out and hung them on the branch. After rubbing her legs she reached for her dress, twisting and squeezing it again.

A wolf howled somewhere far away in the night. She slipped the damp hide over her shivering body, then got down on all fours to explore the ground. She found a fallen spruce tree leaning against another. Its dry branches had caught a pile of dry leaves the wind had blown around. Tatsea, thankful that though the air was cold the wind was light, burrowed into the leaves when the wolf howled again.

Tatsea awoke with a sneeze. Sunlight poked through the black trees. A squirrel scampered along the fallen tree trunk, shaking needles onto her face. Her stomach growled, though hunger was no great concern yet. Another squirrel scampered up the fallen tree. Tatsea almost smiled. She felt about her waist until her fingers pressed down on the strands of sinews she had hidden away for herself when she had been butchering the caribou for her captors. The scampering squirrels appeared to be waiting to give themselves to her.

The firestones had dried overnight and in the daylight Tatsea soon built a roaring fire. After hanging her clothes on sticks to dry beside the flames, she tiptoed a short distance from her camp and set two snares. Drying the hide clothes was not a quick procedure. In order to keep the clothes from hardening while they dried, she kept rubbing them between her hands. The sun passed more than halfway across the sky before she was satisfied that her clothes were dry.

Her snares yielded a hare and a squirrel. She reset those two snares and then set three more before returning to her fire to skin and cook the two animals. The bone knife felt awkward after Blueleg's sharp knife. Without giving it much thought, after setting the carcasses of the small animals to roast on sticks leaning over the fire, she began separating all the parts of the animals that might have some use. In the end she threw only the entrails to two ravens lurking at the edge of her camp.

After eating Tatsea stole back to the riverbank to see what had happened to the canoe.

In daylight, looking down on the rapids, Tatsea shuddered. The water tumbled over round stones, splashing white, split by sharp rocks. She saw where a boulder forced water sideways into calmer water near the shore. The throb of her bruises reawakened, reminding her of her body's slamming into the boulder. She spotted one of the thundersticks poking up from a spray of water and for a heartbeat she felt as if she were in the river with her foot caught in the rocks.

Then she screamed. The river plunged over a small cliff, down on another rapids. In the exploding spray, the canoe jutted up from where it was wedged between two rocks. Tatsea stopped her scream, and clasped her hand over her heart to calm it. She gaped at where she might be had the canoe not flipped, had the boulder not bumped her away from the rapids.

She crept along the riverbank, careful not to get her newly dried moccasins wet. She scanned the water, looking for anything from the canoe she might use, especially Blueleg's knife or his axe. But finding those was a hopeless wish. They would have sunk to the bottom of the river and Tatsea wasn't ready to go back into that rushing water even for a sharp knife. Still, she continued to search the shoreline and the water.

About halfway down the rapids, a brown object floated near an almost white rock. When she got even with it and squinted hard, she saw it could be one of the bundles from the canoe. But it was near the middle of the river, much too far in to be retrieved. Still, seeing the bundle gave her some excitement and hope that she might find something. The hides and the clothes she had made for the men would be good to have. Her captors had not yet put on the new clothes. They had been saving them for the winter.

And the packs of meat would help.

Near the bottom of the rapids, floating in a pool of almost unmoving water, she found one of the paddles. With the help of a stick she was able to pull it out of the river. A little farther on she found another bundle, sunk so that only a spot the size of her hand poked up into the air. With the paddle and the stick she worked the bundle close enough to the shore so she was able to pull it out. Even before she opened it she recognized the bundle of her people's hair.

At first she thought of throwing the bundle back into the river so she wouldn't have to think about the horrible end her people had come to. But then she thought of her mother's hair floating forever in these cold waters so far from her people's land. She must take these scalps back to the people they had come from. And then she remembered an earlier thought—that somehow she must follow the journey of her people's hair to find what strange world had sent these cruel raiders such a long distance to hunt her people for their hair.

Tatsea carried the sodden bundle back to her fire, now just a layer of glowing coals. She gathered more dry firewood and built up the fire. Then she added some greener wood so the fire would burn slowly and long. She set up sticks around the fire and unpacked the scalps and hung each one on a stick to dry. Then she went off into the bush to check her snares.

This second night she was dry and warm. But sitting beside her fire, surrounded by her people's drying hair, she dreaded the snowless darkness around the edges of the flickering firelight. In her people's land it was the season of the bushman.

Tatsea had never yet seen a bushman, but she had heard the stories since she was old enough to listen. Only two summers ago, just before she had had to hide in the menstrual hut, Dienda, her boy friend with the big ears, had come from lifting nets with his father and told of the hairy creature, half man, half bear, that had chased them when they tried to land on the shore to make a short camp to cook a fish. And Tatsea remembered the huge footprint beside the canoe one morning the summer they had camped on Big Island in Wha Ti.

The more Tatsea remembered the stories, the more she shivered and the stranger the night sounds from the bush became. The faraway wolf howl seemed as close as the edge of the flickering flames that caused shadows to dance all around the circle of drying scalps. She huddled close to the fire, fearing to be seen in the firelight, yet afraid to slip into the darkness. Drifting into sleep she felt like she was split into two parts, almost like two birds, two separate hawks, each with a bundle of her people's hair in its beak, one flying home to Wha Ti and her people's bodies on Do Kwo Di, the other carrying the scalps to some place Tatsea could not see, even in her dream. And even as her two hawks flew, pulling her in opposite directions, like a piece of intestine stretched hard between two fighting ravens, Tatsea saw shadows running before her eyes that sometimes looked like Ikotsali and the baby chased by a furry bear-like creature, running upright on two legs like a man.

When Tatsea awoke she was lying beside the barely glowing coals of the fire. A light dusting of snow covered the ground and the rushing rapids had a different sound from the day before. She rose and built up the fire. Then she hurried to the river. Except for the rapids, it was covered with ice.

For the next few days Tatsea busied herself creating a camp to keep her through the winter. She built a shelter by leaning short tree trunks against the fallen tree that had sheltered her during the first night. She covered the logs with spruce branches and leaves. With her bone knife she cut fresh boughs to cover the floor to make a soft bed. She set and checked her snares twice a day and always she caught at least one hare, squirrel, or ptarmigan. She saved everything, allowing only the entrails for the two ravens who spent most of their time around her camp. She never let the fire go out, and when she wasn't busy building or skinning or cooking, she gathered firewood and stacked it up in a pile.

Each day she also checked the riverbank in case something else from the canoe had washed ashore. One day she was lucky. She found the stomach pot spread out on a rock not far from shore. It took some careful manoeuvring with her paddle and a stick but eventually she managed to drag it ashore. For the first time in many, many days she boiled soup.

Each day the weather got colder and the ice got thicker. Tatsea found it harder each day to break through to the water. One day she decided to cross the river. She walked along the edge with the paddle in her hands until she was well downstream from the rapids. Then she crossed over to the other side. She planned to explore the shore beside the rapids for other items from the canoe. Two light snowfalls since the ice formed had brought snow barely deep enough to show a hare's footprints.

A short distance before she reached the open water at the foot of the rapids, she noticed the thunderstick that had been poking up from the rocks was gone. A worrisome thought that Redcoat or Blueleg might have found it crossed her mind, but then a slight change in the riverbank caught her eye and she shifted her attention to what appeared to be a path leading up the bank into the bush.

At first Tatsea wanted to turn back and hide on the other side of the river. A path meant that others might be near. Then she saw her own footprints in the snow; if others were near they would see her footprints and find her anyway. Then she thought about how there was no path on the other side and rapids almost always meant a portage. Often travellers made a camp at a portage and sometimes left things behind when they moved on.

Tatsea crept up the bank, eyeing the ground beside the path. Tufts of grass and low cranberry bushes poked through the thin layer of snow. Tiny tracks led off in many directions, telling Tatsea that she might do well to set snares on this side of the river. The path was narrow and when she raised her eyes, she saw wounds on the tree trunks showing where branches had been chopped off to make it easier for carried canoes to pass. Down beside her, she could hear the rushing of the rapids. Abruptly the path opened into a small clearing. Bare poles from a small tent stood near one edge. In front of it three sharpened roasting sticks stuck out of the ground beside charred logs.

Tatsea looked around for signs of people, then tiptoed to the camp, scanning the ground for tools. At first she found nothing, just a few stones and bits of wood and small tree stumps poking up through the snow. Then her eye caught something leaning against a tree behind the tent frame. Her heart leaped as she hurried to pick it up. It was a stone axe. With an axe she could cut down trees. The edge of the axe blade was dulled from use, but careful chipping with another stone would sharpen it, she thought. Many times she had watched her father chipping away at the special stone brought from the medicine place where Yamozha was born.

Encouraged by her find, Tatsea searched the clearing for other useful things but she found nothing. Still, she was satisfied and about to return to her camp when she spied the path where the portage continued beyond the clearing. Why not go to the end of the portage and explore the riverbank for items from the canoe?

About ten steps along the path a spot of bright light caught her eye. The spot looked like sunlight glistening from water, but she was up on the bank, high above the river. Warily, she tiptoed closer. The spot of light changed when she moved, though it stayed in one place. Gripping the stone axe, she crouched before the shiny object. Flat like a piece of ice, the colour of evening water, it had an unusual shape. Unlike the sharp, jagged corners of a piece of ice broken from a pool of water, this object had four edges, each smooth and straight. Tatsea had never seen such a shape anywhere.

With trembling fingers Tatsea reached out and picked it up. The edges felt hard and sharp. Then something moved inside the shiny surface. She lifted the object a little higher, then dropped it with a cry. A person was hiding inside the piece of water.

CHAPTER NINETEEN

THE SHARP KNIFE CUT THROUGH THE BELLY OF THE WHITEFISH as easily as lard, Ikotsali thought. What strange magic these Enda raiders had. Or was it magic? Once when he was a boy Ikotsali travelled with his father's camp to the quarry far to the north, to the place where Yamozha was born. For days the people chipped away at the walls of the cliff to gather pieces of the cutting stone for their knives and arrowheads. But even the best, most carefully crafted stone knife could not cut the way this enemy knife could. What strange quarry of rock did these Enda raiders have access to? With such sharp tools at hand, what was the purpose of killing his people for their hair? The Copper people, with their soft yellow knives, were fierce and a dangerous enemy. But no Copper man had ever been interested in slashing the hair from a man's head or a woman's. Could some evil medicine in these strange tools make men do deeds bloodier than even those told about monsters in long-ago stories? With a sharp tool like the knife in his hand a man could always kill food; it could not be the madness of hunger that drove these men to slaughter his people.

Ikotsali scooped entrails out of the whitefish and tossed them to a trio of ravens walking around in a circle at the edge of the bush. For a moment the ravens reminded Ikotsali of a very slow drum dance. He grinned and looked at his baby daughter lying on a hide blanket near the fire. He had laid the baby naked on the hide after he had cleaned her up and emptied the moss bag. Now his daughter was enjoying the freedom of kicking her legs and waving her arms. A travelling baby spent far too much time in the moss bag.

A log cracked in the fire; two of the cooking stones glowed red hot. He laid down his knife and reached for the lifting sticks. Deftly he grabbed a red-hot stone between the sticks and lifted it over the opening of the stomach pot and dropped it in. He grabbed the other hot stone, dropped it in, and quickly tied off the opening to keep the heat inside.

The baby gurgled and then called out with a delightful sound. Ikotsali looked at her with a smile; she had grabbed both feet with her hands. "Bebia nezi," he said, clucking his tongue. The baby met his eyes for a moment; then he turned back to cutting up the fish for the pot. All too soon the baby would feel her hunger and all too long before the water would boil to cook the fish.

When he finished cutting up the fish, he pulled the cooled stones from the pot and dropped in red-hot ones. Then he added the pieces of fish and tied off the stomach again. Once he had heard the story of a chief of the Copper people who had a sheet of the soft yellow stone so large he was able to make a cooking pot for his wife, a cooking pot stronger than fire, a cooking pot that could boil water without cooking stones. The water got so hot in the copperstone pot that the wife burned her hand when she lifted the pot from the fire. The pot dropped from her hand and spilled the boiling water on the chief's foot. The enraged chief slapped his wife so hard he broke her nose and when the evil pot cooled down he broke it into small pieces, which he traded for a moosehide canoe. No one had tried to make pots with the soft yellow stone since then. Ikotsali looked at the hard, sharp knife in his hand. Would these evil Enda raiders make pots out of this hard stone?

The baby squealed on the blanket. Ikotsali glanced up from the knife. His little daughter had rolled over on her stomach, pushing at the hide with her hands, bending her knees and kicking her feet in the air. Ikotsali smiled at the patch of blue skin on her bum. "It will soon be time for you to crawl," he said to his daughter. "Just don't run away. Stay on the blanket."

A shadow fell over the baby, a soft shadow like a cloud drifting in front of the sun. Ikotsali kept his eye on his little daughter kicking her legs on the hide. The shadow stayed, so Ikotsali turned to pick up the lifting sticks and glanced toward the bush. His heart almost stopped. The shadow stretched from the baby on the hide across the pebbles of the beach, across the grass and the rosebushes and the fireweed. Between two trees, a creature stood like a man, taller than a grizzly bear, eyes glowing from the furry face like coals from a dying fire.

Ikotsali tried to reach for his baby on the hide, but the glowing eyes fixed on his and looked deep into his eyes, down through his neck, through his heart, all the way down to his toes, eyes that burned him and froze him at the same time. He couldn't move, he was frozen hot with his hands reaching out for the baby. The creature just stood staring into his eyes, staring into his dreams, deep into his heart, sucking at his power.

And then the sun sank behind the trees and Ikotsali felt himself falling, without end as if in a dream, yet the ground pressed up against the soles of his moccasins. He could not move; he could not look away.

Out of the corner of his eye he saw a movement. The baby! The baby crawling! The baby crawled off the hide into the grass. He saw the little blue bum move between a rosebush and a fireweed plant. Slowly, like an endless fall in a dream, the baby crawled unafraid, straight ahead toward the bushman. The baby's blue bum disappeared between the bushman's legs.

The last light disappeared. Even the stars would not shine. Ikotsali stood frozen in the blackness, his hands reaching out for his baby.

CHAPTER TWENTY

ICE COVERED THE RIVER. SNOW COVERED THE HIDE BLANKET beside the cold fire. Ikotsali still stood, reaching out, unable to move. The sky reddened through the treetops. A raven glided down from a tree and tore at the stomach pot with its crooked beak. Slowly sight returned to Ikotsali's eyes. He saw the light covering of snow on the ground. He saw the outline of the empty hide blanket.

He heard the raven squawking, saw it tear at the stomach pot. His hands dropped and he kicked the raven away from the dead fire. The insulted bird raucously flew up to a tree.

With his eyes wide open he saw again how the baby crawled off the hide blanket, between the rosebush and the fireweed plant, through the grass between the bushman's furry legs, into the bush. With his eyes to the ground, he followed the baby's path. Through the thin snow he saw one large footprint pressed into the ground where he had last seen the baby. Larger than the feet of three men, the footprint had six toes. It pointed toward the bush.

Ikotsali sniffed, smelled cold air. He looked at the branches of the trees ahead of him. No telltale bits of fur stuck to any of the branches. Ikotsali stumbled into the bush. His eyes darted wildly from side to side, hoping to see a sign of a track, spruce needles scraped by a dragging foot, a dead branch freshly broken. He ran faster, refusing to duck to avoid the branches whipping his face. He had to find the baby. He had to find the bushman. He had to find the baby before it was forever altered by the bushman's spell. Only his own frog-medicine power had enabled him to fight off the bushman's trance—a fight that lasted all night. And even now, zigzagging through the bush, his darting eyes catching the movements of shadows and birds, he felt drained of his power. But he couldn't stop. He could not let his fear of the bushman keep him from his child.

That's when he heard the drum. At first he thought he heard his own pounding heart. He broke his run and stopped beside a tree. He felt his heart, but he heard the drum, a tiny drum beating quietly. When his own heart slowed he heard the drum more clearly. More clearly—but growing fainter.

Ikotsali looked around slowly. He saw the rising sun through the trees. He saw the scrapes of his footsteps in the light snow. He saw the madness of his run. As if all his knowledge of tracking animals had been wiped from his mind by the bushman's trance, his desperate run had taken him in a giant circle. He was only a few steps away from the edge of the bush, a few steps from the spot where the bushman had stood.

The tiny drumbeat strengthened slightly. Then he heard a cry, a cry so faint he thought it might be a part of the bushman's trance. Then he heard it again. He looked at the spot where the bushman had stood. A short distance from the six-toed footprint lay a spruce bough covered with dry leaves.

Ikotsali stole up to the leaf pile and carefully crouched beside it. With trembling fingers he brushed the leaves aside. His baby huddled naked in the leaves and needles. She cried out again, but her cry was cut short by a fit of coughing. Her little nose was caked with mucous. Gently, Ikotsali lifted the baby out of the leaves and slipped her inside his shirt. Her little body like ice against him, she sneezed. Her convulsing body strained against his shirt, the mucous from her nose sprayed his chest. Cradling the baby in his arms, he stumbled back to the dead campfire.

The stomach pot lay in shreds on the ground, bits of whitefish scattered beside the ashes. Keeping one hand on the baby under his shirt, Ikotsali gathered wood for a new fire. The morning air was still and the thin layer of snow had not wet the wood. His firestones were safe in the pouch at his waist. Soon the fire crackled in front of him.

The baby sneezed again inside his shirt, then coughed and cried out in hunger. He would have to feed the baby soon. But he had no stomach pot. He had no fish. The river was frozen. He had only one birchbark pail in the canoe. Could he hunt caribou with a sick baby inside his shirt? A vision of the noisy widow, Dagodichih, passed through his mind. Should he have stayed in her tent? But his little daughter had refused that woman's breast. The little mouth fastened on his own nipple and he felt a new hardness, a tiny tooth poking out of the lower gum. In his mind he glimpsed Tatsea bending to lift a fat hare caught in a snare.

Ikotsali found the moss bag beside the hide blanket and stuffed it full of dry moss. Then he rummaged through the bundles in the canoe for the little shirt the noisy widow had made for his daughter. When the baby was dressed and comfortably stuffed into the moss bag, he hung it around his neck under his shirt so the baby rested on his chest. Then he found a bundle of sinews in the canoe and he stole into the bush to set his snares.

After he set his snares Ikotsali began the slow process of heating water in the birchbark pail. He had just dropped the first red-hot stone into the water when he heard an alarmed squeak from the direction of one of his snares. He hurried over and found a large hare caught but not killed. Ikotsali grabbed the hare and with a quick movement dug his fingers in under the hare's ribs to stop the heart. Long ago his mother had showed him how to do this, warning him never to kill an animal slowly. Remembering this, he heard his mother's voice telling him a story while she showed him how to drain a hare's blood into a pot, how to crack the skull to scrape the hare's brain into the pot and mix it with the blood. His mother told a story of a man who had saved his dead wife's child with hare's brain and blood.

Ikotsali didn't rush as he remembered this story and when he checked the other snares he found two more hares.

It took a long time for the brain and blood mash to be heated up. Ikotsali set the hare meat to roast on sticks and stirred the mash while the baby sneezed and coughed and cried and sometimes slept against his chest. At last the food was ready and Ikotsali used his finger to shove the thick mash into the baby's mouth. The baby was so hungry she did not refuse the strange food and Ikotsali had a shuddering thought that if only he had let the baby get hungry enough she would have accepted the noisy widow's milk.

But it was too late for that and Ikotsali brushed such thoughts from his mind as he spent the next few days keeping the baby warm and fed. A little back in the bush he built a small shelter, covering logs with spruce boughs, and he checked his snares three times a day. He never let the fire die and always kept a red-hot stone ready to be dropped into the water.

The baby ate and slept and seemed stronger but her cough would not go away. The cough and the sneezing kept getting worse.

One morning the baby coughed so much and her nose was so plugged up with mucous Ikotsali thought his baby would die. He had been too proud, he thought. He had thought he could keep a baby without a woman's warmth. He saw himself stumbling alone into a Dogrib camp. He felt the staring eyes.

He could not let his baby die. He must search deep inside

himself for some medicine to save his daughter's life. A feeling nagged him, something he knew, something that would cure the baby's sickness. But he couldn't remember; he felt as if the bushman's trance had wiped things from his mind. Tatsea must not lose her daughter.

With the baby cradled inside his shirt, he fell asleep beside the fire. He dreamed of Tatsea, her belly big with the child, sitting beside the tent. A pile of red willow branches lay beside her. With deft fingers Tatsea stripped the inner rind from the willow bark and twisted it into long strings to be woven into fishing nets. And then he dreamed of his mother boiling water in a stomach pot, a stomach pot filled with the inner rind of the red willow.

Darkness had fallen when at last he dipped out some of the willow broth with his small drinking cup and let it cool. Then he fed the broth to the baby with the drinking tube.

At first the baby spit out the strange broth. Then she began to swallow. When the cup was empty she fell asleep. After a while Ikotsali heard his daughter's breath flow more easily through her tiny nostrils.

Each day Ikotsali peeled and boiled willow rind. Each day the baby's breathing improved. When not boiling willow rind, Ikotsali used the Enda axe to strip branches from fallen trees to build a more secure shelter. Though the baby was growing stronger Ikotsali decided not to travel.

CHAPTER TWENTY-ONE

TATSEA HELD THE AXE READY TO SMASH ANYONE WHO JUMPED out of the shiny object. But when the strange piece of water didn't move, Tatsea knelt in the snow and waited. She wasn't going to turn her back and let this person attack her from behind. Nothing happened. How could a person get inside such a small object? Had she seen anything at all?

She leaned forward to look again, then jerked her head back. A woman had looked at her from inside the piece of water. A woman like the woman who looked up at her from the lake sometimes. But the woman in the lake was never so clear, so real. The woman in the lake was more like a shadow.

Tatsea leaned forward again. She didn't blink when the woman looked back at her. The woman's hair was black; three thin black lines marked the light brown skin of each cheek. Tatsea remembered how Ehtsi, her grandmother, had poked her cheeks with an awl and rubbed in the blackness from a burned stick to make such lines. Were those lines still on her face? Her fingers reached up to touch her cheek. In the piece of water the woman's fingers reached up to touch her face, too.

"Yexe e?i," Tatsea said. You do like me. And even while Tatsea spoke the woman's lips moved. "Yek'adawo." You tease me. And Tatsea laughed together with the woman in the piece of water.

The woman in the piece of water seemed so friendly Tatsea soon lost all fear of her. Using strands of her hair for thread, Tatsea sewed a little bag from a squirrel skin with the fur turned in to keep the piece of water on a string of babiche around her neck. Then whenever she felt lonely she took out the piece of water and talked to the woman. They looked into each other's eyes and together they untangled their hair with their fingers. Tatsea discovered that by holding the piece of water in different positions, she could see different parts of the woman all the way from her head to her feet. She studied the woman, staring at her nose, her eyes, her lips, her chin. Without thinking she began playing with different poses and expressions on her face and always the woman in the piece of water acted with her like they were sisters. They smiled together and frowned together and sometimes stuck out their tongues at each other.

One day she noticed the zha, the lice, crawling in the woman's hair and the look on the woman's face told Tatsea that the lice crawled in her hair, too, and so by watching each other closely the two women picked the little bugs out of their hair and popped them into their mouths. The zha were plentiful for it had been a long time since Tatsea had been with anyone who would notice the bugs and pick them out of her hair for her.

Tatsea talked to the woman even when she was too busy to hold the piece of water in her hands, sure the woman could hear her where she nestled inside the squirrel bag around her neck. Tatsea told the woman about her baby and her frog-faced husband, Ikotsali. She told her about the camp on Do Kwo Di and how the Enda raiders had killed her people for their hair. What did such men want with her people's hair? But the woman never answered her question. Even when Tatsea pulled out the piece of water and stared hard into the woman's eyes while she asked the question, the woman merely moved her lips, spoke words with no sound.

Sometimes Tatsea talked about her baby for so long that the women cried together and sometimes Tatsea thought the woman's face changed with the tears running down her cheeks. Sometimes Tatsea thought that if the black lines weren't there on her cheeks the woman would look just like her baby daughter. And then some animal cry in the bush made her remember her baby's cry and she would think of the moss bag she had left hanging on the tree and her heart hurt like a cut from Blueleg's hard, sharp knife.

So she would hide the piece of water inside the squirrel bag and go to check her snares or begin chopping down a tree with the stone axe, a task that sometimes took three or four days. At times she almost gave in to knowing who the woman in the piece of water really was but she pushed that thought to the edges of her mind—she didn't want to be all alone again.

As the days shortened Tatsea rose from her bed as soon as spots of light showed through the holes in her shelter. She gave no thought to resting while there was light in the sky. She checked snares and set new ones. She gathered firewood. She strengthened her shelter. Each day her nostrils sensed an increased chill in the air. Each morning more snow covered the ground.

Her collection of hare and squirrel skins grew and she began sewing them together to make a winter coat. She also built a marten trap with logs and a string of babiche tied to a piece of hare for bait. After a while she had enough skins to make a warm sleeping robe. Tatsea never stopped doing things, except in the dark when she slept, or when she needed to talk to the woman in the piece of water. Meat was always roasting over the fire or keeping warm in the stomach pot she hung beside the flames after the hot stones had heated the water. While she set her snares she would keep her eyes open for berries frozen on the bushes.

If only she could kill one caribou, she thought, but she feared letting the fire go out and she didn't want to wander far from her camp in search of the caribou; hunters sometimes wandered for days before they found the animals. Without weapons or anyone else to help her, she feared she might die in the attempt.

More snow fell, so Tatsea cut some saplings and laboriously carved long sticks and soaked them in the open water of the rapids so she could bend them into snowshoe frames. With sinews cut from the small animals' backs, she wove the webbing. When she finally put them on her feet and stumbled around in the deep snow, she thought she heard Dienda, her boy friend with the big ears, laughing at her. Tatsea stuck her tongue out at him, then wondered what had happened to him and his brothers.

With the snowshoes she set her snares farther from her camp and she built more deadfall traps. One day she caught a porcupine in her deadfall; cautiously she pulled out the quills to decorate her new winter coat.

On another day, returning from her snares, Tatsea passed a stand of red willows on the riverbank. She thought of fish and quickly gathered an armful of thin branches and carried them back to her camp. After she had dealt with the two hares and the ptarmigan in her pack, she sat down beside the fire and peeled the bark from the branches. Then she peeled away the inner bark and twisted it into long strings. This was long, tedious work but the thought of having a good supply of strings to make a net in the spring kept her busy. Besides, it was hard to look at the woman in the piece of water in the flickering light of the fire, and sometimes dark winter nights just seemed too long to spend huddled in her shelter, sleeping alone. The fire and the busy fingers made the night a little less lonely and the far-off wolf howl less frightening. And during her peeling and twisting of the willow rind Tatsea talked to Ikotsali, her husband.

In the time since the caribou bull crushed her father's leg and Ikotsali moved into their tent and took her for his wife, Tatsea had hardly spoken a word to this frog-faced father of her child. She had listened to his orders and obeyed his commands. She had listened to the things he told her under the sleeping robes at night, the things he had seen during the day when out hunting in the bush or out on the lake checking his nets. She had listened, but she had been afraid to speak, frightened of his frog face with sores dripping even in the darkness of the night. She never turned away from his touch, she knew what a wife must do, but she had been unable to speak, even when Ikotsali asked her a question and held his breath for an answer. She just lay there in the darkness, holding her breath, too, feeling the warmth and stickiness of his face above her. Then he would slowly release his breath into the darkness and turn away from her and sometimes not speak to her for days.

But he never struck her and as her belly got bigger with the baby he often picked out the tastiest parts of the meat for her to eat. And in the dark his hand on her belly feeling for the baby's kick was as gentle as a feather or a snowflake on a day with no wind. Ikotsali, the only child of his parents, seemed more curious about a baby growing inside a woman than any other man she had seen in her life. The men who took her sisters for wives had never seemed interested in their growing bellies in the same way—except to brag to the other men. At least, Tatsea had never noticed such gentleness in her sisters' husbands, even in those first seasons when a husband lived in his new wife's father's tent. And yet Tatsea could not speak to Ikotsali, could not tease him or tickle him or even return his kisses the way she could have with Dienda, her squirrel boy with the big ears she had played with from the time she was big enough to crawl away from the stinky moss bag.

But now while she peeled the willow bark and twisted the rind into string, she sometimes talked to Ikotsali until her tongue got tired. She told him how many ptarmigan she had caught and that a wolf had howled in the night and that the two ravens fought over the hare guts. She told him about her journey with Blueleg and Redcoat and the boy who attacked her and she told him about the sharp knife at the bottom of the river and the thunderstick gone from where it had been sticking up from between the two rocks in the rapids. Tatsea told him about the woman in the piece of water and how they helped each other pick the zha bugs out of their hair.

She told him about the red willows she was peeling and she told him how she would boil the rinds to make a medicine soup if she got sick. But she was not sick, she was feeling well, and she wasn't hungry. She could eat every day.

And while she talked, it sometimes seemed as if she could see Ikotsali sitting on the other side of the fire, cradling the baby in his arms, the flickering flames casting shadows of light on his face. One evening she heard the baby sneeze and she told him to boil the willow rind to make medicine soup for the baby. And sometimes she heard Ikotsali's voice talking back to her and she answered his voice and they had a conversation and when Tatsea crawled into her hut to sleep she would have warm dreams.

The days got colder; the dark nights grew longer. Snow fell every night. Then a howling blizzard kept her huddled in the shelter, the blowing snow so thick she could barely tell day from night. She moved the fire into the doorway of the shelter and choked on the smoke until she poked a hole in the roof to let the smoke escape. When the storm ended the bush cracked with cold, the animals in her snares frozen stiff.

The days were so short that Tatsea worked from first light until dark, gathering firewood, checking snares, and melting snow for water. She dared not risk dipping water from the still open river, for the rushing rapids sprayed water on the rocky shore and coated it with treacherous ice. It got so cold the animals stayed in their burrows and for several days Tatsea made rounds of empty snares. One morning she found a white ptarmigan frozen solid still clinging to a branch. It took a long time to thaw.

Still, Tatsea had enough to eat because she had gathered food every day and she was comfortable, though during the endless nights she longed for her family's tent with the warm breaths of the other people steaming up the air. One evening as she knelt on the spruce boughs she had spread beside the fire, chewing on a piece of roasted hare, she was startled to see a pair of eyes watching her from the edge of the firelight. She shivered, thinking a wolf had found her and she quickly looked around to see if there was a whole pack. She saw no other eyes. Then a dog sidled into the light, stood for a moment staring at her, tongue hanging down, tail wagging. Tatsea didn't move, uncertain what to do. The dog stepped closer, sniffed, then lay down beside her, head resting between front paws on the boughs. The dog's brown eyes watched Tatsea and the piece of meat in her hand. Gently, Tatsea dropped the meat in front of the dog. The dog sniffed the meat and quickly gulped it down. She reached for another piece of meat roasting on a stick and dropped it before the dog. Again, the dog gulped it down and waited. Tatsea fed the last of her roasted meat to the dog. The dog still eyed her expectantly, but when Tatsea made no move to provide more food, the dog whimpered for a moment, got up, yawned and stretched, then turned and vanished into the shadows.

Tatsea felt a mixture of relief and emptiness when the dog was gone. The few dogs that lived around her people had been no more than a presence on the edges of the camp. They fed themselves, except for scraps of meat thrown to them when the camp had plenty of food. The dogs were a part of the camp, in the way of ravens and gulls. When she was a child she had befriended a dog, until her grandmother scolded her for putting her coat on the dog's back.

Not sure what to think about this dog, she pulled out the piece of water with the woman in it and told her the story about the young woman, living with her brothers, who married a handsome stranger. One night the woman woke up to find herself alone in the bed, her husband gone. The sounds of a dog gnawing on a bone annoyed one of her brothers, who threw his axe at the sound. When the woman lit a fire they found a big black dog in the tent, lying dead. After that, her stranger husband was not seen again. The woman's brothers declared that her husband had been a man by day and a dog by night and they threw her out of their tent and they left her behind when they moved their camp because she had slept with a dog man.

For a long time the young woman lived alone until one day she gave birth to six puppies. Ashamed, she hid them in a sack. Yet she couldn't help loving them and she set out each morning to snare hare for the puppies to eat. One day, returning to her camp, she heard children's voices and she found children's footprints in the snow around the fire. But she saw no children, only her puppies huddled safely in their sack. The next day the woman left as if to check her snares but instead of going to the bush she hid behind a tree and watched the tent. Soon the puppies scrambled out of the sack and when they began to play around the fire they turned into children. The woman leaped out to gather her children into her arms. She caught three, two boys and a girl. The other three children scampered back into the sack and in the darkness of the sack became puppies again. The two boys grew up to be great hunters with strong power. They married their sister and had many children and that was how the Dogrib people began.

After the dog left, the night turned very cold; Tatsea couldn't sleep, so she left the shelter and walked to the riverbank and looked up at the sky. The moon had not yet risen and the stars shone so brightly they looked like they might drop to the earth. Tatsea saw chik'e who, the star of the north that never moved. If she walked at night the star could help her find her way back to Wha Ti.

Tatsea was still thinking about walking back to Wha Ti the next day when she returned to her camp with a marten and two hare. She laid the animals on the snow and built up the fire. But before she set to skinning the animals she pulled the piece of water from its squirrel-skin case and talked to the woman about walking back home at night with the stars helping her to find her way. But as always the woman just mimicked Tatsea's every move.

Sudden voices shocked her, but before she could hide, six men surrounded her, the fur around their hoods covered with frost as if they had been walking for a long distance. Two men carried thundersticks; another, pulling a wooden sled, gripped a spear; the others brandished arrows notched in their bows. Tatsea did not move. No use to cry out, too late to play dead.

Once the strangers determined that she was alone, they lowered their weapons and curiously examined her camp. One man pulled up her snowshoes stuck in the snow beside her hut. He looked at their long shape with pointed ends and laughed, then passed them around to the other men. The strangers wore snowshoes short and rounded like fat beavertails. Another man crawled into her shelter and in a moment had discovered the bundle of scalps and tossed them out onto the snow. They found her axe and her cache of meat and her collection of skins and sinews and porcupine quills. Everything was quickly stuffed into their packs. Her collection of twisted willow-rind strings puzzled these men and one man waved it in Tatsea's face, asking a question with words she did not understand, then laughed and threw it back into the hut.

Satisfied that they had found everything of value, they dropped Tatsea's snowshoes at her feet and gestured for her to put them on. The man who had pulled the sled tied the bundle of scalps to it, then muttered at Tatsea and pointed at the pulling rope. Her thoughts still whirling, Tatsea stepped fearfully into the rope and began to pull. The man laughed and fell into step behind her.

The strangers led her through the bush until the light began to fade and they reached their camp, a circle of skin tents set up in a clearing. Women tended fires and cooking pots that hung over flames, yet didn't burn. Children chased each other through the snow. And Tatsea's heart ached when she heard the first baby's cry since her capture. For a moment she felt like she had come home.

The women gathered around her and the looks on their faces chased the feeling of home away. Even the boy who had attacked her had never looked at her with such hatred as these women did while they examined her face, her clothing, her snowshoes. One woman held her nose and laughed wickedly. Another poked her belly sharply to see how fat she was. A girl, younger than Tatsea, spat in her face.

Then the man whose sled she had pulled growled at the women and they scattered, but not before tossing a handful of snow in her face. Tatsea wiped her face and tried to get a good look at the man who might be a friend, but before she could turn her head he crouched, grabbed her around the knees, and lifted her up. Tatsea cried out when her belly hit his shoulder. The man laughed with a boastful roar, laughed harder when she kicked her legs and pummelled his back with her fists. The men, women, and children laughed and cheered and a snowball hit her ear. Tatsea's tormentor danced in a circle, swirling round and round. Tatsea gulped for air, the people around her a dizzying blur.

Suddenly, a challenging holler roared above the noise of the crowd. The man stopped in mid-circle and let go of Tatsea's legs. When Tatsea hit the snow the challenger rushed at her tormentor and grabbed him by the hair. The wrestling had begun. And Tatsea knew that she was the prize.

All evening long she was shouldered by one man, then another, as fights were won and lost. No sooner had one winner grabbed her and lifted her over his shoulder than another man hollered out a challenge and Tatsea would be dumped in the snow and a new fight would begin. Unlike the boy's fight with Blueleg, this fight involved no weapons; the goal appeared to be to pull the opponent's hair.

Tatsea found herself trapped between the wrestling men and the circle of onlookers. Every time she tried to move farther away from the scuffling men, the women rushed at her and kicked her or tried to pull her hair, even though one of the men always stepped in and chased them back. One woman grabbed her dress at the throat and tried to rip it, but Tatsea's sewing held. Tatsea almost got away, when another woman jumped on her back and reached around to scratch her face.

Just then a tremendous cheer went up from the onlookers and the woman was yanked from Tatsea's back. A fist landed in the woman's face and Tatsea was hoisted up on a winner's shoulders once more. Tatsea hung head down, feeling the blood from the scratch run across her cheek. Too tired to struggle, she closed her eyes to play dead and waited to be dumped in the snow at a new challenging shout.

But no new challenge came and the man carrying her strode across the clearing and dumped her in the opening of one of the tents. He nudged her with his foot and Tatsea crawled into the darkness with her new master right behind.

CHAPTER TWENTY-TWO

IN DAYLIGHT IKOTSALI SNARED HARES AND FISHED THROUGH the ice. Whitefish soup was still the best food for the baby, although she had five teeth now and showed interest in eating the food Ikotsali ate. The Enda axe made it a little easier to chop a hole in the ice. Ikotsali was tempted to attach a long, thin pole to the axe head to make an ice chisel but he feared the axe might fall off when it broke through the water and he didn't want to lose this valuable tool. Likewise he feared that the blade of the knife might break if he used it for a chisel. After studying the axe head, intrigued by the hole for the handle in this strange stone, he decided to risk inserting a longer handle. With the sharp Enda knife he carved a handle that fit tightly into the axe hole. Even so, he tied the head to the handle with babiche to ensure that he would not lose it accidentally.

He did get tired of the taste of whitefish and hare. He longed for a morsel of caribou, wished he had taken more meat when he fled Dagodichih's camp. But he had not wanted to overburden the canoe, for he had had hopes of finding Tatsea somehow. But then the baby became ill and now he wondered if his hope had been a foolish dream.

To push away these thoughts he studied the Enda knife and axe, then carved a handle that would turn the knife into a spear. Imitating the hole in the axe head, he used the knife to dig a hole in the end of the spear handle, into which he shoved the knife handle and then bound it tightly so it couldn't move.

Ikotsali wasn't ready to risk going in search of caribou, but he knew that caribou wandered far in search of food and if they came to his little camp he would be ready. Watching the child sleeping in the swing, he let his mind travel with the caribou. Although his father had never travelled to the place, he had told Ikotsali of meeting Barrenland people who had journeyed from the northern water that tasted like tears. These Barrenland people had said they had seen the place where the caribou gave birth to their calves. The baby stirred in the swing and Ikotsali wondered what a newborn calf looked like.

The little daughter, now recovered from her sickness, grew more active every day, and Ikotsali wished he had stayed with the noisy widow long enough for her to have made leggings and moccasins for the child. He tried to sew something from hareskin but he had no sinew. So he wrapped hareskins, fur inside, around the little legs and tied them with strips of hide. The Enda knife made it easy to cut strips straight and even. Thus the little girl was able to crawl about on the shelter floor, and after a few days was trying to pull herself up into a standing position.

Ikotsali found himself talking to the baby. It helped the time pass and kept his voice from dying. He had spent so much of his life alone, without speaking, that now he found that he would talk so much that sometimes his tongue would get tired. The thought that he was talking as much as Dagodichih, the noisy widow whose talk had driven him crazy, amused him, and the child stopped her crawling and gave him an anxious look whenever he stopped talking.

At first he talked about what he was doing, speaking the thoughts that passed through his mind while he worked at the various tasks he had to do throughout the day. Then he found himself telling stories, especially if the baby crawled into his lap when he sat beside the fire. Some stories told of long ago things—stories of Raven who played tricks on the people and Yamozha who made the world safe for people. He told Raven stories when ravens hopped around his camp and Yamozha stories at night when the fire burned low in the doorway of the shelter. In his wanderings around the camp he had determined that the small lake they were living beside was the lake where Yamozha met the old people with a daughter who became his wife, but the old people were evil and they tried to trick Yamozha into doing dangerous things to get him killed—getting feathers from an eagle's nest, sinew from a mammoth's back, arrowheads from under giant frogs. But Yamozha outsmarted the evil ones and in the end, when his wife changed into a grizzly bear who wanted to kill him, Yamozha had to kill his own wife with his arrows.

But after he had told his child all the stories he could remember about Yamozha, Ikotsali told her stories about her mother, Tatsea, the hawk. One story seemed to bring a smile to the baby's face. It was a story of how Tatsea would turn into a hawk and fly high above the trees until she would spy the baby below in Ikotsali's arms. The hawk would float down like a feather and perch on the log beside them and stare at them with her hawk eyes. Her feathers would drop to the ground and Tatsea would reach out and cuddle the baby in her arms until the sun had risen and set as many times as there were mosquitoes in a swamp. This story made Ikotsali feel so good and became so real in his mind, he began to believe it himself.

But Ikotsali feared the night. Nightmares disturbed his sleep and twice he awakened to his daughter's cry and discovered that he had almost crushed her beneath him as he rolled over in his sleep. He had made a small swing in the shelter but the nights were too cold to leave his child alone up in the swing when there was just one adult in the shelter to warm up the air. In winter people kept each other warm and children slept between their parents. But when he rested the baby on his chest and did his best to fall asleep on his back without moving, the dreams got more terrifying.

Especially the wrestling dream. That was when he moved most violently in his sleep. Yet what could he do? Always the dream began the same way—he was with Tatsea, watching her at the bathing rock, watching her nurse the baby, watching her cut up fish. Or he was sleeping next to her in the tent or paddling in the canoe down the river to the falls to fish for grayling. Tatsea was talking to him or talking to the baby. He heard her voice clearly at his ear, he smelled the woodsmoke in her hair, he tasted her cheek on his lips. Her hand caressed his chest under his shirt, her dark eyes sparkling.

And then an attacker gripped his shoulder, or his throat, and flung him aside face down in knee-deep snow. When he turned over, Tatsea screamed above him where she hung head down over the giant man's shoulder. She pounded her captor's back with her fists, but he paid her no heed as he raised his free arm high in the air and shouted out in triumph. A large circle of cheering women and men surrounded them, their faces lit up by the long, licking flames of a large fire in the centre.

Ikotsali scrambled up from the snow and hurled himself at the huge man. Another man stepped out from the circle and shouted a challenge. Tatsea's captor roared with laughter and dumped her in the snow just as Ikotsali reached for the enemy's shoulders. His hands passed through the enemy as if the man were made of smoke and Ikotsali sprawled face down in the snow again. Beside him Tatsea scrambled to her feet only to be attacked by two screeching women. Ikotsali jumped up and swung his fist but his arm passed right through one woman's head. He yelled at Tatsea and grabbed for her to pull her free, but there was nothing to hold on to.

Again and again Ikotsali flung himself at Tatsea's captors, to no avail. No one noticed him and the wrestling continued and Tatsea was tossed from one man to another. Ikotsali refused to give up and he kept attacking the smoke people until he stumbled and fell exhausted beside the fire, too tired to even close his eyes. He was forced to watch Tatsea dragged by her hair to a tent while the circled people cheered and stamped their feet in the snow.

A burning pain on his hand roused him from the dream. He jerked his hand away from the glowing coals in the doorway of his shelter and for a few breaths he was still in the dream, his eyes on the closed tent flap through which Tatsea had disappeared. He still heard the feet stamping in the snow. Just when the dream faded into nothing, a hawk slipped out from the tent flap and flew away—leaving behind the noise of shuffling in the snow.

The shuffling noise continued outside. Ikotsali sat up, cupping his burned hand. The baby, still cozy in her moss bag, stared at him with wide eyes from the edge of the sleeping robe.

"Etse ile," he whispered. *Don't cry.* Then he crawled outside into the pale morning sun.

Caribou crowded the open ground between the lakeshore and the bush, pawing through the snow to the plants underneath. Ikotsali held his breath and his heartbeat quickened, the nightmare wiped from his mind. For a short time he stood, letting the sight wash over him. *When caribou come to you there is hope, no matter what else has happened.* Then he slipped back into the shelter.

"Ekwo," he whispered to his child as he fastened the Enda knife to the spear handle. *Caribou have come.* The child grinned at him but made no sound.

Ikotsali moved like a shadow through the trees and into the midst of the browsing animals. With no small calves to protect, the cows were relaxed and he was able to slip up beside a good-sized cow and plunge in his spear without spooking the others. He pulled out the knife as the cow sank to the snow, and then he slipped silently up beside another. The knife blade was so sharp, it punctured the hide and plunged through to the lungs so smoothly, the animal collapsed almost before it felt the pain.

It was only after the third cow went down that the bull leading this herd sensed something wrong and called out a warning. The caribou began to scatter into the trees. Ikotsali gave chase to one more cow, but when he approached her flank she swung around and faced him with her antlers. He stopped, his spear ready. The cow bawled, then turned back toward the trees.

Ikotsali looked around. He was alone on the shore with three killed caribou. The child cried in the shelter so he hurried to build the fire to heat the whitefish soup, but his mouth watered for the taste of caribou to come. He sang a happy song as he crawled into the shelter.

"We will make it through the winter," he said to the baby as he brought the fire back to life. And he began telling the child a story about how Tatsea the hawk would find them again.

CHAPTER TWENTY-THREE

TATSEA'S LEGS ACHED. HER BACK HURT FROM THE HEAVY PACK that strained from the tumpline across her forehead. And the rope from the sled she pulled chafed at her hip bones. Tatsea was now the slave wife of Fish Mouth, the man who won her at wrestling. All night long she had smelled his rotting fish breath and in the morning light when she saw his chinless face, Tatsea thought his mouth looked like a fish mouth, too.

No more fighting had happened since then. Night travel kept the band busy. From sundown to sun-up the band followed a mean-looking man who carried Tatsea's bundle of skins on his back. He had a wife with a dog. The wife had tied Tatsea's people's scalps to the dog's back. Two or three other women used dogs to carry loads. For Tatsea, this insulted both her and the dogs. Was there no end to the evil of these people?

At first light Mean Face would choose a spot to make camp

and the women quickly built cooking fires and set up rough shelters to get them through the day.

Tatsea's slave husband, Fish Mouth, treated her roughly the first few nights, but once the band began travelling at night, he hardly even glanced at her. Tatsea knew that the easiest way to avoid mistreatment was to carry her burdens without complaint and not to draw attention to herself. Fish Mouth had another wife some years older than Tatsea, a sullen woman who rarely spoke. When the first wife crawled into the tent on that first night, Tatsea feared the woman would attack her the way the other women had during the wrestling. But after putting the two children to bed, the first wife silently made a place for herself in the sleeping robes on the other side of her husband.

The older woman said nothing to Tatsea, except to gesture her toward the sled when time came to begin the night's journey. Tatsea decided that the first wife must have pulled the sled herself before Fish Mouth brought home a slave wife. Sometimes Tatsea would notice an increase in the weight of the sled and when she looked back she would see the woman had added her own pack to the sled or set one of the children on the load to ride for a while. A few times when the sudden weight seemed more than usual, Tatsea found the first wife herself sitting on the sled, grinning at Tatsea in the moonlight.

Tatsea did her best to keep pulling and the first wife rarely left the extra load on the sled for a long time. Once, Fish Mouth caught the older woman riding on the sled. He snarled at her and the first wife scrambled off the sled so quickly she ended up face down in the deep snow beside the trail.

In the mornings when Mean Face chose the spot to make camp, Tatsea and the first wife quickly gathered firewood and began cooking. The first wife and some of the other women had small cooking pots made of the strange thunderstick stone—cooking pots that did not burn even when hung right over the flames. These women needed no cooking stones to boil water. Tatsea wondered where these pots came from, but she had no way to ask. Blueleg and Redcoat had talked little among themselves and even less to her so she had not learned enough of the language to ask such a question. This travelling band was more talkative, but Tatsea noticed that Fish Mouth's first wife seemed to communicate little with the other women, and so while there was lively conversation on the night trail ahead of her, Tatsea's new family trudged along almost eerily silent.

At first Tatsea didn't care. Those noisy, chattering women pulling sleds ahead of her had attacked her. But then she began to wonder about the first wife and she secretly watched her in the morning light around the cooking fire before they crawled into the tent to sleep through the day. The bones of the first wife's face seemed different from the bones in the faces of the other women. Even her hair seemed a different shade of black.

One morning after Fish Mouth had finished his meal and crawled into the tent with the children, Tatsea caught the older woman gazing at her as she gnawed the last bits of meat from a bone. After glancing over her shoulder at the other women still huddled around the cooking fires, the first wife crawled closer to Tatsea. Kneeling before her, she reached out to touch Tatsea's cheek. Hesitating, uncertain of the correct words, the woman said, "Goni gokwo di." The lines in your face.

Tatsea, startled, didn't understand at first. It had been so long since she had heard her own language spoken. The woman repeated the words and Tatsea replied, "Ayii? Yahti dok'ee? Tlicho?" What? You speak my people's language? Dogrib?

The first wife looked puzzled, but when Tatsea repeated her question the woman seemed to understand. After that the first wife tried to talk with Tatsea whenever she thought the others were too far away to hear. At night she walked beside Tatsea if the width of the trail permitted it. Sometimes she put the children on the sled and helped Tatsea pull it so they could talk. After a few days the woman remembered enough of Tatsea's language to tell her she had been stolen from her people when she was still too young for tattoo lines on her face. But she could not remember the names of her parents, or even her own name from before she was captured. "Ha die yenandi," the first wife said. Cannot remember.

The older woman avoided speaking Dogrib when Fish Mouth or the other families might overhear. And in the presence of the others, she tended to treat Tatsea rather gruffly. However, the older woman began to teach Tatsea the strange words of the enemy language. Astam. Come here. Wiyas. Meat. Tatsea listened but she never spoke these words unless she was alone with the first wife and her children.

Tatsea observed that the greatest part of the loads on the sleds and on the women's backs were animal furs. Helping the first wife put the heavy pack of furs on her back one evening, Tatsea asked, "Tsawo. Edi?" Fur. Where to?

The first wife looked at her curiously. "Necha dechi ko." Big stick house.

"Ayiha?" Tatsea said. What for?

"To visit men with fur on their faces."

"Fur on their faces?" Tatsea shuddered. "You will visit nahga—bushmen?"

The first wife looked puzzled at Tatsea's concern. "Not bushmen. Fur-faced men who live in big stick house. We get thundersticks and cooking pots that don't burn. And we get needles."

"Needles?"

"Yes, needles sharper than a fish bone. Needles that do not break even when I am sewing moosehide." The first wife groped underneath her winter coat and drew out a small bag. She opened it and pulled out a long, shiny sliver, a needle so thin Tatsea could hardly see it pinched between the woman's fingers. The first wife held it out to her and Tatsea grasped it with trembling fingers. It was harder than bone, with a tiny hole for the sinew at one end and a point at the other end so sharp that when she touched it with her fingertip, it pierced her skin. She jerked at the sudden pain and almost dropped the needle. A drop of blood appeared on her fingertip and she sucked it away. Tatsea wanted to test the needle by pricking a hole in the hide of her sleeve, but the first wife took the needle back and tucked it inside the little bag, which she slipped inside her clothes.

One morning Mean Face did not stop at daybreak to choose a spot to make camp. He kept on going, leading the band along the trail until the sun was high in the sky. Then he stopped, but instead of setting up the camp, the people busied themselves with the bundles of furs, unpacking them, sorting them, and repacking them. Mean Face repacked the collection of skins, sinews, and porcupine quills he had stolen from Tatsea's hut.

"What will happen?" Tatsea whispered to the first wife.

"We will trade fur for good things. Maybe even get some burning water. Fun. Dancing. Feast with fur-faced men."

So this was why the Enda raiders dragged animal furs on long journeys across the land. To get good things and to get burning water. Tatsea remembered the burning water log. She remembered how Redcoat smashed the log on Blueleg's head. Frightened, Tatsea looked around at her captors busy preparing their furs. Mean Face's wife knelt before a pile of her people's scalps. She held one of the scalps in her hand and untangled the strands of hair, first with her fingers and then with an object that looked like the fin of a fish.

Tatsea grew more frightened, and angry, too. "What will be done with my people's hair?" she whispered to the first wife.

"Trade for good things, maybe burning water, maybe red blanket. Fur-faced men like long fur from creatures who live in swamps."

"That's hair!" Tatsea said aloud. "THAT'S MY PEOPLE'S HAIR!" She rushed at Mean Face's wife and snatched the scalp from her hands. "YOU ARE CRUEL PEOPLE! YOU HAVE KILLED MY PEOPLE FOR THEIR HAIR! YOU ARE WORSE THAN BUSHMEN!"

For a moment the people were still, startled by the raging words from this woman who had been so silent along the trail. They did not understand her words but they knew what she was talking about. Then Mean Face called out sharply. Fish Mouth and another man grabbed her and though she shouted and fought she was soon dragged out of sight of the trail and shoved up against a tree. Tatsea screamed as her arms were forced around the trunk and tied at the wrists. Fish Mouth slapped her face, then grabbed her hair and yanked it. She choked back her scream and went limp as the other man lashed her legs tightly against the rough bark.

CHAPTER TWENTY-FOUR

EACH NIGHT IKOTSALI DREAMED OF A HAWK FLYING TOWARD THE sunrise until it hovered above Tatsea tramping through deep snow on snowshoes. Each day while he busied himself about his little camp, taking care of the baby, preparing food, mending his clothes, sewing new moccasins for himself and the child, more and more his thoughts were filled with Tatsea and where she might possibly have gone. He began to think of everything he knew about Tatsea and about Enda. He wandered through his memories for stories he had heard people tell, stories of other lands, other people, other ways and things. He remembered one fall caribou hunt when they met a Tets'ot'i band on the Barrenland who told stories of a big water larger than Tindee that brought strange men with faces like snow, who travelled in canoes so large they had trees growing in them, trees so tall they touched the sky. The Tets'ot'i claimed these strange men had many magic things, but strangest of all, these men in the huge canoes travelled without women, though it was said that the Enda from the land of the rising sun would let these strangers use their women.

Ikotsali thought about what he knew of the Tets'ot'i who wandered the lands of the midday sun on the other side of Tindee. He thought of Tlicho, Dogrib people, who had sometimes wandered with the Tets'ot'i and he thought of the story of the Dogrib men who had set off in search of these snow-faced strangers and never returned. He remembered what his father had told him about how the world was and where things were placed on it, how small rivers flowed into bigger rivers, which flowed into lakes and then into waters so large only spirits could cross them—and this water tasted like tears.

And he thought of the story of how the world was made. The first man, Tchapewi, had camped with his family beside a river where he built a fish trap that caught so many fish it blocked the river's flow and the river flooded until water covered the whole world. Just before their camp washed away, Tchapewi and his family scrambled into their canoe, where a collection of fleeing animals quickly joined them. For many days they floated on the floodwaters, looking for signs of land. At last, the waters stopped rising and Tchapewi sent a beaver into the water to search for land. For many days they waited for the beaver to return, only to see the beaver's drowned body floating past the canoe. However, Tchapewi would not give up and he sent a muskrat into the water to search for land. The muskrat, too, stayed away for many days, but at last returned to the canoe, exhausted, barely alive. Tchapewi pulled the poor creature into the canoe and discovered a small clump of earth in its paw. Tchapewi's heart thumped with joy, but before he touched the clump of earth he cradled the muskrat in his arms and warmed it with his body until the animal stopped shivering.

Then Tchapewi took the earth into his hands and shaped it and set it on the water, where it grew until it was a tiny island on the water. He set a wolf on the island, but the wolf's weight caused the earth to sink beneath him so Tchapewi told the wolf to run around to keep the island from tipping. For a whole year the wolf ran around and around the island, keeping it from tilting, until the island had grown large enough so all the people and animals on the canoe could go ashore and stand on dry land again. Tchapewi stuck a stick of wood into the ground, which turned into a fir tree that grew so rapidly that in no time its top reached the sky. A squirrel ran up the tree and Tchapewi chased it but he couldn't get close enough to knock it off the branches. He followed it up so high he reached the stars, where he found a fine plain and a beaten road. Here in the road Tchapewi set a snare made of his sister's hair. Then he climbed down the tree to the earth.

In the morning the sun appeared in the sky as usual, but at midday it got caught in Tchapewi's snare and the world was instantly darkened. Tchapewi's family accused him of having done something wrong when he was up in the sky and Tchapewi admitted this, saying he had not intended to do so. One by one he sent different animals up the tree to cut the snare to free the sun, but the sun's heat burned each of them up before they could reach the snare. At last Tchapewi sent up a ground mole, a grovelling and clumsy creature. The mole burrowed under the road in the sky, quickly chewed the snare, and freed the sun. However, the instant the mole poked its head up into the sun's light it lost its eyes and ever since then its nose and teeth have been brown as if burnt. While all this was going on, the island kept getting bigger and bigger until it grew to the size of the world today. With his fingers Tchapewi traced the rivers and scooped out the lakes so the waters could flow off the land again and leave living creatures a dry place to live.

Ikotsali dreamed of Tchapewi's fingers drawing rivers across the land and each time he dreamed he saw more of how the waters flowed from the big water, Tindee, to a bigger water that appeared to have no end. During the day he found himself staring at the baby crawling about on the packed snow near the fire, wondering if the child was strong enough for winter travel in unknown lands. He thought, too, of the weather, how once the cold was gone the snow would be wet and sticky, dangerous to travel through. It was a troubling decision to make, even while he prepared for a journey, making a sled from the hides of caribou legs, sewing extra moccasins for his feet, for he well knew how quickly footwear wore out when travelling long distances. When he had packed everything he thought he would need on a long journey, he found he had more than he could carry on his back and pull on the sled. So he built a cache up in a tree for much of the meat, but still he was almost too burdened to walk quickly when he finally set off one sunrise, singing to the baby as she bounced with each step in the moss bag on his back.

CHAPTER TWENTY-FIVE

TATSEA CLOSED HER EYES AND LISTENED WHILE THE PEOPLE disappeared down the trail, laughing and shouting. The rawhide ropes cut into her wrists; her hands turned numb and cold. Her mittens had fallen off when she was dragged to the tree. She opened and closed her fists to warm her hands. When she opened her eyes, her breath hung like a big cloud in front of her face. Her cheeks and her forehead tingled. Tatsea tried shrugging down against the trunk of the tree to slide her head into her hood but that didn't work.

A gust of wind chilled her face, and then her legs. One legging had slipped down below her knee and the wind bit her bare skin. It was too cold for a person not able to move.

Tatsea turned her head sideways, looking for something that might offer her any hope. Trees and more trees, trunks black under snow-laden boughs. Still Tatsea peered at each tree. She didn't know what she might be looking for but she kept looking, watching for movement. Off to her left just three trees away a snow-covered bush at the foot of a spruce caught her eye; it had a strange shape, no branches sticking up out of the snow. At first she thought it might be a stump of tree struck by lightning, but something about it made her shudder.

Tatsea forced her wrists apart as hard as she could. She tried rubbing the braided rope against the tree trunk but with her wrists so close together she just rubbed her own skin. She tried to move her feet but the men had tied the rope so tightly she could barely wiggle her toes.

A gust of wind dumped snow from overhead branches; pitching her head she cleared the snow from her eyes to stare straight at the strange bush. The wind had blown the snow off the top, revealing a tattered hood. Another gust dumped more snow on her head. When Tatsea cleared her eyes again, the tattered hood had blown back. A white human skull grinned at her.

Tatsea shrieked, then closed her eyes and listened to her echoing voice.

She screamed again, imagining her voice travelling through the trees to find a human ear. She imagined her voice finding Ikotsali's ear. She filled her lungs for another scream, when a mittened hand clamped over her mouth. Her terror sharpened; through her watery eyes she saw a red-coated man stumbling through snow between far trees. Then a woman's voice whispered, "Gondi ile." Don't talk. Tatsea blinked her eyes. The red coat was gone.

A knife slashed the rope at her wrists. "Run away. Go back to your people. Do not follow me." The first wife took her hand from Tatsea's mouth and slashed the rope at her ankles. "Go back to your people. Do not follow me."

Numb, shocked, Tatsea collapsed into the snow. Before she could stumble to her knees, the first wife vanished into the shadows of the darkening trees.

Tatsea wanted to run after the first wife, but she could barely move. She floundered in the snow until her blood warmed up enough to let her get to her feet. The skull grinned. Tatsea could not look away. She stumbled toward it, trying not to look at the holes where the eyes had been. She brushed the snow off the body. Its arms were lashed to a tree just like hers had been. Tatsea looked around. Three more trees looked like they had bodies tied to them. Tatsea stumbled to each one and brushed away the snow. One skull still had hair and some shreds of skin on its face. A string of babiche hung around the neck bones. Tatsea pulled on it. Out of the snow came a small pouch made from the feet of a swan.

Dienda! He had died with her swan's-feet pouch around his neck.

Tatsea staggered back to the trail. She found her snowshoes where they had ripped from her feet when she was dragged and one mitten trampled in the snow where the band had repacked their furs. She looked back along the darkening trail. She could travel all night and be far away before Fish Mouth would even think to look for her. He probably expected to find her frozen hard as stone by the time he came back, needing another scalp to trade for the burning water. If the first wife hadn't freed her. . . .

As she started walking briskly along the trail, Tatsea wondered why the woman hadn't come with her. Then, after as many steps as there were fingers on her hands, she stopped, remembering Mean Face's wife running her fingers through her mother's long black hair. She remembered the hair piled on the snow. She remembered the dog forced to carry the hair. She heard the first wife say, "Fur-faced men like long fur from creatures who live in swamps."

These fur-faced men believed that her people's hair came from creatures who lived in swamps. And as long as these strange men traded thundersticks, sharp knives, cooking pots that didn't burn, and burning water for her people's hair, the Enda raiders would keep killing her people until they were all gone.

Tatsea took a step in the direction the Enda had gone. She stopped again, wanting to weep and scream. Her baby! And

Ikotsali! Tatsea turned around and began a shuffling run back to her people's land. An appalling thought stopped her in her tracks. All she had were her snowshoes and the little bundle with the piece of water with the woman in it. Fish Mouth had stolen her bone knife and her fire bundle when he groped under her clothes after he had won her in the fights. Even the sinew snares she had carried in her belt were gone. And if she found a way to kill, how would she make a fire without firestones?

Then even darker thoughts raged through her mind. How could her baby not be dead? How could anyone have found the moss bag hidden up in the tree? The Enda would have killed Ikotsali. How could he have escaped? She had seen the Enda chasing him. The Enda would have taken his hair. Tatsea sat down in the snow and she cried. What could she do? If her baby was dead, if Ikotsali was dead, if she had no tools to survive alone, she might as well sit there and wait to die. Softly she began to sing the song her grandmother had sung as she prepared to die that winter when Ikotsali saved her father's life and became her husband. And then she thought about her mother and father and the other people in her camp having no time to sing before they died, how they still lay there on Do Kwo Di without their hair.

Tatsea staggered to her feet, slowly turned around, and trudged along the moonlit trail after the Enda band. Although her head swirled with dreams of Dienda's skull and the red-coated man, she walked steadily without hurrying, wanting to be sure she wouldn't catch up with her enemies or the first wife. Gone from her people for so long, the first wife couldn't leave this band now. She had a husband and children, and when Tatsea thought about this she decided she must do nothing to reveal that it was the first wife who set her free.

In the first morning light Tatsea discovered the edge of the bush. Before her lay a wide open space of white snow and a necha dechi ko, a strange, big, stick house—upright tree trunks close together, tops sharpened as if gnawed by giant beavers. Smoke rose from fires somewhere inside. To Tatsea the thing looked like a monstrous deadfall trap. Off to the side the Enda camped at the forest edge, fires out, silent as death.

Tatsea stole across the open snow toward the giant stick wall. Unsure what she would do when she got there, she knew that somehow she must get inside this house and talk to these fur-faced men the first wife had told her about. The first wife apparently did not fear these strange men and Tatsea decided that if they were not bushmen, then they must be humans, and just maybe she could tell these humans about her people's hair. She had nothing to lose. If nothing else she might be able to steal a knife to help her live in the bush.

Tatsea's long shadow nearly touched the wall when a creaking noise chilled her body. The wall in front of her began to move. Without wanting to Tatsea staggered backwards. The pointed heels of her snowshoes caught in the crusty snow and she fell on her back. The log wall kept moving, squeaking raucously in the frosty air, until the wall had opened up. A fur-faced figure walked out through the opening, then stopped, startled, when its eyes found Tatsea sprawled on the snow. The man carried a thunder-stick over his shoulder.

But Tatsea's eye was caught by the object clenched between the man's teeth. It looked like a drinking tube with a little bowl on the end of it. Smoke rose from this little bowl. The man sucked on the tube, then opened one side of his mouth and blew out a cloud of smoke, smoke that smelled different from any burning she had smelled before.

The fur-faced man looked at her and laughed. He spoke some strange words she could not understand. He pointed at her, then at the Enda tents on the edge of the bush. He waved his hand, telling her to go to the tents.

Tatsea scrambled to her feet, saying, "No! No!" in her own language, but in her hurry she tripped on her snowshoes again, kicking one off as she fell. Her snowshoe landed at the smoking man's feet. The man laughed again, blowing a big cloud of smoke out of his mouth. Embarrassed at her clumsiness, Tatsea didn't move, fearing he would drag her to the Enda tents.

The man stopped laughing. He picked up her snowshoe. Slowly he turned it over in his hands; he ran his fingers over the long pointed frame and the hareskin and guts lacing. Then he looked at her and Tatsea saw the question in his eyes. Tatsea shuddered. She had never before looked into eyes the colour of sky. The fur on his face and the hair sticking out from under his strange flat bonnet were the colour of a red fox.

Fox Face spoke a question in his strange words. He pointed to her and to the Enda tents and shook his head. Then he said in the Enda language, "You are not from them?"

"No," she said, remembering the word the first wife had taught her.

The next thing Tatsea knew Fox Face had helped her to her feet and was leading her through the opening in the log wall. He stopped to push the moving part of the wall closed behind them. Tatsea looked around in wonder. The stick house was so big, other stick houses stood inside it, houses made of logs and mud, it looked like. Fox Face gripped her hand tightly, though not roughly, and led her across the snow to the biggest house. He still held her snowshoe in his hand and Tatsea hobbled after him, her other snowshoe still on her foot.

Fox Face pushed open a piece of wall of the biggest house and pulled Tatsea inside. After the sparkling snow of the dawn, the inside of this house appeared black, like a cave at night, the only light a fire in a cave made of stones. "Stay here," he said in his strange language and he let go of her hand to cross the room to another piece of wall that might open. Fox Face struck the wall with his knuckles three times.

Tatsea's heart beat very fast; so many strange objects lurked in the flickering shadows of the firelight. This fur-faced man seemed friendly, but how could she be sure he wasn't a bushman? This house was strange enough to be a bushman's home.

Yet Fox Face had spoken to her in human language. She had never heard of a bushman speaking in human language before. Still, the language he used was the language of the Enda raiders, the men who killed her people for their hair.

He knocked harder and then a grumpy voice growled from behind the wall. Fox Face called out in his own language, not the Enda language. Then the wall swung open. Tatsea cringed when the white fur-faced figure emerged from the shadows. Fox Face pointed to Tatsea and handed the ghostly-looking man her snowshoe. Looking at the snowshoe, Ghost Face shuffled closer to the firelight, then stepped up close to Tatsea and peered into her face. He came so close that she had to turn away from his breath—sweet smoke and rotten berries. Blueleg's burning water smell.

Ghost Face muttered to Fox Face and Fox Face muttered back. Then both men reached for her coat. Tatsea turned away but Fox Face's strong hand on her shoulder forced her to stand still while Ghost Face fingered the small animal skins she had sewn together to make her coat. Fox Face said something else and let go of her shoulder to crouch before her. He grasped her leg at the knee to examine her leggings and run his fingers over the stitching of her moccasins. At the same time she felt a hand slide her coat up the backs of her legs. Tatsea stiffened, fearing the fur-faced men would use her as a slave wife, but then her coat was lowered again and Ghost Face's rotten berry breath blew on her again while he grasped her chin and, ignoring her eyes, ran his fingertips over the tattooed lines on her face. He muttered again, and Fox Face stood up to scrutinize her tattoos, too. He commented to Ghost Face as he stroked her cheekbone, then slipped his hand into her hair to finger her ear.

"Ile!" she cried, breaking away from the men. No! Her rush of words silenced the men. With a mixture of the Enda language, her people's Dogrib language, and many signs and gestures, Tatsea told the two men she was not a fur animal. As she talked and described how her people had been killed for their hair, she saw the men's faces change. For a moment she feared they were angry with her. Then the two men lifted their shoulders toward their ears and shook their heads at each other. Tatsea stopped talking. The fur-faced men did not understand her story.

Fox Face made her sit on a low stage beside a higher stage on which he had placed a strange bowl with hot soup. He gave her a tool, almost like the strange smoking object in his mouth, made of the same stone as Blueleg's knife.

Tatsea gripped the tool, frightened. Then Fox Face took the tool from her, dipped it into the hot soup, lifted it up, and put the bowl end into his mouth. Then he dipped the tool into the soup again, lifted it to Tatsea's mouth, and slipped it inside before she could turn away. Tatsea swallowed the hot soup. She had not eaten since before she had been tied to the tree. The soup tasted unlike any other she had eaten, but her hunger was so great, she did not refuse when Fox Face kept dipping more soup and raising it to her mouth.

The heat of the soup travelled through her body and each swallow made her feel more tired. Tatsea had not slept for two nights and a day. She felt herself drifting to sleep, still sitting on this strange stage, eating soup. The last thing she remembered was Fox Face grinning at her through smoke puffing out of the side of his mouth.

CHAPTER TWENTY-SIX

TINY CRYSTALS OF ICE HUNG IN THE SKY LIKE MIST AS IKOTSALI trudged across a frozen lake. Four sundogs chased each other around the sun. Ikotsali wiped the frost from his eyebrows and tightened his hood around his face. Bits of ice fell from the hareskin scarf wrapped around his neck. He wished he had taken time to snare animals with better fur before he set off on this journey.

On his back the baby kicked in the moss bag. His daughter was tired of sleeping on his back, tired of being carried. She wanted to crawl, to explore the world. The darkness inside his backpack was not to her liking at all and he felt her struggling to poke her head out from the hareskins he had wrapped around her. Ikotsali understood the baby's discomfort, but what could he do? The wind was light, but in this cold even a wind with the touch of a baby's eyelashes bit like a burning frost.

Shielding his eyes against the sun, Ikotsali scanned the

horizon of the lake for the nearest shore. All directions offered about the same distance to the shelter of trees. There was no use in trying to retrace his steps to find a path around the lake. He might as well go forward. At least he could walk quickly without snowshoes on the wind-packed snow, but he couldn't run, for his lungs could frost up if he moved fast enough to need to gulp air. The cold was but one hardship he had encountered since he had set out from the camp where he cached the meat. On the second day a storm came up at midday, forcing him to huddle with the baby in a hastily erected shelter with no opportunity to gather enough firewood to last for the two days the wind and snow howled around them. After the storm he tore his snowshoe lacing on a sharp stump hidden under the snow, so he spent the rest of the day repairing the snowshoe before he could continue.

With the storm had come colder weather. Although the sky was clear and sunny, the cold made travel difficult and the ice crystals in the air played tricks on his eyes. The lake he was crossing now seemed much larger than it had appeared when he first stepped off the shore. But he couldn't turn back, he had to keep moving ahead, even if the baby complained and struggled on his back.

As the day grew brighter, the ice crystals and the sundogs faded from the sky. But the sun glared off the snow, the blinding whiteness forcing him to walk with his eyes closed; he found himself stumbling this way and that so when he opened his eyes he wasn't sure if he was still facing the right direction. He tried to keep the sun in front of him, but this made it harder to see. He tried to keep looking at the snow in front of his feet and this worked for a time, but after some distance he would find his feet taking him in a circle.

Then his eyes made out a faint mist rising from the lake near the shore to his right. Mist rising in winter meant open water. Open water meant flowing water. Flowing water meant the mouth of a river. A river could take him nearer to Tatsea. Ikotsali adjusted his pack and raised the sled rope so it rested more comfortably on his upper chest. Keeping his eyes on the rising mist, he trudged forward with a quickened step. He began to sing to the baby despite the cold air. For some distance the baby seemed content on his back, trying to sing along with him at first, then falling silent. She is asleep, Ikotsali thought, but he kept on singing. He closed his eyes against the glaring snow, counting his steps through the fingers of both hands before he opened them again. Raising his hand to his forehead, he trudged forward again until the glare stung again and so he closed his eyes for another stretch. In this way he made his way nearer and nearer to the rising mist.

He kept up his singing; it helped him to keep moving, it helped him to think that he would find Tatsea. He kept his eyes closed through a count of his fingers and then another and then another. Far away inside his eyelids a tiny figure stumbled toward him. He quickened his step, nearly running, the snow hard under his moccasins. The baby bounced quietly on his back. His feet hardly seemed to touch the snow. The sled bounced over the hard waves of snow. Ikotsali waved at the tiny figure in the distance of his eyelids. The figure seemed to wave back.

Ikotsali shouted, but he didn't stop to listen. He didn't stop to open his eyes. He was intent only on the tiny figure far in the distance.

Then his feet broke through a crust of snow and he plunged into freezing water.

The baby screamed at the sudden jolt. The mist from the river mouth rose beside them. Ikotsali stood in a watery hole two fallen tree-lengths from shore. The water swirled around his legs, up close to his waist. He had to get to shore fast and build a fire. His only hope was that his bundle of firestones had stayed dry.

CHAPTER TWENTY-SEVEN

A MUSKY STINK TOUCHED OFF A SNEEZE. TATSEA OPENED HER EYES to darkness, except for a spot of weak light on the wall shaped like her piece of water with a woman in it. Her fingers felt for the little bundle around her neck and for a breath she wondered how Fish Mouth and his first wife had not found it and stolen it from her.

The stink came from the sleeping robe covering her. Softer than caribou or bear, with no fur on either side, the robe stank as if not properly prepared with brains and smoke. Still, she was warm under this robe, and the soft robe she lay on felt like a bag stuffed with moss. Her head rested on another stuffed bag, smelling of hair, but not the smell of her own hair or Ikotsali's. In the murky air above her she saw the faint shadows of logs that covered this strange shelter she was in—a log shelter taller than two grown men. The spot of light seeped in through drumskin hide stretched over a hole in the wall.

Tatsea's heart ached for her baby again. She closed her eyes and for a time she drifted through the forest along the rivers she had travelled on. Nowhere did she see Ikotsali and the baby. Even when she neared Wha Ti she saw no sign. She felt like she was hovering over Do Kwo Di. She tried to catch a glimpse of the tree where she had hung the moss bag. As she seemed to drop to the burned-out campsite, she thought she glimpsed the shapes of structures she hadn't seen there before, but then a cold thought slapped her awake. How could Ikotsali be following her if she had left him no signs to pursue?

Tatsea sat up, then fell back. She was not on the ground. She was lying up in the air on a stage.

She was dead!

The fur-faced men had killed her. They were bushmen. Fox Face had killed her with his soup. Tatsea reached up and felt her hair. She opened her eyes and looked around. Bundles of animal furs hung from the walls—more furs than she had ever seen at one time. Her people made clothing from the furs the women gathered—never did they collect more furs than they could use. Why would anyone kill so many animals and then carry the furs across such long distances? Even if she was dead she needed to find out.

Her legs still worked, so she slipped off the stage. She noticed her snowshoes leaning against the stage, but then a fur bundle near the patch of light caught her eye. From a distance in the shadows she had thought the bundle could be the skin of a long-haired hozi ejie, the muskox. But when she touched the fur and sniffed it she knew right away what it was. The first wife was right. These fur-faced men traded for hair.

Voices on the other side of the wall broke into her thoughts. Enda words! And one of the voices growled like the first wife's husband. Fox Face spoke and then the white-haired ghost man echoed his word, "Iskwew." Fox Face repeated the word. Were they talking about a woman? Were the fur-faced men asking the Enda about her?

"Mwac," Fish Mouth said.

"Mwac, no no," Mean Face's voice added.

Before Tatsea could think what to do the wall opened. Ghost Face rushed in, grabbed Tatsea's wrist, and dragged her into the room where the Enda were arguing.

Fish Mouth stared at her, mouth open. Mean Face stared, too, then began shouting at Fish Mouth.

"Astam!" Fish Mouth yelled, waving at Tatsea to come to him. Tatsea tried to hide behind Ghost Face, who still gripped her wrist. Fish Mouth stepped forward, but Fox Face blocked his way. "Niwa!"

"Mona!" Tatsea cried out, remembering the Enda words. "No, I am not his wife!"

Fish Mouth grabbed Fox Face by the shoulders to shove him out of the way when Mean Face laughed. These men will fight for me again, Tatsea thought, but before she could decide if that might be a good thing, Mean Face said, "Winipecapew," pointing at Tatsea. "Winipistikwanew! Wihcekisiw!" Tatsea remembered the Enda women's shouts, the words the first wife had later explained to her. Her face is dirty. Her hair is dirty. She stinks.

Fish Mouth let Fox Face go. Mean Face pointed at Fox Face, then at Tatsea. "Natawenimew," he said. He wants her. Then Mean Face gestured at Ghost Face. "Iskotewapoy?" he asked, curving the fingers of one hand and raising them to his mouth, pretending to drink. Fish Mouth laughed and shouted, "Iskotewapoy! Wihcekisiw!"

Fox Face looked at Tatsea, then spoke to his partner in his own language. Ghost Face answered and released her wrist. As soon as he stepped back into the room where Tatsea had slept, the Enda men started toward her but Fox Face blocked their way, speaking in a firm but calm voice.

Ghost Face reappeared, carrying two cups. Fox Face gestured for the Enda men to sit down at the stage. Ghost Face set the two cups down in front of them. The Enda men gripped the cups and carefully raised them to their lips. Tatsea's nose caught the sweet, rotting smell of burning water and she remembered the fight between Blueleg and the boy. I must escape again, Tatsea thought, and she tiptoed toward the place in the wall where she had entered this strange house of the fur-faced men. She reached the entrance without being noticed, but the wall would not move when she pushed against it with her shoulder. She pushed harder, then heard laughter behind her.

Fox Face appeared at her side, speaking softly in his own language. He laughed quietly, then showed her how to slide a carved piece of wood up out of another carved piece of wood. Tatsea stumbled backwards as the door swung open, then she rushed outside and breathed in the fresh air, sneezing when the glare off the snow struck her eyes. A few steps away from the stick house she squatted to relieve herself.

When she rose she caught Fox Face watching her adjust her skirt, like Redcoat staring at her through the bushes. Fox Face pulled the smoking tube from his mouth, stepped closer, and pointed at himself with his tube.

"McKay," he said. "I am McKay."

Tatsea looked at him, puzzled as he put the tube back between his teeth, sucked, and blew out a thin stream of smoke. When Tatsea didn't speak he pointed the tube at himself again and repeated his words.

"McKay, I am McKay." Then he pointed the tube at Tatsea. She stepped back, fearing some strange power.

Fox Face, sensing her fear, looked down at his tube, then hid it behind his back. With his other hand he pointed at himself and repeated the strange words, "McKay, I am McKay." Then he pointed at Tatsea. "What is your name?"

Tatsea still didn't understand, but when Fox Face gently repeated the word a few more times while he pointed to himself, she decided that she must try to please him so she pointed at herself and tried to repeat the same words he had said.

Fox Face laughed and shook his head. Then he stepped toward her and reached for her hand. Tatsea pulled back, but then she allowed him to take her hand in his and he pointed her finger at himself and said, "Me." He repeated the word three times, pointing her finger at himself each time he said it. Then he turned Tatsea's finger toward her and said, "You." He repeated this three times, then let Tatsea's hand go, and, pointing at himself with his own finger, said, "Me," then pointed at Tatsea and said, "You."

Tatsea smiled, raised her chin slightly, pointed at Fox Face, and said, "Me, me, me," then pointed at herself and said, "You, you, you."

Fox Face laughed and shook his head. Tatsea looked at her finger, puzzled, then looked at him, a flicker of fear in her eyes. Fox Face pointed to himself again and said, "Me." He pointed at Tatsea and said, "You." Before Tatsea could try to repeat what he said, he took her hand, pointed it at her and said, "Me." He let go of her hand. Tatsea looked at her finger, pointed it at herself and said, "Me." Fox Face smiled and nodded his chin up and down. Tatsea pointed at herself again, said, "Me," and looked up at Fox Face, who smiled again, then pointed at himself and said, "Me." Tatsea, puzzled again but just for a breath, looked Fox Face straight in the eye, pointed at herself, and said, "Me," in a determined voice. Fox Face nodded, pointed at himself again and said, "Me." Tatsea pointed at herself and as she said, "Me," in a louder voice, Fox Face, still pointing at himself, said, "Me," at the same time. Tatsea laughed; Fox Face laughed and then they repeated, "Me, me, me," until they broke down laughing.

It didn't take long for Tatsea to learn to point at Fox Face and say, "You," and then Fox Face pointed at himself and said, "Me, McKay." Tatsea grinned, pointed to herself and said, "Me, McKay." Fox Face frowned and shook his head. Tatsea frowned, too, at Fox Face, looked down at her pointing finger, then slowly raised her head, looked into Fox Face's waiting eyes and said, "You McKay."

Fox Face grinned and nodded his head. "Me McKay." He pointed to himself. "You . . . ?" He pointed at Tatsea.

Tatsea looked at Fox Face's finger pointing at her; she looked at her own finger pointing at Fox Face. "You McKay," she said. Then she bent her wrist to point at herself. "Me . . . ?" She paused. What was she? What was McKay? Hawk's wings fluttered through her head. She raised her chin and said, "Tatsea . . . me Tatsea."

"You Tatsea," McKay said, pointing at her with his pipe. Then he stuck the tube in his teeth, sucked, and blew out a cloud of smoke in her direction. Tatsea wrinkled her nose and waved away the smoke. Noticing how her hand pointed to the big stick wall, she said, "You . . . ?"

McKay pointed at the wall and then at the house. "Fort," he said.

Loud laughter from inside the house interrupted Tatsea's attempt to say, "Fort." The wall opened and the two Enda raiders burst through, each with a smoking tube between his teeth. In the doorway Ghost Face called after them in a friendly voice, waving what looked like a big knife longer than a man's arm. McKay hurried over to the raiders, and walked with them to the opening of the outer wall. He spoke calmly to them and, after he opened the wall, the two Enda laughed and slapped McKay on the back as they stepped outside the fort.

The moment the wall was closed again and the wooden bar dropped into place, McKay strode back to the house where Ghost Face still stood, brandishing his long knife. "Come, Tatsea," he said, waving her to the door.

Once inside McKay and Ghost Face talked in serious tones in their strange language to a third fur-faced man sitting on the floor near the fire cave. This man, with face fur the colour of caribou belly hair, rubbed a thunderstick with a piece of hide. How many other fur-faced men lived in this fort?

As they talked Ghost Face picked up a flat stone from the table, sat down, and began to rub the stone along the blade of his long knife. McKay picked up a cup and scooped white powder from a container similar to Blueleg's burning water log, only larger, into a large shallow pot. He shook more white powder from another cup into the pot, then stirred in animal grease and water to make white mud. With his hands he shaped the mud into a flat stone and laid it on the bottom of the pot. Then he hung it over the fire in the little stone cave.

Tatsea watched, still amazed that the pot would not burn. The mud slowly turned from white to brown and unfamiliar cooking smells soon filled the room. The smell grew hotter and hotter until Tatsea thought the mud would burn. McKay lifted the pot off the fire and with a stick tipped the pot so the white mud fell like a stone out onto the eating stage.

McKay set down the pot and pointed at the round, flat mud-stone. "Bannock," he said.

"Bannock," Tatsea said, pointing so eagerly her finger touched the strange stone. She jerked her finger back from the hot surface and sucked on it to soothe the burn.

"Hot," McKay said. "Wait."

Tatsea's tongue picked up the taste of the strange stone, bannock. McKay pulled a knife from his belt and with quick movements sliced three pieces from the bannock. After handing one piece to Ghost Face, he held out another to Tatsea. Hesitantly, she took the piece between her fingers. The bannock, still hot, no longer burned her fingers. She watched McKay and Ghost Face eat their pieces. Tatsea sniffed the bannock in her hand. The smell made her hungry. Then she ventured a small bite. The bannock tasted strange—not like meat or berries or roots or the inside of a caribou stomach. The taste was not unpleasant, though, and because Tatsea had not eaten since McKay's hot soup had put her to sleep, she quickly ate the rest of the bannock from her hand. McKay cut another piece and handed it to her with a smile. Then he pointed to her and said, "You Tatsea." Tatsea stopped herself from biting into the bannock, pointed at him, and said, "You McKay." McKay then pointed at Ghost Face and said, "You Dougal." Tatsea repeated his words. Then McKay pointed at the belly-hair-faced man who was aiming his thunderstick at the roof, and said, "You Smith." After Tatsea repeated his name Smith pointed at the thunderstick and said, "Musket."

"Musket," Tatsea repeated, watching him lower the weapon and lean it against the wall. "Musket kills my ears," she said in Dogrib. Smith raised his eyebrows at her words, then, from a ledge on the wall, he picked up what looked like a flat black rock the shape of Tatsea's piece of water with the woman in it. He picked up a small cooking pot, dropped the black rock in, and hung it over the fire. Then he picked up a larger pot, the size of a bark water pail, and dipped water from a container like a log for burning water, a log bigger around than any tree trunk Tatsea had seen. Smith set the pail down and sat down on a small stage to watch the pot he had hung on the fire.

The smell of this cooking frightened Tatsea like Blueleg's hot thunderstick resting on her shoulder. Still, she needed to know what would make Enda haul furs for such a long way so she stepped closer to the fire cave to see what was happening in the pot. The flat black rock was melting into thick black water.

Beside Smith a black tool lay on a piece of hide spread over another small stage. When all of the rock had melted, Smith reached out and lifted the small pot from the fire, set it down on the floor in front of him. He grabbed the tool from the hide. The black tool became part of the man's hand, as if the man's thumb and forefinger had grown into long black claws. The man dipped the claws into the small pot and pinched. In one quick movement he lifted the pinched claws out of the pot and dipped them into the large pail. Tatsea heard the sizzling of hot cooking stones dropped into water. When the sizzle stopped, Smith lifted the claws and opened them over the hide-covered stage. A small black pebble fell to the hide. Quickly Smith dipped the claws into the small pot again and repeated the motions until a second pebble dropped on the hide. By the time he had dropped as many pebbles on the hide as there were fingers on her hands, Tatsea had decided that Smith was making black pebbles for a thunderstick.

By this time McKay had shaped another white mud stone and was hanging it on the fire. A scraping noise caught Tatsea's attention and she stepped back a little to watch Dougal sitting at the eating stage, holding up his shiny knife longer than a man's arm. He stroked a stone along the curved tip of the blade, then ran his fingers along the edge. Suddenly a mouse scampered onto the table. Dougal swung his knife and cut the mouse in half so fast the front end of the mouse still ran two steps before falling over.

Before Tatsea could gasp a larger creature leaped up on the table and devoured the two halves of the mouse. At first she thought it was a baby nonda, a lynx, because the creature's ears were not tufted like an adult lynx, but then she saw the creature's long tail. No lynx had such a long tail. Once the creature had eaten the mouse, it arched its back and then leaped again—up onto McKay's shoulder. Tatsea thought McKay would fight off the nonda, but instead he stroked the animal's fur as if it were a child. Then McKay looked at Tatsea with a grin on his face. He turned so the creature could look at Tatsea. Tatsea had never looked into the eyes of a lynx. The one time she had caught a lynx in her snare the animal had been frozen hard in the cold.

McKay crouched and set the creature on the floor. Before Tatsea could move the creature lurked beside her foot, rubbing its neck on her moccasin leg. Tatsea kicked at the creature and it scrambled back to McKay. McKay laughed and gathered the creature up in his arms and stroked it. Then he calmly walked toward her. Tatsea looked around the room. All the men had stopped to watch her. She didn't think she could dash for the door before one of the men would grab her.

McKay stopped stroking the creature's fur, pointed at it, and said, "Cat." Then he reached for Tatsea's hand and gently pulled it toward the creature's fur. The fur felt soft like a lynx, warm like a hare still alive in the snare. Then she felt trembling under the fur and heard a sound like Ikotsali's snoring, only this snoring did not come from the creature's nose—it seemed to come through its fur.

For the rest of the day Tatsea saw so many strange things she almost forgot about the bundle of hair she had found in the room she had slept in. Other places in the walls opened, and behind these openings Tatsea saw more rooms with more strange things.

McKay took down a little house hanging from the roof on a notched stick and set it down on the table. The walls of the little house were so clear Tatsea could see a white stick poking up inside. McKay opened one of the clear walls, then lit a stick from the fire in the cave and carefully stuck the flame inside the little house and set fire to the top of the white stick. After he tossed his burning stick into the fire cave, McKay closed the little door. Then, carrying the little house, he beckoned Tatsea to follow him through an opening in the wall.

The fire in the little house cast shadowy light over curious items piled on ledges on the walls of the room. McKay hung the little lighthouse on a notched stick. Then he opened another hole in the wall about waist high so that light from the fire cave also shone on the goods on the ledges. Thundersticks. Horns like Redcoat and Blueleg had carried. Cooking pots that would not burn. Knives. Axe heads. Blankets like snow with a stripe the colour of blood.

Then a flash caught Tatsea's eye and she stepped over to one of the ledges. A piece of water with a round wooden frame like a drum stood on the ledge. When Tatsea stepped closer she saw movement in the water and then she recognized the same woman she carried inside the piece of water in the bundle around her neck. Puzzled, she reached inside her clothing for her bundle and pulled out her tiny piece of water. Even in McKay's dim light the woman in her piece of water looked the same as the woman in the piece of water on the ledge.

McKay took the lantern from the notched stick and stepped closer. The light appeared in the piece of water beside McKay's face. She looked at McKay, then back at the piece of water. McKay's face grinned beside the woman's face. Tatsea shivered. Her aching loneliness overwhelmed her as she stared into her own black eyes, giving in to the knowledge that she really was all alone. Her eyes stared back at her so intensely they filled with tears and she didn't notice McKay hang his lantern on the notched stick again.

Then his hand appeared beside her hair, holding an object like the fin of a fish, an object like Mean Face's wife had used. McKay slipped his other hand under her hair and began to pull the fish fin object through her hair. Tatsea was so shocked she stood frozen until the fish fin caught on a tangle and a sharp pain shot through her scalp.

"Ile!" she screamed, wresting herself from his grasp. Without thought she snatched a knife off the shelf and whirled to plunge the blade into McKay's neck. McKay dodged, knocked the knife from her hand, then circled her neck with his arm and choked her just enough to stop her struggle.

The other fur-faced men crowded to the openings in the wall and Tatsea quickly gave up and stopped her screams. Dougal blocked the doorway with his long knife. McKay relaxed his hold a little and spoke calmly in the language she could not understand. Dougal replied sharply and pointed toward the outside door with his long knife. Tatsea cringed, thinking Dougal wanted to send her outside to the Enda. Then, as McKay spoke again, his voice still calm, she felt his fingers stroking her hair.

Tatsea wrenched herself free, the force of her fury stunning the traders. "Gokwigha!" she screamed in Dogrib. "Gokwiwho! While!" Hair! Hair stripped from head! No more! She screamed the words again, staring down the astonished traders. She grabbed her hair with both hands, strained to remember the words in the Enda language. "Westakay?" she tried. "Namwac westakay! Mona, mona!" Hair? No more hair! No, No!

McKay pulled the funny flat hat off his head and, with his other hand, pulled at a clump of his hair. "Westakay?" he asked. "Hair?" He pointed to Tatsea's head. "Hair?" Then he pointed at Dougal's head. "Hair?" Tatsea pointed to her own hair and said, "Hair. Gokwigha. Hair."

McKay spoke to the other men, but the only word she understood was hair. How could she make them understand? She had to show these men that the hair on the wall in the room where she had slept was hair. Dougal still blocked the door with his long knife. Smith stood at the waist-high opening. She watched their faces while McKay spoke. Even though she had attacked him with a knife, McKay's face and voice seemed the most willing to try to understand her. She waited until McKay paused in his speech. "You McKay," she said, pointing at him, then at herself. "Me Tatsea." Then she pointed past Dougal to the opening to the room she had slept in. "Hair," she said. "Gokwigha. Hair." She beckoned McKay to follow her and she stepped through the doorway with hardly a glance at Dougal's long knife. Without looking back to see if McKay was following, she scurried across the main room, pushed open the door to the room full of furs, rushed to the wall, snatched the bundle of hair, then stepped back into the main room, holding out the hair. "Gokwigha! Hair! Gokwiwho! While! Namwac westakay mona mona!" Pointing at her own hair, then at the bundle, she repeated her words in all three languages.

While the three men gaped, she carried the bundle of hair to the entrance door and pointed in the direction of the Enda camp. Even though she knew they could not understand her words, she told them anyway how the Enda had come to their camp with thundersticks and sharp knives to kill her people for their hair. The puzzled looks on the faces of the fur-faced men frustrated Tatsea. She had to make them understand. In her arms she held the hair of many dead people. Desperately, she searched through her mind for something she might do. Then she crouched and laid the bundle of hair on the floor. With trembling fingers she found the knots that tied the scalps together. She loosened one and separated it from the bundle. Then she stood tall and placed the hair over her own. "Hair. Done hair," she said. People hair.

Dougal leaned on his long knife, staring at her along one side of his nose. Smith grinned through a puff of smoke. McKay pinched the hair on his chin, amusement in his eyes. A melting black rock sizzled in Smith's pot on the fire. Black smoke floated above their heads. A drop of sweat dripped from Tatsea's nose. She couldn't breathe. How could people live all day inside such a hot shelter? Tatsea pulled the scalp hair from her head and laid it gently on the bundle on the floor. Without looking back at the fur-faced men, she turned and lifted the bar from the door and slipped outside into the darkening air.

CHAPTER TWENTY-EIGHT

THE BABY STAYED DRY! THIS THOUGHT REPEATED ITSELF OVER and over while Ikotsali danced barelegged beside the fire. His backpack with his spare moccasins had also stayed dry, so his feet were warm while his leggings, tall moccasins, and parka hung on sticks to catch the heat from the flames. Ikotsali kept dancing to keep his blood warm in the frosty air. Any side of him facing away from the fire would chill to the bone as fast as a sharp knife slicing through fresh meat.

On his back the baby cried and laughed and cried again. The stomach pot hung from a stick turning slowly beside the fire. Ikotsali looked around for more dry wood. The snow was deep here and hard from the wind whipping off the lake. The thin sticks he had been able to find burned quickly. He had found no bigger logs that would burn long. Ikotsali feared the fire would burn down before the broth in the stomach pot warmed enough for the baby. He feared the fire would die before his clothes could dry.

A birch tree caught his eye—a tree struck by lightning, its trunk broken at the height a man could reach. The treetop hung down. Ikotsali stumbled toward it, breaking through the snow, falling once. He grabbed the branches and pulled and twisted with all his might but the treetop would not break free. Snow filled his moccasins; his fingers scraped raw on the frozen bark. The baby howled on his back and, near enough to make him shudder, a wolf howled in answer.

He staggered back to the fire, the thin, dry sticks now a few glowing coals. He touched his leggings. They were still moist, but if he moved quickly he might be able to keep the hide from freezing stiff. The bottom of his parka was still quite wet but the dry upper part would give him warmth. His tall moccasins were still too soaked to wear.

Ikotsali dressed as quickly as he could. The baby had fallen asleep on his back and the stomach pot still felt cold to his touch. He packed it again and then he set off along the riverbank, looking for a spot where he might make a proper camp.

At first he felt much warmer now that the wind wasn't cutting into his bare legs. His movement created heat, the baby slept, and so he kept on going even though he passed a number of spots that might have worked for a camp. Ikotsali feared to stop until he was sure he had the right place. If he stopped at the wrong place it might well be the last place he stopped at.

Ikotsali sneezed and the baby cried out on his back. In the fading light he sneezed again, his nose stuffed up, dripping. A hard edge dug into his back. He felt very, very foolish.

The Enda axe! The sharp Enda axe. He could have chopped the broken tree. How could he have forgotten about it?

He stopped and pulled it out of his pack. He took a moment to look in at the baby and tell her that it wouldn't be much longer. Then he trudged on, eyes darting from side to side, noting every bush, every gap between the green-needled trees. Once a flock of ptarmigan took wing before him and vanished before he could count them all. Then the bush was silent, except for the muffled sifting of his snowshoes in the snow.

Squawking ravens drew his attention away from the riverbank and he headed toward their sound. He stepped into a small clearing; in the fading light three ravens pecked at a snow-covered mound. He yelled to scatter the ravens, rushed forward, then stopped. A man, eyes pecked out, a ragged hole in his face.

Ikotsali brushed snow aside to reveal a boy dressed in summer hide clothes different from those worn by Dogrib people. Another mound lay nearby and when Ikotsali brushed off the snow he found another man, face down. This man wore leggings the colour of sky.

Ikotsali's first thought was to flee; the dead men's spirits might do him harm. But the baby cried loudly enough now to keep the ravens at the edge of the clearing. Pieces of flat, curved wood lay near the blue-legged man.

With the help of the sharp Enda axe, he gathered a pile of dry wood for a good fire at the edge of the clearing. Once the fire was roaring and he had hung the stomach pot to warm beside it, he began to strip off his leggings, now quite stiff from the frost. Then he stopped and looked at the bodies in the clearing. He tiptoed back, chased the ravens away again. He avoided the boy with the half-eaten face and pulled the moccasins off the blue-legged man. The blue leggings felt strange and Ikotsali almost turned away in fear, but the leggings might be warm, so he felt up along the legs until he could reach up under the man's hide shirt.

Ikotsali nearly bolted when he saw how unusual these leggings were at the waist. Never had he seen leggings joined and closed in to cover a man's backside before. Then the baby's cry forced him to his task and he stripped the odd leggings off the dead man's legs and hurried back to the fire.

He peeled off his damp leggings and moccasins, and, after stumbling down into the snow a few times, he found a way to get both his legs into these strange blue leggings at the same time and he pulled them up over his buttocks. Then he quickly pulled on the dead man's moccasins.

The sky had darkened by the time he finished building a shelter out of spruce boughs and packed snow. He fed the baby, ate some roasted meat himself, and built up the fire with a mixture of dry and green logs. He crawled into the shelter with the baby, warm in the blue leggings, but he woke often through the night to scratch his legs, for this curious blue hide itched his skin more fiercely than a swarm of mosquito bites.

In the morning light as he fed the baby, Ikotsali got a good look at the dead man's moccasins on his feet. Their shape was different from those his own people made; then he noticed the mending. The stitching around the mended spot looked familiar—the same kind of stitch his mother had always used, Dagodichih, too—and Tatsea.

Could Tatsea have mended these moccasins for her captors?

After the baby was fed Ikotsali searched the clearing for clues. He was puzzled by the site. There was no sign of a campfire or shelter. The men wore summer clothes but he found no trace of a canoe or footprints in the snow other than his own.

If Tatsea had been with these men, how had she escaped? Had his little wife killed these men? If Tatsea had been here, then at least he had some hope of finding her.

Ikotsali decided to keep following the river. He didn't feel comfortable camping with his daughter so near the dead men. But before he set off he kicked at a bump of snow and found a bundle of small animal furs.

For four nights he tramped along the river, sleeping and feeding the baby during the day. The first two nights passed quickly and he covered long distances on the frozen river in the clear moonlight. On the eve of the third night, however, he woke up sneezing and coughing. The weather was warming and the snow on the river ice going sticky. On the fourth evening, if the baby hadn't complained of hunger, Ikotsali might have remained asleep in the little shelter he had hastily thrown together that morning. Once he had fed the baby and satisfied his own hunger with hot soup, he decided to set off again to find a better camp.

His coughing grated his throat and his sneezing wrenched his body. Time and time again he stumbled sideways after his eyes had closed. He sang for a while to keep himself awake but then he dozed off again and stumbled to his knees before he woke up.

Mist and the sound of rushing water surrounded him. Rushing water meant rapids, open water, thin ice. The mist hid both banks. Keeping the sound of the rapids on one side of him, he crawled across the river ice, the sled behind him, the baby on his back.

When he crawled up the bank ravens squawked. Fresh hare tracks led in many directions from the river. Ikotsali's nose twitched at a faint whiff of burnt wood. With tentative steps he followed the scent to a tiny snow-covered hut. Ikotsali crouched to peer into the dim inside. A tangle of twisted willow bark strings lay on a bed of spruce boughs, moss, and dry leaves.

CHAPTER TWENTY-NINE

NO ONE FOLLOWED HER OUTSIDE AND FOR A SHORT WHILE THE cold air and the dark sky comforted her. No moon, just the stars. Tatsea recognized chik'e who, the star of the north that never moved. Would that star ever help her find her way home? Soon the weather would warm up and the sky would be too bright to see the stars, even at night.

After she relieved herself she wandered over to the outer wall, wondering if she should try to get away. Dougal had looked ready to send her to live at the Enda camp. What might have happened if she had succeeded in stabbing McKay with that knife? Surely they wouldn't have stood by and watched her kill one of their own. And what if Dougal were to throw her out of the fort? What would happen to her then?

As she wandered along the wall she could hear voices from the camp. When she came to a gap between two poles she bent to peek through to the other side. Cooking fires lit up the tents and she could see women tending pots while children ran around. Tatsea recoiled at a sudden stirring in front of the hole and flattened herself against the wall. For a moment just her pounding heart—then whispering—with Dogrib words!

"Come, I must talk to you." The first wife lurked on the other side. Trembling, Tatsea put her eye back to the hole. In the darkness she could not see the first wife clearly. All she could do was trust the voice she recognized, the voice that spoke her language.

Tatsea asked, "Is the man who is your husband with you?"

"No, my husband sleeps."

In the dim light of the starlit snow, a face moved in front of her eye, then an eye stared back into hers. Tatsea had not heard anyone with the first wife. Could the woman really be alone?

"I want to talk to the fur-faced men," the first wife whispered. "Open the wall for me."

"McKay?" Tatsea said, trying out the strange name she had learned.

"McKay, yes, with hair like a fox. Open the wall and I will help you to speak with him."

The answer to Tatsea's frustration at not being able to make the fur-faced men understand her swept over her. Yes, the first wife would help her. The first wife had freed her from the tree and now she would help her with these men. Maybe these men would then help both of them get back to their own people.

"I will open the wall," Tatsea whispered. Starting toward the place that opened, she glanced at the house. Faint light from inside shone through a hide-covered hole. No one had come looking for her. Why not? What might they want with her anyway? Why had McKay taken her into the fort instead of sending her to the Enda camp? All she knew was that he had been curious about her snowshoes. For a moment she thought she should go to McKay first before she opened the wall. But what if he were waiting with his knife? What if the fur-faced men still did not understand and wanted to kill her? The only way to make the fur-faced men understand was for the first wife to help her tell her story.

The log that fastened the opening in the outer wall was much larger and higher up than the carved bar at the door inside the house. It was heavier, too, and Tatsea had to rise on her tiptoes and push with all her strength to raise it out of the hooks. Trying not to make a sound, she lowered the log to the ground. Then, remembering the noise she'd heard the first time she'd seen the wall opening, she pulled gently, opening the wall just enough for a person to slip through. She could see no one. Motionless, she waited for the first wife to reach the opening. When the first wife did not appear Tatsea stole forward to look around the corner. Hands grabbed her ankle and yanked her off her feet. She screamed and hit the snow. More hands grabbed her other ankle. Then starlit snow rushed past her cheek as her head bounced over the icy ground.

How could the first wife have tricked her like this? Why hadn't the woman just left her tied to the tree? Tatsea would have been frozen by now. She got her answer as she was dragged into the light from the fires of the camp. Between the legs of the women crowded around her kicking snow at her and yelling insults in their language, she glimpsed the first wife huddling in the doorway of a tent, one side of her face swollen with a bruise so big her eye had disappeared.

They will kill me now, Tatsea thought. I will never see Ikotsali and my baby again.

Before she could close her eyes to play dead, she had been lifted to her feet. Then she stood alone in a circle of five screaming women, Enda men grinning behind them. One woman darted at her, slapped her face, then darted back to the circle. Another woman slammed into her from behind so she sprawled face down in the snow. The women whooped as Tatsea scrambled to her feet.

Tatsea looked around the circle, trying to see which woman would attack next. One of her tormentors had a louder voice than the others. She was also shorter. Out of the corner of her eye Tatsea thought she saw movement on her left side. With all her might Tatsea rushed at the shortest woman, causing her to jump aside in fear. Tatsea twisted in the opposite direction and dashed in the direction of the fort. But before she had run more than a few steps, a huge man stepped out of the shadows so quickly to block her path Tatsea slammed right into him.

The man laughed when she hit him and mumbled words that sounded like the words the fur-faced men used. Tatsea looked up at a face covered with black hair as long as the hair hanging down from a muskox chin. He embraced her with his strong arms and Tatsea wondered where he would take her. Behind her she could feel the Enda women waiting to see what the man would do. He pulled her to him, squeezing against her. His teeth gleamed through his black face hair. He jerked his body against her three times, provoking raucous laughter from the Enda.

Then with a rumbling laugh he spun her around and shoved her back toward the waiting circle of women. At once she was surrounded again, the women, spurred on by the fur-faced man's action, more bent on hurting her. The largest woman knocked her down. Before Tatsea could scramble to her feet, the shortest woman hit her from behind. Tatsea lay in the snow, wondering if she should play dead, but two of the women grabbed her under the arms and stood her on her feet. When she tried to go limp, she received a sharp kick to her calf and she was forced to stand.

An open hand smacked the side of her face and when Tatsea whirled to hit back, another woman hurled herself at Tatsea's attacker. Just as Tatsea recognized the first wife rolling in the snow with the other woman, she was kicked in the back of the knees and again she sprawled face down in the snow.

A man's holler cut through the shrieks and then feet stomped through the snow near her head. Fearful, Tatsea raised her head. McKay gripped a musket with both hands. The women who had surrounded her faded back toward the tents. Only the first wife didn't stir from where she had been wrestling Tatsea's attackers.

McKay spoke sharp words, both in the Enda language and his own, but Tatsea understood nothing except that the trader was angry. She saw how the first wife watched McKay like a trapped animal.

Then Tatsea felt McKay's hand on her arm and she heard him speak her name. She struggled to her feet and followed as he led her away. Then she stopped and said, "McKay." She turned and pointed at the first wife still kneeling in the snow. But before Tatsea could beckon the woman to come with them, one of her children crawled into her lap and put his arms around his mother. The first wife embraced her child and gazed at Tatsea but made no move to follow. Aching for her own child, Tatsea turned her back on the Enda camp and let McKay lead her back to the fort.

Rumbling laughter greeted them when McKay opened the door and led her into the house. The man with the muskox face sat at the eating stage, holding a cup between his hands. Tatsea's nose picked up the faint smell of burning water.

He rose from his seat, his laugh rumbling loud, and put his fists up as if he wanted to fight McKay. He looked at Tatsea and said something in the traders' language and laughed again. McKay didn't speak, but Dougal spoke sharply and Muskox Face sat down again and drank from his cup. He locked eyes with Tatsea, then slowly licked his lips. Smith noticed the exchange of looks, then pointed at the new man and said, "You Ross." Tatsea didn't need to repeat the name and she plotted how to get a knife for the night.

CHAPTER THIRTY

DURING THE FIRST DAY AT THE CAMP BESIDE THE RAPIDS, THE baby appeared content, happy to crawl about the shelter and outside beside the fire while Ikotsali cooked meat and boiled the willow bark strings to help him cure his coughing and sneezing. With the furs he had taken from the dead men, he fashioned warmer clothing for the child. As she played at his feet, he kept studying the sewing on the dead man's moccasin, wanting to believe it was a clue to Tatsea's whereabouts.

He felt Tatsea's presence in this camp, though the only usable item left behind was the willow bark rind. Could Tatsea have made that? The child, too, seemed to sense something here, looking about as if expecting someone to appear.

During the night Ikotsali had dark dreams—dreams in which he heard Tatsea's screams. He could see nothing but darkness, only Tatsea's cries and voices speaking words he did not understand. Sometimes the voices laughed, sometimes the voices snarled. Sometimes he glimpsed a flicker of fire quickly darkened by a shadow.

At daybreak the child was restless. After eating she did not want to crawl about the camp. Ikotsali had thought to boil more willow rinds, but the baby kept crawling to the moss bag he carried her in while travelling. His dark dreams still haunted his waking mind and he didn't pay attention to the child's activity until she began to cry with the same rage that once had convinced him to leave the comfort of Dagodichih's camp.

He picked up the baby, pressed his nose to her nose, then put her into the moss bag and settled her inside the front of his coat. Hastily he packed his sled and his backpack, and set off along the riverbank down what appeared to be a trail. Only then did the child's crying cease.

When he no longer heard the rushing of the rapids, he thought he heard a man's shout far behind him, but when he checked over his shoulder he saw nothing, and the baby whimpered until he again faced ahead down the trail.

CHAPTER THIRTY-ONE

TATSEA CROUCHED BEHIND A BUSH WATCHING IKOTSALI preparing to call a moose. On her back the baby stretched her legs in the moss bag so she could look over her mother's shoulder. Ikotsali had told Tatsea not to move, not to let the baby make a sound. Tatsea struggled not to laugh as she watched her husband. He was bending and twisting his body into different shapes. Never before had she seen him do such a thing. Each shape made him look more like an animal. Then he froze. His mouth opened and he called softly like a cow moose. He called again, louder so the sound floated through the trees. Tatsea watched him draw more breath and then the world around her exploded with such a raucous, evil noise she sat up from her dream so fast she almost fell off the sleeping stage. Her ears buzzed.

Abruptly the noise stopped; for a moment all was deathly still. Then the fur-faced men's voices murmured on the other side of the wall. Until she had become too sleepy to stand up the previous evening, she had watched the four fur-faced men organize the goods McKay had tried to show her before she panicked when he touched her hair. After he rescued her from the Enda women, he had showed her how to use the fish-fin tool and piece of water and for a while she almost forgot the fight with the Enda women while she ran the fish fin through her hair, discovering how to undo the tangles so the fish fin did not tear at her hair. McKay took the time to teach her how to say "comb" and "looking glass," but mostly he was too busy working with the other men. The other men ignored her, except for the times when she looked up from the looking glass to see Ross licking his lips as he caught her eye. However, no one had paid her any heed when she slipped into the fur room to go to sleep.

Something was going to happen today with the Enda people. Tatsea still doubted that the fur-faced men understood her story about the hair. And she could not depend on the first wife to help her tell her story again.

Tatsea pushed open the wall and slipped into the main room. She halted when she saw Dougal standing in the middle of the room wearing a dress, almost like a woman, with a coat and a bizarre hat. His long, curved knife hung at his side. In his arms he held what looked like a stomach pot with huge drinking tubes. Smith, also dressed like Dougal, held a long stick with a piece of hide on the end of it, coloured red and white and blue in a pattern of crosses. Ross, wearing a red coat similar to the one Blueleg's companion, Redcoat, had worn, carried a musket almost straight up so it leaned back on his shoulder. Fixed to the top tip of the musket stood a knife.

Only McKay still wore the clothes he had worn the day before. His only change—the smoking tube in his mouth was almost as big as a caribou leg bone.

McKay opened the door for the three men and they stepped outside. Tatsea hung back, then stole after them as McKay led the men to the outer wall. When the men got to the gate, Dougal stood very straight and put one of the tubes sticking out of the stomach pot into his mouth. His cheeks puffed out and the noise that had roused Tatsea from her dream filled the air, only now it was even noisier than a flock of ravens squawking at once. McKay removed the bar and slowly pulled open the gate. Still making the horrendous noise, Dougal walked through the door with a kind of step that would certainly be no good in the bush for hunting. Smith followed, carrying the strange hide on the stick so that the wind opened it up like the wall of a tent. Beside him Ross carried the musket with the knife.

Tatsea tiptoed up beside McKay to watch the men march down to the Enda camp. Enda—men, women, and children—scrambled out of the tents. Mean Face raised his arm and the people brought out their bundles of furs and lined up behind him. Dougal stopped marching and stood in front of Mean Face. He continued to make the terrible noise until all the Enda had lined up. Then Dougal and his men turned around and, with slow steps like a crane walking along a water's edge, led Mean Face and his Enda people back toward the stick house.

When Tatsea saw the Enda coming toward her, she turned and darted back into the main house and watched through the partially open door. It was only then that she realized McKay was no longer at the gate. He was in the house behind her with a red coat in his arms and a funny hat in one hand. With a smile he placed the hat in her hands. Tatsea almost dropped it, gaping at the red and green feathers decorating the hat, feathers fine and soft as if from a baby bird. McKay gently nudged her aside to step through the doorway and wait for Dougal to lead the Enda up to the door.

Dougal stopped marching, though he continued the terrible noise with the stomach pot thing. McKay stepped up to Mean Face and helped the Enda leader slip his arms into the coat. Then McKay motioned for Tatsea to step forward. She was so surprised she forgot to be frightened and she carried the hat to McKay. He took the hat and set it on Mean Face's head. Mean Face turned around and the Enda cheered, admiring the red and green feathers flickering in the breeze.

Dougal stopped the terrible noise. Smith, Ross, and McKay hurried into the house. Suddenly fearful again, Tatsea ran in after them. She glanced back over her shoulder. Dougal was leading Mean Face and his wife into the house. Panicked, Tatsea scurried into her sleeping room, then turned to spy through the crack in the door.

Dougal disappeared into the room full of goods. Smith held out a flat pot covered with slices of bannock. Mean Face and his wife each took a piece, then Smith hurried outside even as Mean Face's wife reached out for a second piece. Ross followed him, carrying an even larger pot of bannock.

Dougal opened the window in the wall so that Mean Face and his wife could see the goods in the trade room. McKay carried a small table out of the trade room and set it down so it blocked the doorway. On the table lay a flat, black, four-sided object, beside it a small black pot and a flat brown box. McKay reached back into the trade room, brought out a stool, set it down behind the table, and sat down. He opened the brown box, took out a large feather, and using a tiny knife he sharpened its tip. Then he opened the lid of the black pot. Next he unfolded the flat black object and for a moment the layered white insides made Tatsea think of the gills of a fish. McKay patted down the white layers so they lay flat, then he picked up the feather with his thumb and two fingers and carefully dipped the tip into the small pot. When he raised the feather the tip had turned black and McKay used the black tip to make tattoo marks on the white surface. Then he looked up at Dougal and waited.

Mean Face placed his furs on the window ledge one at a time. Dougal examined each fur carefully, then held up a finger, sometimes two. Mean Face would hold up his own fingers to match those of Dougal. Sometimes Mean Face would hold up two fingers when Dougal held up one and the two men would stare hard into each other's eyes until one of them would change his fingers.

Mostly it was Mean Face who would change from two to one, but once Tatsea saw Dougal slowly raise a second finger.

Every once in a while Mean Face would point at something on the other side and say something in the Enda language. Dougal would shake his head and then Mean Face would pull another fur from his bundle and place it on the ledge and point again. At last Dougal moved his chin up and down just slightly and he gathered up the furs on the ledge and set them down behind the wall. Then, passing a musket to Mean Face through the opening, he spoke to McKay in his own language and McKay dipped the feather into the pot again and scratched more tattoo marks on the white surface.

Mean Face's wife watched without a word, clutching a bundle in her arms. Once Mean Face had his musket, the trading proceeded more quickly since fewer furs were needed for cooking pots, needles, and blankets. Tatsea watched in fascination as the trading took place. She wondered if the bundle of furs the Enda had stolen from her would have been enough to get her a musket. Did she really want such a frightening thing? Would it be better to have a pot that didn't burn? Or a hard knife? A needle? For a breath or two she found herself dreaming about cooking for Ikotsali with a pot that wouldn't burn. Then she noticed that Mean Face had stopped putting more furs on the ledge, even though he appeared to have more in his pack. Instead, he motioned for his wife to step up to the ledge.

Tatsea found this so interesting that she didn't notice right away what it was that Mean Face's wife had pulled out of her bundle. Then she saw the scalp of long black hair spread out on the ledge. Dougal reached out to stroke it. His face was in shadow and Tatsea could not see what he was thinking. McKay, who had been silently making tattoo marks during the trading, murmured to Dougal, then laid the feather down in the brown container. He rose and stepped to the window to examine the hair.

Could these fur-faced men still not know?

With a piercing scream Tatsea burst open the door and

charged the Enda woman so fast that neither of the Enda moved when she snatched the bundle of hair from the woman and darted back to the centre of the room before she turned to face her foes. Her heart hammered so hard she hardly heard her own words while she explained again that this was her people's hair.

Mean Face made threatening gestures with the musket, but even Tatsea had noticed that he had not yet traded for a powder horn or the little black pebbles that killed. Dougal and McKay looked at each other, then at Tatsea, with faces that made her believe that had she not acted they would have accepted the hair for trade. Their faces also told her that they had known all along that this was people hair.

Now Dougal looked sternly at the Enda couple, pointed at the hair still on the window ledge, and asked a question in the Enda language. Mean Face glared at Tatsea, then with gestures and Enda words tried to convince the traders that the long hair came from creatures with long pointed tails who lived in swamps far away. Dougal and McKay listened but with Tatsea right there clutching the hair, they could no longer believe the story of the swamp creatures.

Dougal and McKay looked at each other, then faced the Enda couple and together shook their heads. Mean Face protested, though he made no more threatening gestures with the musket. McKay pointed at the furs the Enda leader had yet to trade. Mean Face snorted, snatched up the bundle of furs, and turned his back on the traders. His wife did the same. Together they marched to the door using the same crane-like steps Dougal had used when he led the people into the trading post.

Dougal spoke to McKay and McKay followed the couple outside. A moment later Smith and Ross entered. Tatsea heard McKay speaking to the Enda in his calm, firm voice. A woman's voice cried out amidst a clamour of Enda voices. McKay uttered a sharp rebuke. The door pushed open. McKay shoved Fish Mouth's first wife inside, then barred the door behind him. With her one unswollen eye the woman glanced fearfully around the room. She turned away from Tatsea's shocked stare, as McKay led her to the eating table and sat her down on the bench.

Tatsea clasped the bundle of hair to her chest, dizzy now that her chance had come. She glanced at McKay, who had stepped back from the table. Meeting her glance, he shrugged his shoulders. Tatsea took a deep breath and stepped in front of the first wife. The woman's open eye widened when Tatsea laid the bundle on the table. "Tell them," Tatsea said in Dogrib. "Tell them this is my people's hair."

The first wife trembled. A tear squeezed from her swollen eye and leaked down the bruise on her cheek. Tatsea felt the woman's fear of speaking. The people she lived with still shouted outside. Her children were out there, too. Fish Mouth and Mean Face waited.

Dougal muttered and Smith stepped out into the room where Tatsea had slept. Tatsea sat down on the bench across from the woman and leaned across the bundle of hair. "You must tell the fur-faced men about my people's hair," Tatsea said.

Smith returned and set a cup of burning water in front of the woman. Warily looking around at the traders, she raised the cup to her lips. She avoided Tatsea's eye.

Tatsea leaned in closer and whispered, "Trade hair for burning water. You said that."

The first wife raised the cup and drank again. When she set the cup down, McKay grabbed it, and, holding the cup high, he spoke to her in the Enda language. He pointed to the hair, then to Tatsea. He lowered the cup and set it between her hands. The first wife took a sip before she looked at Tatsea. She said in Dogrib, "Tell me what to say."

And so Tatsea told her story again, a small piece at a time, pausing so that the first wife could tell it in the Enda language. The traders listened. Sometimes, Dougal or McKay interrupted with questions about the land Tatsea had come from, what kinds of animals lived there, and how many days' travel were needed to reach the land where her people lived. Sometimes the first wife asked Tatsea to repeat her words until she remembered the meaning. Tatsea talked for a long time, until she had no more words to say. She gathered the bundle of hair back into her arms and listened to Fish Mouth's wife repeat the last piece of her story in the Enda language.

When the first wife stopped speaking, Dougal stepped over to the window ledge, picked up the scalps that still lay there, and laid them on top of the bundle in Tatsea's arms. Then Dougal spoke to his men in the traders' language. When he finished speaking he nodded to McKay and McKay stepped outside. Tatsea heard his firm, calming voice through the open door. A shadow appeared in the doorway. Tatsea and Fish Mouth's wife flinched when Fish Mouth stepped inside with a bundle of fur in each hand. Fish Mouth scowled and spoke sharply to his wife. Tatsea cringed, sharing the woman's fear, only to be puzzled when the first wife's face broke into a grin. The woman picked up the cup of burning water and held it out to Fish Mouth. He laughed, dropped his furs, and reached for the cup. As Fish Mouth drank the burning water, the first wife looked at Tatsea with her open eye, and winked.

Dougal took the empty cup from Fish Mouth and, speaking jovially in the Enda language, pointed at the bundles of fur on the floor, then waved at the open trading window. The first wife rose from the bench and joined her husband as they peered at the goods in the dim room beyond the window.

Tatsea slid off the bench and, still clutching the bundle of her people's hair, knelt on the floor, and, watching the first wife tell Fish Mouth what to trade for, she had a feeling that despite her bruises the woman knew how to survive.

CHAPTER THIRTY-TWO

IKOTSALI'S DARK DREAMS TORMENTED HIM, EVEN IN DAYLIGHT AS he trudged through the unfamliar bush. Mostly he felt the dreams or smelled dream things. Or stranger still, in the dreams he seemed to be inside Tatsea's skin—feeling things that were happening to her, smelling things she smelled—but he could see nothing. He felt icy bark on her legs. He tasted hide on her mouth. He smelled unusual cooking—some made his mouth water, some made him spit like a sick man. He smelled very peculiar smoke. He shivered when something scratched at a tangle in his hair.

With every step he grew more concerned that something terrible would happen to Tatsea before he could reach her. Thunder exploded in his head. The cold blade of an Enda knife pressed his skin.

Long ago he had become a frog—but only he escaped. He had

not saved the other Dogrib boys from Enda axes. The power in his arms had led the Enda canoes to the falls—but he was not in a canoe now. And again he had protected only himself.

And now he was not alone. Would any power he might use work if he had a child on his back? If he changed into a frog, how would he carry his child? If he moved into the power world, would the child come with him? Or would the child be left alone, floundering on the cold snow?

And then the baby would stir and he would wake from the dark dream, all his senses awake to the bush around him. And he would sense he had heard something . . . then the silence would overwhelm him as if the world were dead. In such moments of dead silence Ikotsali's thoughts floundered like a caribou in deep snow. He should turn back, return to Dogrib lands. This was not his bush, not his trail. But then like a chill fog, the loneliness of his life before Tatsea would wrap around him, and he would shudder with the memory of how alone he had once been in the camp of his own people. But now he had touched a different life. Turning back offered him no hope.

He tramped on. From time to time he spotted snowshoe tracks not quite covered by new snow—rounded snowshoes of a different people. Then, in a place where people had made fires, he spied the print of a single snowshoe—pointed at both ends.

He spoke Tatsea's name and, scanning the campsite, he repeated her name again and again until it settled into a chant in his head and the dreams now revealed shadowed shapes forming in the blackness. But still he could not see clearly.

The baby began to complain because he had stopped moving forward down the trail but a dreaded thought stopped him from going on. Something was going to happen to Tatsea in the shadows, and tramping through the snow would not get him there in time to help her. Her chanting name grew louder in his head; the baby struggled in the moss bag. He wanted to go on, but his eyes kept being pulled back to the snowshoe print, and then to the cold remnants of the fires. He must not leave this place yet.

Something here might help. Perhaps if he built a fire and cooked he could calm the child.

Once the fire crackled and the meat and the stomach pot had been hung in place, he took the child from the bag and, speaking to her softly, set her down on the snow. Immediately, the child climbed into his lap and without thinking about it he began to tell the child the story of the time all the caribou had disappeared and the people in the camp had no food. Day after day the hunters came back with nothing and the people got hungrier and hungrier. Only the Raven seemed to be content when he flew off into the sky each day. The people became suspicious. One day a man saw a vision of the Raven approaching long before the bird reached the camp. The next day the people asked the man to follow the Raven in his vision to see where he went. At first the man was able to follow the Raven, but then his vision lost its power. He asked the people to rub ashes from the fire on his eyes. Soon his vision power returned and he saw the Raven fly into a huge tent far out on the Barrenland. When the man came back from his vision he told the people where the Raven went and the hunters set out for the Barrenland with the women and children moving their camp behind them.

Ikotsali's voice continued to tell the story of how the people found all the caribou trapped in the Raven's huge tent on the Barrenland, but his mind was thinking ashes. He fed the child and chewed some roasted meat himself, letting the fire die down. He began to chant Tatsea's name while the flames shrunk into glowing coals and as the coals faded he heard the baby's tiny voice join the chant. More than once he reached out and almost touched the ashes, but he stopped each time the warmth touched his fingertips.

The child was asleep on his lap when at last he dared dip his fingers in the ashes. Trembling, he closed his eyes and rubbed the ashes on his eyelids. Cradling the child, he sat without moving until long after his ears and his nose had told him that darkness had settled on the surrounding bush.

Something moved inside his head. Feathers caressed the sides of his skull. Claws clasped his hair. Wings thrust wind into his ears. His eyes followed the shadow up past the treetops.

Then he waited for daybreak, chanting Tatsea's name, the child snuggled against his chest, warm and real.

CHAPTER THIRTY-THREE

TATSEA TIED THE LAST STRIP OF HIDE TO THE CORNER OF THE burial stage. McKay had helped her wrap Dienda's body and the bodies of his brothers who had been tied to trees and left to die. At first she had worried that the spirits might be upset that their bodies had not been wrapped in caribou hides. However, the traders had no caribou hides, and now when she looked at the wrapped bodies she felt certain the red stripes along the edges of the white blankets would surely amuse the spirits and keep them from abandoning the dead in this strange land. Tatsea longed for a drum to help her sing for these Dogrib men, but it was the wrong season to make one. So she closed her eyes and listened to the drum inside her head, thinking about Ikotsali and her baby as she softly began to sing the death song.

She had sung only a little of the song when Ikotsali and her baby appeared so clear in her head that the song changed from the death song to a song of hope with words not from old songs she remembered but words from somewhere deep inside herself and from the hawk she felt hovering in the sky, even though the season for hawks had not yet returned.

A cough broke into her song. She opened her eyes and looked over her shoulder at McKay, who leaned against a tree, waiting to show her how to shoot a musket. Her musket weighed on her back. She remembered Blueleg's musket going off beside her ear. Though her deafness hadn't returned since her canoe spilled in the rapids, did she really want such a frightening thing? Dienda, her friend, had died looking for these thunderstick muskets the Enda used to kill her people. McKay had promised muskets for her people if they brought furs to the traders. But a musket would be useless if she didn't know how to use it.

Tatsea closed her eyes again, to get back into the song, to get back the vision of Ikotsali and her baby. But even the hovering hawk was gone. Even with McKay and his musket behind her she felt alone.

Slowly she turned to face McKay. He beckoned her to come closer. Tatsea stiffened her back and walked toward him, eyes on his musket. Back at the fort McKay had been teaching her musket words—barrel, stock, ramrod, lock, trigger, hammer, pan, flint—and she recalled them now, but at first his strange words confused the workings of the musket. Finally she had convinced him to let her watch him work the musket and then let her do it for herself. And so she had learned how to open and close the pan, pull back the hammer, aim by looking along the barrel, and squeeze the trigger. McKay had also showed her the ramrod, the lead shot, the larger horn for coarse powder, the smaller horn for fine powder. But today he would show her how to load the musket and shoot with lead shot.

"Ready, Tatsea?" McKay said, giving her an encouraging smile.

"You do, Tatsea see," she said.

"I do, you see," McKay agreed. Reaching into his shot pouch, he pulled out a lead ball and cupped it in his left hand. Then he pulled the stopper from the tip of the larger horn and poured coarse black musket powder to cover the lead ball in the palm of his hand. Closing his hand so the powder wouldn't spill, he pushed the stopper back into the horn. Then he opened his hand, plucked the ball out of the powder, concealing it in his other hand, leaving fingers free to grip the musket barrel firmly as he poured the powder from his hand down the barrel. Then he pulled the ramrod from the wooden stock under the barrel and inserted it into the barrel mouth and packed the powder at the bottom of the barrel. McKay wrapped a piece of paper around the lead ball, put it in his mouth to wet it with spit, then inserted it into the barrel and rammed it down with the ramrod. Now he lifted the musket and balanced it horizontally on his arm. He flicked back the flint hammer halfway and flipped up the lever that opened the pan. He pointed to the little hole leading from the pan into the barrel and Tatsea saw that the hole was clear. From the smaller horn he poured a small amount of fine powder into the pan, then lowered the lever to close the pan.

Tatsea kept her eyes on the flint hammer and the iron lever when McKay raised the musket, setting the butt of the stock against his shoulder. Back in the yard of the stick house, McKay had used a piece of flint striking steel to show her how the spark would explode the powder. Tatsea wanted to see the flint hammer strike the steel lever.

McKay pulled the flint hammer back until it locked, then he placed his finger on the trigger, closed one eye, aimed the barrel at a circle carved in the bark of a tree, and squeezed the trigger. Tatsea watched the flint strike the iron, thought she glimpsed a spark, then staggered back as the shot echoed through the trees. When she looked at the tree, she saw the splinters in the bark where the shot had hit.

Tatsea took a deep breath and slipped the musket off her shoulder. Without a word, McKay watched her measure the coarse powder over the lead ball in her palm, pour it down the barrel, and pack it with the ramrod. She spit into the snow after she had wet the paper-wrapped ball in her mouth and tried hard not to swallow the awful taste while she rammed the ball home. Cradling the musket in her arm, she half-cocked the flint and opened the pan. She shook the fine powder from the smaller horn into the pan, closed it, and raised the musket to aim at the target on the tree. She had just pulled back the hammer to the full cock position and was lining up the barrel with the target, when she noticed a movement out of the corner of her eye. Without thinking she shifted her body, musket and all, to meet the movement. A todzi, woodland caribou, stood pawing at the snow.

Tatsea's arms trembled, then she tightened her grip and pushed the stock firmly against her shoulder. She pointed the barrel at the spot behind the animal's ribs where she would plunge a spear. The musket barrel wanted to waver and she shifted her feet to get a more solid stance. Then, when she got the barrel aimed at her target again, she squeezed the trigger. The powder exploded, kicking the musket into her shoulder, her ears plugged by the force of the sound. She lowered the musket and waved away the black smoke. Her ears cleared. Through watering eyes she saw the caribou had fallen onto its side in the snow, its legs pawing desperately. Tatsea looked for the wound behind the ribs, but saw none. Instead, a spot of blood oozed on the side of the animal's neck.

How come the lead ball had hit the neck when she had aimed at a spot behind the ribs? Then, considering how the musket almost kicked her off balance, she decided only luck had made the ball hit the caribou at all. Could she trust this thunderstick musket?

Still, a freshly killed caribou waited to be butchered. How it had died no longer mattered.

Tatsea caught McKay's eye as she slung her musket onto her shoulder and pulled her knife to approach the caribou. His face showed disbelief and admiration.

With two sharp knives the butchering went quickly. McKay understood how to skin and cut up an animal. However, he watched curiously when she deftly stripped the hide from the caribou's legs and with the four strips of hide fashioned a sled that glided smoothly over the snow, even when loaded with the meat they couldn't pack on their backs.

The smell of caribou ribs cooking in the large pot over the fire tickled Tatsea's nose as she knelt on the floor, organizing the goods she was packing for her journey home. Dougal had agreed to allow McKay to accompany Tatsea for part of the way to her people's land as long as he returned in time to take the furs to the fort by the big water for the coming of the big canoes from across the water that tasted like tears. McKay wanted Tatsea to take samples of trade goods back to her people to encourage them to trap animals and bring furs to the post to trade. Dougal wanted her to take one item of each type on a sled—including his largest pot, a red coat, white powder for bannock, a log of burning water, and pipes and tobacco leaves for smoking. Smith had tried to teach her how to smoke but Tatsea coughed so hard she thought she would die. The smoke from musket fire was hard enough to live with, but at least it had some kind of purpose.

Tatsea insisted that she only take the goods she could carry on her back—once the snow was gone, a sled would be useless and the canoe she would have to build too small to carry all those goods. So Tatsea thought carefully about each item she chose to take. Was the item useful enough to carry on her back all the way to Wha Ti?

Two small cooking pots. A hard knife. A sharpening stone. An axe head. An ice chisel head. Two blankets with red stripes. A package of needles. A spool of thread. A bag of coloured beads. A thimble. A comb and a looking glass with wooden edges. Flint and steel for firemaking.

One other thing she selected was a coil of rope made from

what looked to be twisted grass. Tatsea thought this would be useful on her journey. Once she was back with her people, she could easily braid her own rope from strips of hide.

Almost she decided against taking a musket—it hurt her ears, it frightened her, it was clumsy, and a heavy burden to carry. McKay caught her staring at it, shaking her head. Then she noticed the musket Ross had carried in the trading ceremony—the musket with the knife on the end of the barrel. Such a musket would be of more use. If the musket ball missed the animal or did not kill it, a hunter could use the musket like a harpoon. Tatsea pointed at the musket with the knife where it leaned on a table beside Dougal's noisy stomach pot thing. McKay gave her a puzzled look, then he stepped into the trade room. He reappeared with a musket knife in his hand. He showed her how to fix it to the barrel of the musket for use and how to attach it for safe travel.

McKay also supplied her with a full pouch of lead balls, two full powder horns, and a few sheets of paper for wrapping shot. She seemed to be all set for using the musket, but something seemed to be missing. She looked inside the bag of shot. Then she looked at McKay and pointed at the black claws Smith had used to make the lead balls.

McKay grinned, but shook his head. He told her that they had no more claws or lead to trade. When her people brought furs to trade, they could get such things then. Tatsea pretended disappointment, but she had already determined that all the things she needed to use a musket would soon be used up. And then the musket would just be a heavy stick. At least hers had a knife on the end of it.

Tatsea had packed everything except for food when a sudden barking of dogs erupted outside. Since the Enda had packed up their camp and disappeared into the bush with their few dogs, Tatsea had heard no animal sounds near the fort. Smith and Ross hurried outside. McKay and Dougal, too, stepped to the door to look.

Then Dougal and McKay made way for two frost-covered men who appeared to have travelled a long distance. One man looked like an Enda person, the other a fur-faced trader. Dougal and McKay seemed surprised by the sudden arrival of these men, especially the fur-faced man, though their surprise quickly turned to welcome and they set hot food in front of the visitors.

Outside the dogs continued to bark. Tatsea tiptoed over to the door. In the moonlit yard a row of dogs tied in pairs stood barking in front of a large sled made of strips of wood. Smith pounded stakes into the trampled snow with an axe while Ross untied dogs from each other and retied them to the stakes. When Smith had driven in enough stakes, he opened a bundle on the sled and began tossing fish at the dogs. Although Tatsea had never seen such a thing before, it was clear to her that these dogs were slaves used to pull the sled. Was there nothing these men respected?

After Ross had tossed each dog a fish, he turned toward the door. Tatsea ducked back inside and was kneeling at her pack when Smith and Ross came in and joined the men at the eating table.

Much of the talk was in words Tatsea could not understand, but the attention seemed to be on McKay. At one point in the conversation McKay turned to look at her, concern on his face, and then Dougal shrugged his shoulders and gestured toward Ross. Ross glanced at Tatsea and slyly licked his lips.

Tatsea tried to hide her fear, and carefully filled her pack with food. After she tied up the pack she was about to carry it into the room she slept in when a thought made her hesitate and she carried her pack over to where her snowshoes stood against the wall near the door. She laid her musket, powderhorns, and shot pouch on top of the pack.

Then McKay crouched beside her. Speaking slowly, he explained that he had been called to the fort on the big water and would have to leave with the two visitors in the morning. However, Dougal was allowing Ross to accompany her for three days on her journey to her homeland.

Tatsea nodded to show that she understood, but she said nothing. She didn't argue, she didn't scream; she didn't look into McKay's eyes. Instead, she yawned and laid her head on her pack. She closed her eyes and began to breathe as if she had fallen asleep. She heard McKay return to the table and rejoin the conversation. Her nose picked up the scent of burning water. She tried to stay awake but the drone of the men's voices remained soft and she found herself drifting into sleep, becoming a hawk hovering on the wind. She flew just above the treetops, looking down on a trail tramped down by snowshoes. The trail met a river and then followed its bank until she saw the mist of rapids. And then through the misty air she glimpsed the little shelter she had lived in alone and her nostrils twitched at the scent of woodsmoke in the mist.

Tatsea opened her eyes into darkness, feeling that some sound had awakened her. The two visitors appeared to be asleep in the faint glow from the coals in the fire cave. Barely moving her head, Tatsea's eyes scanned the entire room. The other men must have retired to their beds. Tatsea took a long, slow breath, smelling the dead smoke from the men's pipes. Without a sound, Tatsea gathered musket, snowshoes, and pack, and slipped outside. The door thumped as she pulled it shut behind her.

Snow fell in large, fluffy flakes. She could barely make out the mounds where the dogs slept under the snow, silent, except for a low whimper or a groan here and there. Fearing to rouse the dogs, Tatsea stole toward the gate like the shadow of a hovering cloud. She was groping along the wall for the bar that fastened the gate when her nose caught a whiff of fresh pipe smoke. A hand clamped over her mouth and wrenched her face down to the snow.

Tatsea kicked and tried to scream but her attacker stopped her mouth and rolled her on her back, pinning her down with his weight. The mass of hair on his face scratched her when his lips sucked on her cheek. Ross! Then she felt the flat, cold blade against her neck. "Sh, sh," he breathed into her ear. The knife pressed harder. Slowly he slipped his hand off her mouth. Tatsea gulped for air without a sound. The knife grazed lightly off her skin.

Ross pressed his hairy mouth on her mouth and began pawing at her clothes. Tatsea stiffened, afraid to play dead. She cringed when his hand found her skin. Her ear detected the flap of a silent wing. A shadow slammed Ross's head, knocked loose his hold, flung him onto his back. Ross flailed at the hawk, claws clenched on his mouth, shrouding his face with its wings.

Terrified, Tatsea heard the hawk chirk softly, the sound like a dream. Then she knew she couldn't wait. She gathered up her things and scrambled for the gate. One dog barked, and then the pack joined in. Frantically, she heaved up the bar and wrenched open the gate enough to slip through. She scurried across the clearing into the trees, then stopped to arrange her pack and her musket on her back. After tying on her snowshoes she peered ahead through the falling snow and set off down the trail at a brisk pace. The dogs' barking faded and Tatsea hoped the traders were too sleepy to bother getting up.

The snow had stopped falling by the time she reached the burial stages for Dienda and his brothers. The moon, now low in the sky, shone soft light on the trail. The going was a little easier, but Tatsea also knew that her tracks showed clearly in the fresh snow. She needed to run as far as she could before daylight forced her to find a place to hide. She bent to check the bindings on her snowshoes, then resumed the rhythm of her half-walk, half-run that allowed her to travel steadily without tiring too soon. She called up the little piece of dream, the brief glimpse of her little hut, and fixed it in her mind.

The hawk's shadow moved on the snow in front of her as she moved. Daylight had come. Tatsea didn't look up to see the hawk in the sky, she just looked at the shadow, wings spread, hovering, leading her on. From time to time she glanced around for a hiding place where she might sleep, but then she returned her gaze to the hawk's shadow and trudged forward. She had to find Ikotsali and her baby. Without breaking her stride she pulled off a mitten, reached back inside her pack, and found one of the ribs she had packed. There had been no time to make drymeat, lighter to carry, but as she chewed she felt the meat fill her with strength, and she thought she might be able to keep on going until the sun went down again.

Faint barking, far behind her, shook her out of her dreamwalk. At first she thought a wolf pack had picked up her scent, then she reasoned that wolves would track her in silence. For a few steps she heard nothing more and then barking again.

A fallen spruce tree rested on its branches some distance off the trail. Twice her snowshoes broke through the crust of the deep snow before she was able to conceal herself behind the branches. Tatsea's hands seemed to move like clouds while she loaded the musket; the distant barking rose and fell. At last she closed the pan and rested the barrel on the fallen tree at a spot that gave her a good view of the track she had made from the trail; her thumb was ready to cock the gun.

Woodsmoke teased her nostrils. Woodsmoke with a hint of cooking. At first she thought this was part of her dream. She looked over her shoulder. The smoke seemed to be coming from beyond a ridge back in the bush. If nothing else the ridge was farther away from the trail and might be a better hiding place. And it would be best to know who else was around before the dogs arrived.

Her musket at the ready, she crept up the ridge, then paused behind a tree to peer down the slope. A small shelter huddled at the centre of a clump of four trees. A stomach pot hung turning beside a tiny fire.

Tatsea saw no one near the shelter, heard no activity from inside it. Stealing from tree to tree, musket half-cocked, she reached a tree next to the shelter. Food smells wafted from the stomach pot. A twig snapped. She caught a movement out of the corner of her left eye. She swung toward it, aghast to see tatters of red stumbling toward her. The blurred figure she had seen was real. Redcoat! With a musket!

Eyes shifting wildly from side to side, he staggered knee-deep through the snow. Frostbitten black skin stretched over his face bones, grisly like a dead man's skull. Only once, when she was very young, had Tatsea seen such a starving man stumble into a camp. How had Redcoat made it this far?

Swallowing the taste of lead, Tatsea nearly gagged as she wrestled her musket to her shoulder. The eyes in the black skull found her, but showed no sign of recognition. Redcoat staggered to a stop, his musket swinging as he struggled to aim. A black finger pulled the trigger.

Before Tatsea could duck, she heard a sizzle and then Redcoat's musket exploded, flinging him backwards into the snow. A chunk of musket barrel shot past Tatsea's head. Black smoke hovered over Redcoat's crumpled body; splinters of musket and bone lay scattered over the snow. A bloody hand twitched halfway between them. The flint hammer stuck out of one side of Redcoat's face, his jaw a mess of blackening blood.

Tatsea gaped at her unfired musket, appalled by its potential treachery. Would it blow up in her hands, too? Had these fur-faced traders put bushmen's spells on the goods they traded for furs?

An anguished cry shattered Tatsea's thoughts. She whirled to face a figure in blue leggings stumbling past her, a snared hare in hand. Blueleg? Tatsea raised her musket, pulled back the hammer to full cock. Blueleg paid her no mind, determined to reach the shelter. He's going for a musket, Tatsea thought. She had to shoot. But her finger froze on the trigger.

The dogs yelped somewhere beyond the ridge. Blueleg scrambled into the shelter. Then a baby's cry. From the shelter. Tatsea's head swirled; she staggered. The musket started to slip from her limp fingers. Blueleg had her baby! No!

No! Tatsea stiffened, regripped the musket. She charged

toward the shelter, screaming in Dogrib, "My baby! Give me my baby!"

"Ile!" a man's voice shouted from inside the shelter. No! Tatsea stopped, confused. Blueleg speaks Dogrib? The man in the blue leggings appeared in the entrance to the shelter, brandishing a harpoon with a trader's knife on the end. For a long breath they eyed only each other's weapons. Then they took in each other's faces.

Tatsea lowered her musket.

"Could you be the mother of my child?" the man said in Dogrib. "Tatsea?"

"Ikotsali?" Tatsea said, the sores on her husband's face the most beautiful sight she had ever seen.

"Bebia?" she asked, suddenly terrified.

Ikotsali gestured behind him. Tatsea dropped her musket and scrambled past Ikotsali into the shelter. A wide-eyed little face stared at her over the edge of the swing strung up over Ikotsali's bed. Tatsea fell on Ikotsali, hugging and kissing him, saying his name over and over and over again, until a faint thump and a gurgle made her stop. She looked past Ikotsali's astonished face. The baby had climbed out of the swing and tumbled down on Ikotsali's bed. Tatsea gathered the child in her arms, hugging and kissing, weeping. She fumbled with her clothing and put the baby to her breast. She winced when she felt the baby's teeth, saddened when she realized her milk would not flow. It had been too long. Still, she wanted to stay there forever, wincing while the baby tugged at her dry breast.

The dogs woke her from her reverie. The baby still sucked in her sleep. Gently, she tucked the baby into the swing. Then she crept outside and snatched up the musket. Firming her stance, she raised the musket to her shoulder. The first dogs topped the ridge. Then she saw them all, hauling the sled, a fur-faced man on the back of the sled wielding a long whip.

Tatsea was about to squeeze the trigger when the musket barrel wavered in her hands. She stiffened her knees to keep from falling; the weight of the musket wanted to push her to the snow. What if her musket, too, exploded in her hands, now when she had found her baby? She had loaded the musket in a hurry. What if she had made a mistake? Behind her the baby cried. The dogs had frightened her baby.

Tatsea steadied the musket. Redcoat's musket had been stuck many days in the spray of the rapids. Her musket was new. She looked along the barrel at the man on the sled. Ikotsali stepped up beside her, his harpoon ready. Ross would not get her now.

Tatsea squeezed the trigger. Crack! The lead ball struck bark, echoed, the dogs suddenly silent. Through the musket smoke, a voice.

She missed! Furious at the betrayal, Tatsea raised the musket to fling it away. But no, the knife. The knife was her only hope.

The voice called again. "Tatsea, me McKay." McKay stepped off the back of the sled and slowly walked toward them, his arms slightly spread. He made no move to take the musket from his back. Tatsea looked at the sled and saw he was alone. She set the musket stock down in the snow and fixed the knife in the travel position. Behind her the baby cried. She handed the musket to an astonished Ikotsali. Turning her back on the two men, she crawled back into the shelter.

CHAPTER THIRTY-FOUR

AFTER MUCH GESTURING AND MANY CONFUSING WORDS TATSEA and Ikotsali allowed McKay to coax them onto the sled. Tatsea could not find enough words that McKay would understand to explain to him why her people might find using dogs as slaves to haul sleds offensive. How could she tell the story of how her people came to be when she could use only words like lock, barrel, and stock?

McKay had promised not to take them far. Dougal wanted him back at the fort. And the man who owned the dogs was waiting. As it was, McKay took them west down the trail until near nightfall, and even though Tatsea was seated in between Ikotsali's legs with the baby in her lap, the whole journey in the sled reminded her of being tossed from rock to rock when her canoe had tipped in the rapids.

Yet, many days later, long after McKay had left them to return to the fort and they were building a canoe to take them the rest of the way to Wha Ti, Tatsea spoke to Ikotsali about how the riding in the sled pulled by dogs had been like riding in a canoe when she had been too small to help with the paddling.

Ikotsali kept his grip steady on the pieces of canoe frame so Tatsea could tie the joint with sinew. "How would we carry a pack of dogs in our small canoe once the snow was gone? A man would have to hunt just to feed the dogs. The women and children would cry with hunger."

Tatsea had an arguing thought and started to reply, but then she stopped herself. She thought about the Enda camp packing up when the trading was done. In her mind she could still see the first wife bent under her pack, the burdened sled behind her, trudging after her husband through the sticky snow to gather more fur.

That's what McKay and Dougal wanted her to do—snare small animals and make long journeys to trade for muskets and powder for bannock and dried leaves to suck in smoke and burning water to make people shout and scream and fight with each other.

Many times after McKay had turned his dog team around to return to his fort, Tatsea had considered dumping the heavy musket into the river to lighten her load. Although Ikotsali watched intently when she showed him how the flintlock worked, when she offered him a chance to try it out he shook his head. Tatsea sensed that if she dropped the musket beside the trail, Ikotsali would not pick it up.

Yet, Tatsea could not bring herself to abandon the musket. Muskets had been used to frighten and kill her people. Dienda and his brothers had died trying to get muskets. She had seen enough of the trade at the fort to understand that someday the fur-faced traders would reach Wha Ti. If her people were lucky it might be McKay; if not, it might be Ross.

McKay had told her how Smith had found Ross stumbling about the fort, wild-eyed, mouth open, unable to speak. There were no marks on him to show he had been attacked. The Enda guide with the man from the fort on the big water had suggested that a bushman had wrestled Ross for the woman and won, dragging Tatsea off to the bush with him. McKay laughed when he told her this and said that, of course, he knew that Tatsea had decided to set off on her journey alone and that Ross had just drunk too much burning water and would be fine after a good sleep. "Those Enda people see spirits behind every tree," he had said.

For a few breaths Tatsea had looked into McKay's amused eyes. She remembered his fingers in her hair when he had showed her how to use the comb and looking glass. Yet, she knew that if she tried to tell her story of Ross and the hawk, McKay would laugh.

The dogs tugged restlessly at their harnesses, but McKay seemed to be waiting for something from Tatsea. She didn't understand what he wanted; greetings and farewells were not part of the Dogrib way. The baby squirmed on her back, trying to look over her mother's shoulder at this strange creature. Behind her Ikotsali had slung the heavy musket over his shoulder; he gripped his axe, anxious to find a good camp before dark. Tatsea bent to check her snowshoe binding, then turned and quickly broke into a wide-legged run behind her husband. She didn't look back when McKay shouted his command to the dogs and cracked his whip.

When Ikotsali stopped to make camp a short while later, the bush was so silent McKay and his dogs seemed like a vanished dream. But in the darkness of the shelter with the baby sleeping peacefully in the swing overhead, words spilled out as Ikotsali and Tatsea clung to each other. Through the night and long into the next day they talked and listened in the shelter, bringing the baby down from the swing to snuggle between them. They told each other nearly everything while they lived and journeyed back to Wha Ti—everything that could be told.

Ikotsali listened intently when Tatsea told him about Ross and the hawk. He was about to tell her about how he had sent the hawk from his head when Tatsea added how McKay had laughed when he told her how Ross had been unable to speak in the morning because of drinking too much burning water.

Ikotsali felt his tongue stopped; he could not speak of the hawk. A fearful uneasiness settled over the shelter and they clung to each other in silence until the warmth of their bodies awakened their desire and love pushed their fear deep into the shadows.

When they woke they talked again. They talked all day, tramping toward home, talked to their daughter when they stopped to make camp, talked as they built the canoe, talked as they paddled upstream until they found the river that flowed into the big water, Tindee.

At last they reached Wha Ti and found a camp of Dogrib people, and Tatsea and Ikotsali became known as goxoho elexegots'edo, the lovers who talk to one another. Her people's hair was returned to Do Kwo Di and Tatsea told Dienda's mother how her sons had died.

The musket was useful as long as the black powder lasted. In its last days Tatsea used pebbles instead of shot and green leaves instead of scraps of paper, but without the black powder the weapon could not work. For a few seasons the musket was dragged along from camp to camp and then was mislaid.

After many fires, holes did melt into the cooking pots that didn't burn and Tatsea used birchbark pails and stomach pots again. Even the hard knives, axe heads, and ice chisel wore down with repeated rubbing on sharpening stones, but the tools were still in use in the camp on the big part of the lake beyond Do Kwo Di and Big Island when word came that fur-faced men who lived in a mud and stick house like a beaver house were trading ice chisels for fur at the far end of the lake where the tall spruce tree stripped of branches halfway to the top marked the opening of the river to the falls.

Tatsea questioned the messenger, asking if the traders might be McKay or Ross, but she was told the chief trader called himself Leroux and he was not from the big water that tasted like tears.

Tatsea and Ikotsali decided they didn't need to travel to the other end of the lake to trade. They still had the knives, axe heads, and ice chisel, and caribou were plentiful on the way to Sahti, where their oldest daughter had found a husband with the people of Dagodichih's camp. Tatsea did tell the people travelling to see the traders the worth in skins of a musket or a knife. Above all, she warned them not to trade for burning water.

On the trail to Sahti, in the tent that night, Tatsea and Ikotsali clung to each other, feeling again the fearful uneasiness they had pushed away to the edges of their dreams. Then Ikotsali spoke in the darkness and told Tatsea about how he had sent the hawk from his head to find her and how he had been unable to speak of this after she had told him about McKay's laughter. Tatsea took his hand and placed it on her belly that had given him more children than there were fingers on one hand. He felt the kick of the coming child.

"We must speak our stories and dreams or our children will die," Tatsea whispered. "But we must choose carefully what we speak. The fur-faced men will not believe us."

ACKNOWLEDGEMENTS

IN 1983 MY WIFE AND I MOVED TO THE NORTHWEST TERRITORIES to teach at Mezi Community School in Lac La Martre, a Dogrib community midway between Great Slave Lake and the Mackenzie River. Frustrated by the dearth of printed learning materials relevant to the lives of the students, the school staff under the enthusiastic leadership of principal Jim Martin embarked on a reader project in which school staff wrote stories based on the life of the community. During the Lac La Martre Reader Project, Mike Nitsiza told me the story of how the Dogribs got their first rifle and the story of how a Dogrib medicine man led pursuing Cree raiders from Man's Bones Island down the La Martre River and over La Martre Falls. Mike Nitsiza and Frances Zoe guided us on a trip down the river to the falls, a trip that planted many images in my imagination, which resurfaced when I was writing the novel. Frances Zoe also told the story of the boy who turned into a frog and introduced me to stories of Yamozha, the man who wandered around to make the world safe for people. Frances Zoe's translations of the raven stories as told by David Chocolate also hovered in the background during the writing of this novel. Mike Nitsiza's translation of Menton Mantla's account of a musketless caribou hunt provided the inspiration for *A Caribou Hunt With No Bullets*, a reader I wrote in 1984, which later worked its way into this novel. Although these stories I was told are set in a time when the Dogrib people were being attacked by raiders who had contact with white traders, the responsibility for combining the stories into one narrative and imagining the characters Tatsea (taht say ah) and Ikotsali (ee koh tsah lee) is mine.

Other sources that proved useful in constructing this narrative include Kerry Abel's *Drum Songs: Glimpses of Dene History*, Samuel Hearne's *A Journey from Prince of Wales's Fort in Hudson's Bay to the Northern Ocean, 1769-72*, George Blondin's *When the World was New* and *Yamoria the Lawgiver*, Emile Petitot's *The Book of Dene*, and the work of June Helm, which has now been collected in *The People of Denendeh* and *Prophecy and Power Among the Dogrib Indians*.

The two editions of *Tlicho Yati Enihtl'e A Dogrib Dictionary* published by the Dogrib Divisional Board of Education were invaluable in inumerable ways and I hope my likely incorrect use of the Dogrib language is at least somewhat forgiveable. And thank you Frances Zoe for teaching me the Dogrib vowel sounds. If only these Dogrib dictionaries had been around when I lived in Lac La Martre.

The Cree language reference I used was *Ininimotan: Becoming a Successful Cree Evesdropper* as well as a few words I learned from the Bakers, Bighettys, Birds, Merastys, and Morins when I lived in Granville Lake, Manitoba.

And thank you, William Nitsiza, for the cassette of a live recording from a drum dance, which played in my headphones for hours as I wrote the first draft.

I must also thank the Manitoba Arts Council, which funded the Rural Writer-in-Residence program at the Parkland Regional Library in Dauphin, Manitoba. The resources of the library and the Fort Dauphin Museum provided many little titbits of information and inspiration as I was writing the initial draft. And special thanks to Joe Kostachuck, who showed me his collection of historical artifacts and taught me how to fire a musket.

And thank you, Susie Moloney, for coming along at just the right time to give me the kick that enabled me to write through to the ending, which had eluded me for so long.

And finally, mahsi cho to the people of Lac La Martre, now Wha Ti, for putting up with my teaching there for six years and giving me the daughter for whom I had to write this novel.

—Armin Wiebe, Winnipeg, January 2003

GLOSSARY

DOGRIB WORDS AND PHRASES USED

Ayiha—why
ayii—what
Ayii? Yahti dok'ee? Tlicho?—What? You speak my people's language? Dogrib?
bebia yewaedi—Feed the baby
chik'e who—north star
Dagodichih—noise duck
dechita gojie—wood buffalo
Dienda—ground squirrel
Do Kwo Di—Man's Bones Island - This name and the spelling was given to me by Mike Nitsiza when he first told me the story of how the medicine man led the Cree enemy over the falls.
edi—expression of the expectation of more information
Ehke—to be twisted, sprained

Ehtse—grandfather, old man
Ehtsi—grandmother
ejiet'o—milk
ekwo—barrenland caribou
Enda—Cree; southern natives
ets'aetla—make a turn; turn around
etse ile—cry no
gokwigha—hair
gokwiwho—scalp removed from the head
Golo Ti Dee—Marian River
goma—stink; smell
gondi ile—speak no; don't talk
goni gokwo di—face, lines in skin
goxoho elexegots'edo—lover, talk to one another
ha die yenandi—cannot remember
Hatl'ode—Hay River
hozi ejie—muskox
Ikotsali—medicine man frog (the author coined the name)
ile—no
Nahga—bushman; enemy
necha dechi ko—large stick house
nonda—lynx
Sahti—Great Bear Lake
Tatsea—type of hawk; falcon
Tets'ot'i—Chipewyan people
Tindee—Great Slave Lake
todzi—woodland caribou
tsawo—fur
wekwi ejiet'o deghaa—have milk enough
Wha Ti—Marten Lake (also Lac La Martre)
Whati Dee—La Martre River
while—no more
Yamozha—man who wandered the world in the time of the giant animals and made the world safe for people. Many landmarks in Denendeh were created by Yamozha.
yegho naxoʔa—trick her
yek'adawo—tease

GLOSSARY

yeniwo hanide—wants that way
yexe eʔi—be like; mimic
zha—lice

Adapted from *Tliicho Yati Enihtl'e Dogrib Dictionary* (1992) and *Tlicho Yatii Enihtl'e A Dogrib Dictionary* (1996), published by the Dogrib Divisional Board of Education. For simplicity I did not use tonal marks for the vowels. Dogrib is part of the Na-Dene or Athapaskan family of languages, which includes Slavey, Chipewyan, Apache, and Navaho.

CREE

astam—come here
iskew—woman
iskotewapoy—whiskey
mona—no
mwac—no
natawenimew—he wants him
namwac—not
niwa—my wife
westakay—hair
wihcekisiw—he stinks
winipecapew—his face is dirty
winipistikwanew—his hair is dirt
winsisk—dirty ass (as explained by the children of Granville Lake)
wiyas—meat

Adapted from *Ininimotan: Becoming a Successful Cree Evesdropper* (no date), published by Manitoba Association For Native Languages, Inc. For simplicity I did not use tonal marks for the vowels.